A FATE FAR SWEETER
Title
Passion & Peril In Ukraine
By Roger Turenko

TO DIMITRI BUDANA and all the innocents who have died as a result of the brutal Russian invasion of Ukraine.

When discussing well-known public figures and other matters, the subjective opinions of the characters may not represent the actual viewpoints or conclusions of the author or the publisher. Although the names of cities, places, and some background events, such as the Russo-Ukrainian war may be real, all characters, names, and events in the storyline are fictitious. Except for well-known public figures specifically referred to by name, any similarity to real people, living or dead, is coincidental and not intended by the author.

Copyright © 2024 by Planetary Book Company, Las Vegas, NV

Planetary Books believes that authors and other creative people should earn a living from their work. Copyright laws are intended to motivate writers and artists to create works that enrich our lives and culture. Their work shouldn't be stolen. Scanning, uploading, or distributing this book without permission is theft and violates the author's rights. You may use limited excerpts (up to 2,000 words) for review purposes. For permission to use additional material, please contact the publisher at info@planetarybooks.com

Preface:

After 20 years of service, I retired from the US military, expecting to be happy. Instead, I found myself feeling useless and depressed. I had no wife or children. No foundation to build a civilian life. I had no direction or purpose anymore. But, everything changed in April 2022 when Ukraine's President called for experienced foreign soldiers. I became a volunteer in the Ukrainian Foreign Legion to combat Russia's full-scale invasion.

General Rutanov, Supreme Commander of the Ukrainian Armed Forces, personally assigned me a crucial mission: infiltrate Russian-occupied Crimea and destroy a massive missile storage facility. Those rockets, left undisturbed, would surely terrorize innocent people in Ukrainian-controlled territory. We had to destroy them. Despite the danger, I felt compelled by duty and moral conviction to act.

Little did I know that passion and unexpected love would find me. Nor did I anticipate how my choices, made in the name of duty, would profoundly affect both my life and the lives of others…

1

When a man is slain,
Words cannot resurrect the dead.
But, for the sake of life,
Must we bow and obey?
The dictates of a tyrant?
For death is a fate far sweeter than tyranny.
Source: *Aeschylus' Oresteia (458 BC), Agamemnon*

A thick fog enveloped the southern shore, making everything moist and slippery. A relentless rain fell from the heavens, with no sign of stopping. I learned that such weather was typical for this region of Ukraine in the spring. It was deep into the night, hours before dawn, and darkness prevailed. Even the moon was obscured by gloomy clouds. For a while, there was a spooky quietness. Then, the shrill scream of air raid sirens ripped through the atmosphere. Those were the conditions during the early morning hours when I embarked in the tiny craft that had been jerry-rigged by Ukrainian marine engineers, rebuilt from an underwater drone to a one-man mini-submarine.

My name is John Kovalenko. That's not my real name, of course, because I must conceal things for security reasons. But let me tell you something about myself. I served in the United States Army for twenty years and still consider myself an American soldier, even though I am retired. I joined the army as an officer at 22 and left at 42 after fighting in two wars: one in Iraq and the other in Afghanistan. It was a tough and exhausting career, but I earned an honorable discharge and a pension. Then, I joined the fight to defend Ukraine in April 2022, as a volunteer in the Ukrainian Foreign Legion, one month after I retired from the US military. Since then, I have fought many battles. I helped to defeat the Russian invasion in Kharkiv Oblast, and I assisted in holding the line in Bakhmut.

But as the warm winds of early May 2023 swept away the cold of the previous months, a twist of fate flung me far to the south, hundreds of kilometers away, to a mysterious port that lies somewhere between the cities of Mykolaiv and Odesa, and it was from here that I embarked on my journey to Crimea. The tiny underwater boat was designed to reach a top speed of 32 knots when submerged, which equals about 60 km/hour. That would have let me reach my destination in less than five hours. But top speed doesn't translate into actual speed.

It took slightly over 12 hours and two charging cycles, during which I had to surface for a time, to use diesel generators to recharge the sub batteries. But, finally, I reached Cape Tarkhankut and anchored the sub about 500 meters from the shore. The Cape is in the northwestern part of the Crimean Peninsula, and its coastline consists of high cliffs that rise at an almost 90-degree angle from the water. There are only a few narrow, rocky places to rest onshore, at the base of the cliffs. Mostly, the cliffs simply meet the water, without the benefit of even a pebbly beach.

The name "Tarkhankut" is Tatar. The Tatars originally inhabited Crimea before the Russian Tsars conquered it. Today, they constitute only a small minority of Crimea's population. When translated, Tarkhankut roughly means "Devil's Corner," and it is an apt description of the place. The nearby waters have always been perilous to navigation, especially in the days of wooden ships. The nearby sea has many hidden underwater boulders and rock outcrops and has been filled, over the years, by shipwrecks. Locals say that the ghosts of countless souls who died near this rugged shore haunt the surrounding seas. Tumultuous waters, towering cliffs, mysterious caves, and rugged promontories characterize the forbidding landscape. This scenery gives observers the sense of entering "hell" on earth.

But, for me, the cliffs were majestic. A thing of beauty.

The sun was still high in the sky because, to avoid Russian surveillance, I had left the Ukrainian-controlled shore long before dawn. The sub was very cramped, and I had been inside for a long time. Yet, I was hesitant to leave. To come ashore during daylight hours could be dangerous. There was the possibility of observation, and my arrangements required that I meet a representative of the local partisans in the dark, at the base of the cliffs. So, I stayed put for a while, trying to decide what to do. After about twenty minutes, however, my patience was at an end. Freedom from the cramped sub was around me. The waters just outside the submarine would allow me to stretch my arms.

A wiser man would have stayed on board in spite of the discomfort, but I am not always wise. I simply couldn't endure it anymore. I wanted out! Furthermore, I was already dressed in a wetsuit, and all I needed to do to make my escape was to don a scuba tank and some breathing gear. In the narrow space, that was a challenge, but I managed it. In a few moments, I was ready to go.

The mini-sub, as I told you earlier, was a Jerry-rigged underwater drone. It didn't have a proper escape trunk, so there were only two ways out. One was through the top hatch. But, since I had not surfaced yet, I couldn't use that method. The incredible weight of the water above made the top hatch impossible to lift. Even if, by some miracle, I managed to open it, the result would be flooding. The only other way was through a mini-torpedo tube, at the front of the craft.

I collected several waterproof bags which I had stuffed with my things before leaving, and opened the torpedo hatch. It was a tight fit even with the bags trailing behind me. But, the plan had always been to use the tube to exit. So, that's what I did. I squeezed myself in, the hatch shut automatically behind me, and I used the interior manual release to trigger the mechanism that opened the outer hatch of the tube. Suddenly, I was propelled forward, into the frigid water outside, the waterproof bags came trailing after me, tied securely by nylon ropes.

The wetsuit shielded me from the full shock of the cold water, though I felt brief discomfort as seawater seeped through gaps in the neoprene. This initial chill quickly subsided as my body heat warmed the water trapped between my skin and the suit, with the neoprene acting as insulation. My neoprene hood offered some protection, but parts of my face remained exposed to the icy touch of the sea. Despite the discomfort, it was a welcome change from the cramped confines of the submarine. I knew I'd have to brave the cold waters eventually. It was simply a matter of now or later. There was no avoiding it. This was the job, and it had to be done.

Swimming under the water was a liberating experience. I relished the newfound freedom, for several moments, propelling myself forward and back, without purpose, just for the sheer enjoyment of it. Upward, sideways, downward. It didn't matter. I had no particular place to go. Not for several hours at least. So, I repeated this process until, finally, my head broke through the surface. Blood raced through my veins and my heart pounded. I felt alive again!

A large, colorful fish glided past me, oblivious to my presence. It disappeared as it swam away, deep into the murkiness of the water. I turned to look back. I could barely see the small submarine, but it was hard to see anything through the murky water. I didn't know whether this was "normal" for this part of the Black Sea, but it was just as well. So long as the water remained this murky, the submarine would be well hidden. I might need it, again, as it would be just as difficult to leave by land as to enter. It would be even more difficult because after I completed my destructive mission, Russia would be trying hard to find me.

Several hours of daylight remained. I had two tanks of air. Each one represented about 45 minutes worth of underwater breathing. I needed to save one tank for the return trip. Otherwise, I would be forced, when and if the time ever came, to swim back to the sub on the surface, exposing myself to all the difficulties that would represent. So, in reality, I had only 45 minutes of underwater time. I raised my head above the surface to get my bearings. Just as I'd been briefed, a narrow, pebbly beach hugged the base of the cliffs ahead. I faced two choices: swim ashore immediately and then wait for my contact at the cliff's base, or remain in the water until nightfall. The decision was straightforward. Treading water for hours would be too draining.

I began swimming toward the sliver of beach, hoping to find a partially sheltered spot to await my local contact. This was our only possible meeting point on the shore, so I was confident he'd make his way there too. But, as I swam, my mind wandered, and memories began to surface...

I had received a summons to Kyiv from General Rutanov, who was, to say it mildly, an atypical military leader. For one thing, he was a lawyer rather than a graduate of a military academy, but he held the rank of General. His journey into the military began in 2014, fueled by patriotism following Ukraine's "Revolution of Dignity," which led to the ousting of the intensely corrupt President Yanukovich. Recently promoted by President Zelensky, Rutanov commanded respect.

Physically short, like many Ukrainian men, Rutanov bore the legacy of post-Soviet malnutrition. However, this didn't hinder him. Sequential crises, in the midst of war, showcased his unwavering competence, offering hope to a nation teetering on the edge. Unlike those who climbed the ladder through connections, Rutanov's astute planning and decisive actions defined him. In peacetime, such men often remain unnoticed, but during wartime, they surge ahead.

Upon my arrival, I saluted him, but he remained engrossed in his work and didn't even seem to notice I was there. His green T-shirt was a departure from the formal uniform. It was a type of dress that was also preferred by his President, and it seemed to add a bit of rebellious flair to his otherwise stoic demeanor. He pored over a map of a war zone, strategically positioning troops for Ukraine's expected summer counter-offensive. Finally, he looked up from the map and saw me saluting. Instead of returning the salute, he reached over his desk to shake my hand.

"I'm glad to see you, Colonel Kovalenko," he said, finally. "Foreign volunteers are important to us. Not only because of your valuable knowledge and experience but because you represent international support for Ukraine at a critical time."

"Thank you, sir." I started. "You asked to see me?"

He nodded and resumed his seat. General Rutanov exuded authority, and it wasn't just from the insignia on his uniform. It was mostly his commanding presence, and his deep, resonant voice. Once he gave an order, there was no room for doubt or hesitation. The man was confident and inspired confidence in others. Amazingly, despite being born and educated in Ukraine and never having set foot outside the country until middle age, he spoke impeccable English.

"Yes, I did." He replied.

He gestured with an open hand toward one seat in front of his desk.

"Please sit down."

I sat.

Being addressed as "Colonel" always felt a strange. In the US Army, the highest rank I had achieved while commanding soldiers was Major. It was only in the months before my retirement that I had been promoted to Lieutenant Colonel, but I hadn't held that rank for very long. Technically, Ukrainian Foreign Legionnaires can hold no rank above Sergeant, as only Ukrainian citizens can serve as officers. However, the Ukrainians, including the general, always referred to me as Colonel, out of respect, even though it was not my official capacity.

I had spent over a year fighting on Ukrainian soil, and many of my Ukrainian comrades were like brothers. I periodically commanded soldiers and trained Ukrainian forces. I viewed myself as an American soldier serving on foreign soil, even though it was without the active participation of my government. My identity, memories, and experiences were rooted in the US Army. I was pledged to defend Ukraine but I still felt like a US Army Major.

General Rutanov is known for bluntness. He gets straight to the point and is rarely afraid to say what he means. That's exactly what he did, when I met him, that day.

"I need something spectacular," he said, without elaboration.

"Spectacular?" I asked.

He nodded.

"Yes," he said. "Both a real and an informational victory. We need to show a victory, separate and apart from the counter-offensive because, frankly, we don't know how well that's going to go. You know as I do how deeply the Russians are dug in, the huge minefields they've set and the trenches. It'll be tough to get through. But, we still need to show our Western allies that we're taking the fight to the Russians, whether the counter-offensive succeeds or not. Do you remember when you proposed a plan to blow up a missile storage area in Crimea, back in April 2022?"

"Sure," I replied. "I remember."

Nothing had ever come of my plan. It was never approved. Until that very moment, I thought the top brass in the Ukrainian armed forces had just dumped it into the trash and forgotten about it. But it wasn't so.

"My predecessor didn't think much of it. And, to be honest, we were so busy pushing the Russians out of Kharkiv and Kherson, that we couldn't devote any attention to it, back then. But, now, things have settled down into something of a stalemate. The Russians keep building up the number of missiles, and we need that informational victory I talked about. Sooner or later, they're going to use those missiles to destroy Ukrainian property and to kill a lot of innocent people...unless we destroy them before they can launch. I've taken a fresh look. I like your plan, and I'm going to approve it. It's time we did something proactive, deep behind Russian lines. So, if you're still willing, go ahead and destroy that Russian missile storage depot. We'll back you 100%. Blow the damn thing to hell if you still think that you can..."

"I know I can," I insisted.

He smiled, nodded, and said,

"Good."

Many people don't understand that war is more than just two armies engaging in combat. Morale and motivation play a pivotal role. Victory is not determined only through triumph or defeat on the battlefield. Logistics and propaganda are equally important. The most effective propaganda victory occurs when the enemy discovers that they're vulnerable. And, in a war where foreign assistance plays such an important role as it does in the conflict between Russia and Ukraine, it was equally important to show some impressive "wins" even if we couldn't advance very much, yet, on the actual battlefield. That's what the general was talking about when he spoke about an "informational victory."

"As you know," he continued, "our goal is to cut Russian supply lines in preparation for our counter-offensive. We want to blow up storage areas like this, harass them behind their lines, and, ideally, turn the Russian people against the war. We can save the lives of a lot of soldiers by defeating Russia with a thousand little cuts, rather than one big blow."

"Understood, sir," I said. "It's a good plan."

"We've tried to blow up this particular storage facility several times but their defenses always stopped us cold. The only way we can do it, I think, is by following a plan like yours. We need to physically infiltrate and blow it up, close in, right under their noses. Once we do that, they'll feel insecure everywhere. The goal is to make them feel very unsafe even in Russia, itself, so that they'll be motivated to withdraw and end this war against us. With respect to Crimea, and the other land they stole in 2014, we'd like to see them in total panic mode."

He was smiling now, no doubt thinking about the aftermath of a successful attack.

"I understand and agree completely, sir." I said.

"Good."

The general's gaze drifted momentarily. Yet, the intensity by which he was staring at nothing betrayed that, in reality, he was in deep contemplation. It was his way of digging into the labyrinthine recesses of his thoughts. A moment later, he turned back to me, refocusing his attention on the here and now. His voice resonated with newfound clarity.

"It's your plan, of course," he stated. "But, frankly, your American accent is obvious. You speak good Russian, but the accent could mess things up. There are a lot of Ukrainians who can speak Russian almost like the Moskali themselves. But, you have some unique skills. You know how to scuba dive, fly airplanes and drones, pilot submarines, you're an explosives expert, and you've gone on enough covert operations that you won't panic if there is a major setback, while you're carrying it out. And, of course, you've been actively participating in training the new Ukrainian Special Forces units. But, as you know better than anyone, we don't have anyone with your particular skill set who is ready for this kind of assignment..."

"Thanks for the compliments, sir," I said, once he paused.

"I don't have the manpower or physical resources to send a whole squad." He explained. "I don't even think it would be a good idea to do that. This is a job for one very capable man, and you'll have the assistance of the local partisans. They'll be notified that you are arriving. They're all patriots, but they're not professional soldiers. So, they won't know how and where to place explosives for maximum effect, for example. You'll have to teach them, and show them how to use whatever high-tech equipment you bring along. If you want to reconsider, I'll understand. But, we don't have anybody else to take your place..."

I didn't hesitate even a second.

"No, sir, I don't need to reconsider," I replied. "I'm ready to go, and I appreciate your confidence."

"Good," he replied, stamping a printed paper sheet with the official rubber stamp that lay on his desk. It now bore the blue imprint that made it "official" and he handed it to me.

"These are your orders, Colonel Kovalenko," he said. "My aide will provide you with all the rest of the details. We've got some specialized equipment ready for you, and you should feel free to order whatever else you need and we can supply."

With that, the general seemed to retreat into his strategic domain again, fixating back on the intricate map unfurled on his desk. Without uttering a word to conclude our discussion, he shifted mental gears, digging into the depths of the imminent counteroffensive that had occupied most of his thoughts until I arrived. I couldn't help but feel a surge of exhilaration at his having considered my plan worthy, and I felt excited at the prospect of being involved in what might turn out to be a pivotal operation if all went as planned.

"Thank you!" The words slipped out of my mouth excitedly.

The general's eyes snapped up, startled by my continued presence. A mysterious glimmer danced across his calculating gaze, momentarily betraying the shrewdness that lay within. A smile, as inscrutable as a secret code, crept upon his lips.

"Oh, by the way...do you have a wife or a steady girl?" he asked.

"No," I admitted.

"Of course, you don't," he concluded, with a sly smile. "Because if you did, she wouldn't have let you come here. You wouldn't be fighting in my army! So, here's my suggestion. Go pay a visit to the River Palace. That's what I would do. I mean, you never know what might happen. You might as well have a pleasant memory to take to heaven with you, just in case..."

The River Palace is a landmark of post-Soviet Ukraine. It's been around for a long time. It's a huge boat, floating at a permanent dock on the Dnieper River. A place where loud music can be found playing into the wee hours of the night. A combination of nightclub and discotheque, it hosts one of the finest selections of professional girls in Kyiv. They earn their living pleasing men. There are plenty of gray-haired grandfathers there, mostly foreigners but also a few rich Ukrainians, who go to be fawned over by nubile 18 – 25 year-old beauties. The Palace is the finest whorehouse in eastern Europe.

I returned his smile with some sly thoughts of my own. I had gone to the place, on several occasions, with friends who had gone for the girls. He probably had a point about the good memories. Everyone I knew who had taken one of the girls came out with a good memory. But, I took a pass, nonetheless. I'd never paid for sex in my life, and I wasn't about to start doing so in Ukraine. But, I didn't say that, of course, because I thought it might make me seem like a wimp. Instead, I returned his banter with my own.

"Girls are too demanding…" I said, chuckling, "I don't have time for a woman now. But, a Palace girl might work at that. They always say it's better to rent than to own…"

We both smiled at that and he nodded.

"Agreed!" He said, "Unfortunately, I already own. I have a nice fat and happy wife. She spends every cent of my salary every week, conspiring to leave me nothing for pleasures like the River Palace. But, then, what can I say…I guess I love her, so it's alright.

The light smile disappeared as he turned back to his work. His mind, I am sure, was once again far from the River Palace. He was drifting back to the battlefield. Countless lives were dependent upon the strategy he would come up with and a profound responsibility rested on his shoulders.

Then, he rose from his seat, and extended his hand.

"God speed!" he exclaimed.

I gripped his hand, feeling the weight of our shared purpose in that brief connection.

A surge of deep respect compelled me to also offer him a salute. It was an act that had both ceremonial and actual meaning. There were no spectators of course. Our encounter had been an intimate one, and the general, himself, had made a deliberate effort to discard the significance of rank. There was no one to impress. Beyond that, it was already clear that he didn't expect, want or need me to salute him. But my admiration for him was immeasurable, and saluting was my way to express it.

2

As an Army Special Forces soldier, I never served in the Navy SEALs, although I've heard that it is an outstanding institution. Had I been in the Navy or with the SEALs, arriving by water might have felt more natural. Truth is, I'm not the greatest swimmer in the world. Yet, this aquatic approach was my only option. I had to make do.

When I finally resurfaced, I was gasping for air, my heart racing. After removing my scuba gear, I took in my surroundings. The narrow, pebbly beach stretched before me, barely a few feet wide at its broadest point. Rocky outcroppings from the towering cliffs above interrupted the shoreline, creating a rugged, isolated landscape.

The massive cliffs fronted the beach directly and soared upward, defying gravity. The top of the cliffs, I knew, from reviewing a topographical map several days before, opened up into a mostly flat plateau. My breathing was finally slowing down, but I remained very tired from the effort.

I sat down, periodically laying down, on the small beach. For what seemed almost like an eternity, I mostly just sat there, staring outward, toward the sea. I fell asleep for a few moments, every so often, despite the daylight. But, then I would wake up again. Finally, darkness fell and the night began.

I had chosen the safest spot on the peninsula for a clandestine landing. Everywhere else, where the land met the sea more gently, via sandy beaches or sheltered coves, massive defensive fortifications now stood. Anti-tank ditches and concrete "dragon's teeth" lined the shore. Mostly, they were designed to impede mass landings and wouldn't have significantly hindered a lone scuba diver like myself. However, along with the obstacles, such areas are heavily manned and watched, making them poor choices for coming ashore. This location, with its rugged terrain, remained unguarded—perhaps because of its inhospitality.

Suddenly, a clattering of falling rocks caused me to glance up toward the cliff top. In the distance above, I could just make out a silhouette: a figure equipped with a headlamp, skillfully rappelling down the sheer face using ropes and anchors. Having just arrived in Russian-occupied Crimea, I admit to feeling paranoid. Yet, no Russian soldier would descend so openly and steadily towards me. If it were the enemy, I reasoned, they'd have likely opened fire by now. If he was not the enemy, he had to be the partisan contact I was expecting.

As the man's feet touched the pebbly beach, he paused at the cliff's base, his headlamp's glare momentarily blinding me. Sensing my discomfort, he switched it off, plunging us into darkness. Moments later, he activated a lantern at his waist, providing a soft glow that allowed us to see each other clearly. He was an older man dressed in rugged attire, still tethered to his climbing ropes. A satchel filled with supplies hung over his shoulder. After a brief moment of observation, he spoke.

"You are John Kovalenko?" he asked, his accent initially striking me as Russian. I later learned it was the distinctive cadence of Crimean Tatars speaking Russian.

"I am," I confirmed with a nod.

He smiled and, without untethering himself, extended his hand.

"Welcome to Qirim!" he said warmly. "I am Mustafa Azmetov."

Mustafa, I realized, was a Crimean Tatar partisan, and "Qirim" was the Tatar name for Crimea. According to my mission brief, he would be my guide to the other resistance members. He had an olive complexion and was considerably darker than the average Ukrainian, but no darker than the average Sicilian from Italy. His hair was short and gray and his face was marked by deep wrinkles and scars, but even at 68 years old, he seemed agile. He had climbed down the cliff with ease. Underneath a slight paunch, he was still very muscular, a strength carved out of a lifetime of working hard with his hands. While slightly chubby, he was not significantly overweight, especially for a man of his age. Neither his age nor weight seemed to hold him back. As I later learned, he had been scaling these cliffs since boyhood.

"Zdravstvujte," I said in Russian as I shook his hand firmly, which is the formal way of saying, "Hello."

He smiled.

"Hello," he replied in Russian.

"You know my name, I see..." I mused.

"It's in my mission brief," the man explained. "It's an honor to have you fighting alongside us. We'll have much to discuss."

A sense of deep relief washed over me. Everything seemed to be going according to plan.

"Thank you, Mustafa," I said. "I've heard a lot about your successes down here and I'm honored to meet you as well."

That was a white lie. I had no information about the partisans, other than the fact that one of their representatives would meet me at the bottom of the cliffs. But, I was mindful of the need for solid diplomacy and good rapport. He reacted as I expected, with a smile. His eyes sparkled with pride at the idea that an American military man had not only heard of his team and their exploits, but was impressed by his operations.

"It is night, John Kovalenko," he said, gesturing at the cliffs towering above us, "and the path up is difficult. You are, no doubt, tired and there will be no one watching us here, now, or in the morning. No one ever comes here. Halfway up, there is a cave, carved into the sandstone in ancient times. Some say it was the Amazons, a race of women warriors, who carved the caves. I don't know. But, I do know the way to one of them. I doubt anyone else knows it even exists. We can eat and rest there. And, in the morning, we can continue our journey..."

It seemed like a sensible idea. I gazed up at the cliff, assessing the climb. Unlike Mustafa, my cliff-climbing skills were poor. Getting even halfway up would be difficult, but getting some sleep, after the long journey that started in the middle of the night, the night before, seemed like an attractive idea.

"Just lead the way, Mustafa." I replied eagerly.

The man had brought extra climbing equipment for my use. He unwrapped it now and handed it to me. There was a large amount of extra rope that could be physically attached to the pulleys and ropes he was already using, a supplemental harness, a hammer, extra stakes for hammering to the rock face, and more.

"Here," he said, "you probably won't need most of it. Follow close behind me, on the same path. But, you have the stakes, if you need them."

Mustafa gathered my scuba gear and other belongings, the sack containing my high-tech drones and so-called "invisibility cloaks" (which I'll tell you more about later on), and put them all into a much larger fabric bag. He closed the big bag, hooked a rope to it, connected the opposite end to a hook on his belt, and began to ascend, as I just watched from below. His movements were graceful and self-assured. I followed behind as best I could, muscles straining as I climbed. It was not something I enjoyed doing.

Inch by inch, we made our way up, gripping rugged rocks and crevices as we climbed. About halfway up, we reached a ledge and a few feet off that, toward the left, there was a cave opening. Moving toward the left, swinging slightly off the path he had taken on the downward trek, we turned and arrived, one after the other, at the entrance to the ancient cave. A moment later, we were both inside. He unslung the winch and pulley system from his satchel, expertly anchored it to the cave floor, and connected that to the rope he had attached, earlier on. Then, he pulled all my belongings up to the cave with ease.

Soon, when my stuff was safely inside the cave, he took some wood from a corner, where he'd probably piled it up long ago, and filled a stone-edged fireplace near the entrance. With some help from starter fluid and a simple lighter, the cave became illuminated by a flickering flame. The sound of the crackling wood filled the air. Whoever built this cave, so many eons ago, had built well. There was an outgoing draft coming from somewhere in the back of the cave and it pushed the smoke outward, bringing in fresh air

Mustafa took a metal grill that had been sitting in the corner of the cave and set it over the fire. And, then, plastic pouches of seasoned meat came from his backpack. He set it on the grill and soon it was being barbecued over an open flame.

He gestured toward a large rock big enough for me to sit on.

"Please, sit, relax..." he said.

I took my seat and stared at the dancing flames as he tended the meat. After a few minutes of silence, I leaned toward him.

"Mustafa, tell me about your people," I said. "I'd like to understand their history, their struggles."

He didn't answer immediately. But, then, after a minute or so, he turned toward me and spoke.

"There is so much to tell that there is nothing to tell…" he answered.

"What do you mean?" I asked.

He took two skewers worth of the smaller pieces of meat, put them onto a wooden platter and came closer, sitting cross-legged on the rock floor, eating one with the help of a rag that prevented his hands from being burnt. He offered me the other, with the metal on that one also covered with a rag.

"Eat." He urged.

So, I ate, and it was delicious. It wasn't my first experience with so-called "Shashlik," a dish made from barbecued meat that was a favorite throughout Ukraine, but the Tatar version had some spices that were different from the shashlik made in mainland Ukraine.

"Our history is long," he said. "For centuries, we faced oppression, forced deportations, and the threat of losing our culture. But, now we are fighting back."

He laughed.

"Don't you see it?" He asked.

"What?" I replied.

"It is a fire in our eyes that demands justice." He said. "And, I see that fire in your eyes, too, even though you are not one of my people..."

I smiled back and said, "I've read that Tatars were exiled by Stalin, after WWII."

"That is true," Mustafa agreed. "My family spent decades in Kazakhstan. My father, Allah rest his soul, decided that we would return, in 1975. He bought a small house far from the city, where I've lived most of my life. But so many Russians were brought into Crimea to replace us that we are now strangers in our own homeland."

"What about the Russian takeover in 2014?" I asked.

"Many were unhappy about it, including me," he replied. "Some protested and were arrested, never to be heard from again. About 15,000 to 30,000 people fled. Tatar TV channels were taken off the air, our cultural and religious buildings were vandalized, our mosques raided, our homes painted with crosses. Anyone attending seemingly pro-Ukrainian gatherings was arrested. Beyond that, not much changed."

He stopped for a moment, but then continued,

"There was no point in fighting them, back then. So, I kept my head down, said nothing, and continued working. Resistance got you nowhere other than jail, and there was no organized opposition. But in 2022, when the Ukrainian army actively went to war with Russia and with Western support, the time to evict the Moskali finally arrived. That's when I joined the resistance..."

I nodded. "I think you played your cards right," I commented. "And, by the way, I'm impressed with your rock climbing."

He smiled at that, as he turned the remaining shashlik on the fire.

"I have been coming to Tarkhankut for many years," He said, "I've been climbing these cliffs since boyhood. My father taught me. Now, it is second nature to me. I know every nook and cranny, like this cave, for example."

"You live close?" I asked.

"Not really," he replied. "An hour and half drive, partly because of the bad roads."

"So, you drive here from your house?" I asked.

"Yes," he replied. "Many people don't have cars, but I have one. A piece of crap, I have to admit. An old Jigoli. The smallest car ever made. You will see. It was my father's car before it became mine. One of the last products of the Soviet Union. Shitty car, made in a shit hole. But, it gets me from place to place. It uses very little fuel and, when it breaks down, which is often, it is cheap to fix."

"How did you find this place?" I asked.

"The cave?" he clarified.

I nodded. "Yes."

"By accident," he replied. "I discovered it as a child. It became my secret hideout." He paused, his eyes distant with memory. "No one has come here for a thousand years. Only me, I think. There are many other caves and few are known. This one is the best. I used to come here when I was upset. It is a peaceful place where I could gather my thoughts."

Then, focusing on our current situation, he added,

"You can safely leave your gear here until you return to Ukrainian-controlled territory. No one will find it."

"Sounds good to me," I replied.

"Tomorrow, we will climb the rest of the way to the plateau," he explained. "After that, we drive south."

My belly was full from the meat and the fresh bread and the cave, warmed by our fire, provided cozy shelter. Perhaps, it was once equally welcoming to ancient people. We had the modern luxury of foam mattresses to soften the hard rock of the floor, but I mused that even with simpler bedding like straw, it would have made a decent resting place.

Exhaustion began to overtake me as the warmth and fullness lulled me to sleep. Despite the unfamiliar surroundings and lack of a pillow, my eyes grew heavy. Within moments, I drifted off, the day's fatigue finally claiming me.

3

I awoke the next morning, my body aching all over. The discomfort wasn't from sleeping on the foam pad atop the stone floor, but rather from the lingering effects of spending 12 hours in the cramped submarine. Thankfully, I'd managed a solid eight hours of sleep. I felt relatively refreshed and alert despite the muscle pain. A couple of ibuprofen would do the trick. I fished the pills from my med pack and washed them down with a long drink of water from my canteen.

We rekindled the fire and prepared a pot of "ovsyanka," the Russian term for oatmeal. After breakfast, we tackled the remaining climb up the cliff. A short walk brought us to Mustafa's "Jigoli" car, which was waiting for us. He hadn't exaggerated—it was possibly the smallest vehicle I'd ever seen. The Jigoli earned the nickname "people's car" in the Soviet Union due to its fuel efficiency and affordability. Its tiny engine produces 30 horsepower. Some, like Mustafa, continue to drive these vehicles to this day.

Unfortunately, I am over 6 feet tall, and it took some work to squeeze myself in. But, soon, we were both inside the little car, driving south toward the partisan's camp. About halfway to our destination, we came across expansive open fields of sunflowers, and I immediately realized that it was the perfect place to test my drones. It would be easy to go deep into the fields, far from the main roads, where there was no chance of observation. This opportunity might not have presented itself again, any time soon.

"This place looks fairly deserted," I commented.

"It is," Mustafa confirmed.

"I wouldn't mind stopping here for a short time, if you don't mind," I said, "I'd like to test my drones where no one is likely to see."

He nodded his understanding.

Of all the things I had brought with me, the micro-drones were the most critical. They had to be working properly, or there was no point in even trying to go forward with the operation. It was much safer to test them now, rather than wait until we were near a city or any area with a substantial population. There was no sign of other cars, pedestrians, or any other humans. The expansive sunflower fields were ideal.

We turned off the pavement and began driving down a gravel side road. The "road", if you can call it that, ended after a short time, turning from gravel into dirt. Eventually, we were simply surrounded by an endless sea of sunflowers. That's where we stopped and got out, making our way a little further into the heart of the field on foot, gingerly stepping over irrigation channels filled with running water. After walking together in silence for a bit, Mustafa spoke.

"No one will disturb you here," he announced.

We stopped walking and squatted down as I opened and emptied the drone parts. I tried to continue making conversation as best I could.

"Most of the grassy areas in Crimea seem brownish," I commented. "But, here, all the leaves are brilliantly green. And, the sunflowers are intensely yellow..."

"The grass is brown because we get little rain," Mustafa said. "Not enough to grow such crops."

"There seems to be no lack of water," I pointed to one of the nearby irrigation canals, as I began to assemble the first drone.

"Da," he replied, "...but none of it comes from Qirim."

"Where does it come from?" I asked.

"From the Dnieper," he replied.

"Mainland Ukraine?"

"Da."

"Hmm..." I mused.

"There is a reservoir called "Kakhovka", north of us," he explained.

"I've heard of it," I commented. "The Russians control it."

"They do now," He agreed. "But, only since 2022. It is the largest dam in the world...well, maybe, the second largest. In Soviet times, these fields were part of a collective farm. Very big. The dam was built to bring water here and to other dry areas in southern Ukraine. When the Soviet Union collapsed, all farms, like this one, were divided among the workers. Each worker received a small plot. That was in 1991."

"Interesting," I said. "It doesn't look like anyone ever built any fences or divisions of any kind."

"You're right," He continued. "Because it's all still one big farm. Most workers have moved to Simferopol, Yevpatoriya, Yalta, and other cities. They wanted to sell their plots of land, but it was not possible because Ukraine had no land transfer laws. Much of it just fell out of use. Other plots were rented out to big farming companies. In 2014, when the Russians invaded, Ukrainian farm operators who did not swear loyalty to the new regime were expelled."

"The Russian government took the land?" I asked.

"Some of it, yes," he replied. "Most of it was just abandoned. Kakhovka reservoir was north of the new border. Ukraine cut off the water flow and the fields became worthless. Under Russian law, land could be sold, but there were no buyers."

"You say Ukraine shut down the water supply?" I asked, surprised.

"Yes," he replied. "But, in 2021, in spite of that, a group of wealthy Moskali oligarchs began buying land. They bought everything. And, people were happy to sell even for almost nothing because, without water, the land had become almost worthless. The Moskali paid very little and they bought it all, plot by plot, piece by piece. By September 2021, they owned everything. But, the land was still dry and worthless. They looked stupid. But, now, there is more water than anyone needs. This year, Crimea will have the biggest harvest since Soviet times. More money will be earned from this year's crops, alone, than all the money they paid for the land. That is because, when the Russian army took over Kakhovka dam, in February 2022, the water began to flow again."

"You think the oligarchs knew?" I asked.

"Of course, they knew." the man replied. "That's how people become oligarchs. By knowing. In advance of everyone else. Connections. Cheating. They always cheat. The full-scale invasion of Ukraine in 2022 didn't suddenly happen. It was planned for years. For Putin, it was about restoring the Russian Empire, but for the rest of them, it was only about money. About agricultural land like this, oil, minerals, and a whole host of other things that Ukraine has and the rest of the world wants. The Moskali seize and exploit every resource, and line their own pockets."

"Why did Ukraine shut down the water?" I asked.

"Poroshenko said the Russian Navy was using the water it?" I asked.

"Yes." He replied. "But, also, for us to drink, and to grow food. When Zelensky replaced Poroshenko, he promised to reopen it. But, Ukrainian nationalists objected. It stayed closed."

I had almost finished snapping the pieces of one drone together, so I looked warily around, once again, confirming there were no other people who might witness what I was about to do.

"You're certain no one is going to notice what I do here?" I asked.

"As certain as I know the sun will set this evening." He replied.

"How can you be so sure?" I asked.

"Because I know the manager," He replied. "His father, actually. A pro-Russian asshole. Outside of that, he wasn't so bad. In Soviet times, he was one of the collective's managers. In 2014, he supported the Russian takeover. When the Oligarchs started buying land, he helped find and convince the owners. The Moskali eventually hired him to run the place again. But, he spent his entire life drinking, so he died of liver failure a few months ago. His son runs things now."

Then, man's expression conveyed a sense of disgust, and he continued;

"The son is a bigger alcoholic and a bigger asshole than his father. He even hires his drinking buddies to help run the place. Right now, they'll all still be sleeping. When they wake up, it'll be hard for them to even stand up. They won't bother investigating a few sounds in the fields, even if they hear them."

"I hope you're right," I commented.

"Do people drink alcohol in America?" he asked.

"They do.' I answered. "We've got our share of alcoholics. Less than here though."

"I don't drink." Mustafa insisted.

"Why not?" I asked.

He shook his head.

"The Prophet warned us against this poison."

"Not drinking is a good thing..." I commented.

"Yes, alcohol is of the devil," He agreed, "But, the Russians are allies with the devil, and they put down their bottles twice a year, once for sowing and the other for harvesting."

"Are Tatars opposed to alcohol?" I asked.

He paused for a moment.

"In theory, yes." He replied. "But most drink anyway. Alcoholism is a problem. Many Tatars watch the Moskali. Then, they ignore the Prophet's warnings. Even my own nephew, Muhammad...he thinks of himself as an Islamist, but he is an alcoholic."

I murmured acknowledgment, but I was more focused on setting up the drones than on his critique of alcohol consumption. Mustafa sighed and continued,

"Many have caught this Slavic disease... It is contagious." He said.

I smiled reflexively, but quickly stopped when I glanced at him. His expression conveyed deep sadness; the topic clearly depressed him. But, it only took a short time before his demeanor changed. He turned, surveyed the surroundings, smiled, and took a deep breath, exhaling with audible pleasure.

"The air is good, yes?" he asked.

The air did seem exceptionally clean and fresh. I snapped together the last piece of the first drone and turned to him.

"Yes," I replied.

"It is the sunflowers."

"You think so?" I asked.

"Absolutely," he insisted, "they clean the air."

I smiled.

"They breathe in carbon dioxide and breathe out oxygen," he continued. "That's what gives this air its freshness."

I wasn't inclined to argue.

"I see," I said.

"That is why we must have water," he said. "Without water, Qirim is a desert."

"With water, Qirim is a paradise." He continued without prompting. "The one good thing that the Russians ever did was to bring the water back."

This positive comment about Russia surprised me. Was it a hint of support for Russia? He was, after all, supposed to be a partisan. For an instant, I wondered whether to question his reliability. But, there was no choice anymore. He was privy to the most intricate details of my mission plan."

"The water also makes Russians richer, doesn't it?" I pointed out, eager to see his reaction.

"That is true." He agreed.

"So, maybe, Russia had cause to invade Ukraine? After all, didn't the Ukrainians shut off the water supply?"

But, he shook his head violently.

"It was never Russia's water!" he exclaimed.

"Then, Ukraine did the right thing to block the canal..." I stated.

"No," he replied.

"But, how else could they put pressure on Russia?" I asked.

"Water is life." he insisted, again. "It should never be cut off."

Mustafa and his group were approved by the top brass of the Ukrainian armed forces and he had gone to great lengths to meet me at Cape Tarkhankut. If I couldn't trust him, my plan was already doomed. The fact that Russian troops hadn't arrested me was really proof enough. Hearing complaints about Ukraine's alleged misdeeds was unsettling, but it seemed to me that he simply exemplified the nature of Ukraine, a vibrant democracy, where people had a wide range of opinions and felt free to express them. Furthermore, technically, he was right. Ukraine should not have cut off the water, since most of it supplied the civilian population of Crimea.

The partisan movement had started out consisting of Crimean Tatars. Now it included Ukrainians, ethnic Russians and many others. Its members shared a common hatred of the Putin regime, each for their own reasons. As a Tatar, Mustafa had obvious reasons. So, I decided to stop asking questions to test his loyalties. But, he wasn't particularly concerned about my asking or not asking. He was going to tell me anyway. He wasn't done making his point or with explaining his position.

"Water is the blood of Qırım," he continued without prompting, "Without it, the land and the people wither. But, freedom is the heart. Without a heart, blood cannot be pumped. When we were united with

Ukraine, we had blood and a heart to pump it. United with Russia, we have blood and no heart. The one, without the other, is of no value. Do you agree?"

"Absolutely," I said. "That's why I'm here...to help you free yourselves."

He nodded and spoke again.

"I believe you," He said.

In response, I smiled again and finished setting up the first quadcopter, which was now ready for its maiden test flight. Mustafa stared at the drone skeptically.

"It is very small..." he said, seemingly disappointed.

I nodded.

"Small, but effective," I confirmed. "We call them dragonflies."

"America makes such drones?" he asked.

I nodded.

"Yes."

"You have used them before?" he asked.

"Sure," I replied. "I've been using them for reconnaissance for several months."

"But, we need drones to blow up Russian missiles." He pointed out.

"Yes. And, that's exactly what they'll do. I'll use them as kamikazes..."

He continued to look skeptically at the tiny aircraft.

"I don't understand," he said, simply. "The walls of the bunkers where the missiles are stored are made of solid concrete. How will such a tiny drone even make a hole in the wall?"

"It won't," I explained.

"But, don't you want to blow up the missile storage area?" He said. "It is a large facility."

"These carry more than enough explosives to do the job." I replied.

"How can that be?" he asked.

"The key is precision, not weight," I replied, "They can be placed just right."

There was a pause for a few seconds.

"I don't understand," he said, finally.

"Each one of these drones carries one of these," I said, taking a round metallic ball, about the size of a ping pong ball, from my utility belt.

He shook his head skeptically.

"Also, made in America?"

"Of course," I said.

"But, it's not much bigger than a large bullet," he complained.

"It's a lot bigger than a bullet..." I pointed out, "More like ten bullets. About the size of a standard grenade. In Iraq, we used them all the time."

"Against missile bunkers?" He asked.

"Mostly to kill individual terrorists," I replied.

"But, a warehouse..."

"It will work fine." I insisted.

Mustafa looked very worried.

"Are they miniaturized atomic bombs?" he wondered.

I laughed and shook my head.

"No," I said, "They're just very high-precision explosives filled with IMX-101. One drone, acting alone, can't blow its way into a hardened bunker. But, if we get one or two of them inside the bunker...the Russian army's obsolete methods will do the rest. The Russians habitually pile up warheads, artillery shells, plastic explosives, and so on. Lots of them, all in one place, and all filled with TnT and similar outdated technologies."

"Outdated?" he wondered.

"Yes," I confirmed. "It was invented in the 1860s and it's highly unstable. Newer explosives, like IMX-101, explode when exposed to an electrical charge. TnT explodes the moment anything nearby explodes. Since the Russians still use TnT, I can destroy an entire Russian missile bunker with just one or two of these dragonflies, so long as I land them in the right place. When it blows, the warhead blows along with it. Then, nearby warheads also explode. And, they cause other nearby warheads to explode, and so on. It's a chain reaction. Within a few seconds, the entire facility will go up in smoke. Poof!"

Mustafa stared at me for a moment, shocked and expressionless, needing a moment to wrap his mind around what I'd explained. But, a few seconds was all it took. Suddenly, his craggy old face lit up with a broad grin.

"Velikolepno! This is why I love America!" he said, enthusiastically. "A brilliant plan!"

"Thank you," I replied.

"Tell your government we also need this IMX-101..."

"I'll do that," I promised him.

In truth, however, I was on my own. The US government did not support my presence on the ground, and it wouldn't offer any support. Whatever I managed to get, from contacts in the military, was sent unofficially, and had to be delivered in such small quantities that the auditors would never notice it was missing.

"How far can these little drones fly?" he asked.

"They're powered by silver batteries," I replied. "They fly longer than those that use cheaper lithium technology. But, probably, no more than about 4 kilometers."

"Hmm..."

"In good weather..." I added.

"And, in bad?"

"Depends on wind speed, direction, and so on..."

"We should have good weather for many days..."

"I'm counting on it," I said.

"But, the air base is more than 30 km from our camp..."

I nodded.

"I know," I said, "We'll just need to travel a bit."

"It won't be easy." Mustafa cautioned. "Thirty kilometers is almost an hour's drive given the bad roads. Police and military patrols are on high alert now, because of our success. You know about the success of our operations?"

"I've heard," I said, although, in truth, I had heard nothing.

I had been instructed to meet a partisan contact person and to rely on his help. That was it. All I really knew about them was that they were mostly native Crimean Tatars, some other minorities and a few Russians. My knowledge base was about to expand. Mustafa was determined to tell me more.

"In November, 30 Russians in an Ak Mecit hospital never returned to the battlefield. We killed them with a bomb." He informed me.

Ak Mecit is the Tatari name for Simferopol.

"A month later, we set fire to a barracks, filled with Russian soldiers," He continued, "They all died in their sleep. Burned to death. In January, we killed two Russian National Guardsmen in an open gun battle. In February, we traveled to occupied mainland Ukraine, and killed 4 Russian soldiers in Nova Kakhovka, with a car bomb, not far from the reservoir we talked about. In March, we killed the deputy head of Nova Khakovka's occupation administration. In April, we blew up a National Guard checkpoint near Oleshky, killing 5 Russians. A few days later, we killed two occupiers in Velyki Kopanii. And just a few days ago, we reached into the heart of Russia. Our group in Nizhny Novgorod, deep inside western Russia, almost managed to kill the filthy Moskali imperialist Zakhar Prilepin. He escaped. But, we got his driver."

"That's an impressive record," I said, although frankly the idea of killing injured soldiers in hospital beds didn't seem honorable. It felt like something the Russians might do. But, suddenly, I realized that this was exactly why they did it. It was biblical-style justice. Eye for an eye, tooth for a tooth, and so on. At least, they targeted only the occupation administration and soldiers. They didn't go after ordinary Russians. Meanwhile, the Russian armed forces deliberately attacked and terrorized Ukrainian houses, shopping centers, hospitals, museums, and churches virtually every day.

I reminded myself that it was unfair to judge these partisans by American military standards. They were fighting for survival against an incredibly brutal regime, forced to match fire with fire. However, my mission in Crimea wasn't to attack injured soldiers in hospital beds. My objective was to destroy the weapons they were relying on and deal a blow to Russia's military efforts. I resolved to keep my new companions focused on the plan, steering clear of any diversion into personal vendettas or revenge.

I was finally ready to test the drones. The controller app was loaded and one of my phones was up and running, with the drone controls displayed on the screen. I leaned the phone against one of the largest sunflower stalks and picked up the drone.

"Where is the controller box?" Mustafa asked.

"It doesn't exist," I said. "They're designed to work from a smartphone. The camera sends the video back in real-time. I only need this joystick to guide the drone. The drone also has an autopilot based on artificial intelligence. It can make its own independent decisions, including recognizing and landing on a target."

Four sets of tiny helicopter blades began to whir as I pressed the "start" button displayed on the phone's screen. The buzzing little quadcopter sounded like a very large bee. It rose vertically until it was above the level of the sunflower stalks. I moved the joystick and slid my finger across the controller screen to change the angle of its ascent. Now, it flew upward at a lesser angle, but climbed ever higher until it was so far away that it disappeared from sight. But, the fact that I couldn't see it, didn't mean it couldn't see me.

I set the drone to hover overhead. I could still hear the continuous buzz but the sound was so low that it now sounded more like a big fly. I adjusted the camera, pointed it down, focusing directly at us. The picture was clear as a bell, but we weren't in it. Instead, we were hidden under the flower tops. Increasing the magnification didn't help.

But, I clicked on a red button on the phone's display, and the camera switched to infrared mode. That changed everything. Now, I could now see both of us, squatting in the field. We were emitting heat, just as every human body does, against the backdrop of relatively cool flowers. The guidance systems were working perfectly.

I brought the drone back down and snapped together parts to build a second one, testing it the same way. Then, the third, fourth, fifth, and sixth. All proved to be in perfect working order. The testing boosted my confidence and I turned to Mustafa.

"I'm finished," I said, disassembling the drones and returning them to their carry bag. "It's just a matter of giving the batteries a full charge, and getting them to the right place."

"Good," he commented, rubbing his belly and grimacing. "Because I am hungry, and it is time we visit my good friend. Svetlana. She is excited to meet you."

"My arrival is supposed to be on a need-to-know basis..." I pointed out.

"Don't worry," he assured me, "she needs to know."

For a moment, I was at a loss. He read my expression and understood my concern.

"She is our leader," He informed me.

I had wrongly assumed that their leader was a man. That's because Crimean Tatars are Muslims. During my service in Iraq, Afghanistan, and other parts of the Middle East, I had never found a woman in a leadership position. But, Crimean Tatars don't put such stringent limits on their women. They are extremely liberal compared to other Islamic cultures. While women still fulfill traditional roles, they also take on broader responsibilities and leadership positions.

"Sorry..." I said, feeling somewhat foolish. "I look forward to meeting her."

He smiled.

"As you should," He replied, "because she is an excellent cook..."

4

The resistance base camp was in a rural area and occupied a vast expanse of grassland. Several basic cabins were constructed in a central layout resembling a town center and other cabins fanned out on every side, out from there. Each cabin was tiny, with space only for two bunk beds. None had private amenities like toilets, running water, or cooking facilities. They all relied on a shared facility at the center of the compound.

The site resembled a substandard US Army barracks in some respects. But, unlike the immaculate facilities on American bases, most of the structures were in significant disrepair. To put it frankly, the so-called "rest complex" which the rebels used as their makeshift headquarters hadn't been properly maintained for years. It was falling apart.

Surrounding the living area were mostly withered fruit trees, and there were a few neglected vegetable plots now overrun with weeds. The former inhabitants had once lovingly cared for those vegetable plots, growing potatoes and other essential crops that provided sustenance in a communist society where Soviet collective farms seldom yielded enough food to meet basic human needs.

Food rations had once been rigidly enforced in the former Soviet Union. Citizens could spend an entire day waiting in line to receive a basic weekly allotment of potatoes. Dachas and rest complexes, like this one, were once owned by state organizations and intended for the leisure and recuperation of workers and their families. Most of them were located in rural areas, and included plots of land that could be planted. In a time when there was little food, they were a lifeline. Soviet citizens augmented meager rations with self-grown produce.

Fortunately, circumstances changed. In modern Russia and Ukraine, capitalism has brought many benefits in terms of lifestyle, leisure, and economics. Rest complexes, once important to survive in the midst of widespread food shortages, are no longer important. The market economy provides access to many other food sources.

The idea of "rest" also underwent a huge transformation. Previously, taking a "vacation" meant exchanging a cramped city apartment for a dilapidated rural bungalow. Now, both Ukrainian and Russian citizens take trips to resorts and coastal destinations just like Western Europeans. Vacations to Turkey, Montenegro, the Black Sea coast of Bulgaria, and Romania are the norm. Dacha communities and "rest complexes" have lost their appeal.

This rest complex was a remnant of the bygone era. Only elderly former employees of defunct Soviet enterprises still come to such places. And, even they seldom bother. The specific rest complex that served as the headquarters of the local partisans had once been the prized property of the now bankrupt "Weights & Measures Institute" in Yevpatoriya. The complex was overgrown with weeds and underbrush. Nobody cared. It was better to keep the place in its ramshackle condition because, then, it would attract less attention.

We completed the final stretch on foot. As in the sunflower fields, Mustafa's little Jigoli was ill-equipped to handle the rugged dirt road. After a 15-minute walk beyond where he parked, we caught the scent of a delightful aroma wafting through the air. The enticing smell of barbecued shashlik caressed our noses. Seasoned barbecued meat is a signature specialty with Tatar roots, adored throughout the nations that were once a part of the former Soviet Union. Despite the dreary surroundings, the mouthwatering scent left me feeling hungry.

We walked by a row of cabins, and I noticed a slender man with a shaved head and a thick red beard streaked with gray. He was sporting a pair of wire-rimmed glasses and they gave him a distinctly nerdy appearance. That general impression was complemented by a Star Wars T-shirt and a pair of cargo pants adorned with multiple pockets. He was seated on a stool, surrounded by an assortment of electronic scrap. As we approached, he seemed to be paying meticulous attention to a particular project, carefully soldering and running silver lines across various circuit boards.

Beside him sat an open laptop, its screen displaying a series of complex codes and diagrams. He seemed totally immersed in his work, even though, at the same time, he was listening to and humming along with some sort of music through a pair of headphones. He finally looked up as we passed, paused what he was doing, smiled, and took off the headphones. Then, he laughed.

"Mustafa!" he exclaimed, laughing louder, "I knew it would be you! You can smell food from 20 kilometers away!"

"True enough, my friend..." Mustafa replied, smiling, "Unfortunately, I can't eat like a pig and never gain weight, like you..."

"Ah," the man said, dismissively, waving his open palm, "it isn't true. If I ate like you, I would also be fat!"

The space around the man was cluttered with an array of electronic gadgets, most of which I couldn't even identify. Amid the sea of technology, he had wires, cables, batteries, and tools scattered all over the wooden table and floor. He didn't seem to notice the dust, the flies, or the mess. The man's eyes lit up with curiosity as he studied me. He adjusted his glasses and stroked his beard. A smile was on his lips, and I sensed he was brimming with questions, but he didn't ask any of them.

Mustafa smiled as he sparred verbally with his friend.

"John, this is Sasha Melnyk," Mustafa said, enthusiastically. "One of our most valuable assets. He is half-Russian, but we forgive him for that, because he is one of our most dedicated freedom fighters and, definitely, our biggest eater!"

"On this, we disagree." Sasha said, "I'm looking at our biggest eater!"

Mustafa leaned in close and whispered in my ear, acting as if he were sharing a profound secret. He spoke loud enough so the other man would hear every word.

"If you didn't know better, you would assume him to be a full-blooded Tatar, wouldn't you?" Mustafa said.

"I heard that!" Sasha quipped.

"Did you know," Mustafa continued, no longer pretending to whisper, "that my friend, Sasha here, was once the best smuggler on both sides of the Azov Sea?"

Sasha shook his head.

"That was long ago." He insisted, setting the record straight. "Now, I am an IT specialist."

Mustafa waved his palm, dismissively.

"Once a criminal, always a criminal," he said. "Thankfully, he now dedicates his basic criminality to helping us free the peninsula from the Moskali. He is our resident hacker. All these things you see around him are parts of something new he is creating for us. What is it, Sasha?

"An early warning system." The man replied. "It will detect the unauthorized approach of unknown people."

"How, will it know friend from foe?" I asked.

"Artificial intelligence." He replied quickly.

"Ah, yes," Mustafa said, motioning to the man, first and then to me, "Did I tell you that this inquisitive person is John Kovalenko, the American we talked about?"

He gestured toward me.

"Svetlana Yurievna told me," Sasha commented.

He turned toward me, and added,

"I hope you help us kill more of Putin's men!"

"I'm here to destroy one of Putin's biggest missile bunkers," I replied, wanting to make it crystal clear, "If that means killing some of Putin's men, then so be it. But, disrupting Russian logistics is the goal, not killing Russians."

"I see," Sasha said, turning back to his electronics, "My goal is just to kill them. The more dead Putin lovers, the better..."

Mustafa turned to me and spoke.

"You wouldn't believe it, but as I said before, he is half-Russian," he said.

"I am not half-Russian." Sasha snapped.

"Your father was Russian, was he not?" Mustafa pointed out.

"Being Russian is not about genetics," Sasha insisted, "There's not a scientist on Earth who can tell Russians and Ukrainians apart from one another, based on genetic testing. The difference is not in the biology, but in the heart..."

He tapped the left side of his upper chest and then pointed to his head.

"And, also, of course, in here..." he continued.

"In your head or your heart?" I asked, confused.

"Both," He replied immediately. "Because even though the Soviet Union is long gone, Russians, inside their heads, won't admit it. They look to the past. Ukrainians look to the future. I was born speaking Russian. But, I speak Ukrainian now, and English too, and I hate Vladimir Putin and all the backward-looking things he represents. I renounce any part of me that was ever Russian, if there ever was any..."

"Well said," Mustafa turned to me and praised his friend, "He has a beautiful way with words, doesn't he?"

Then, he turned back to his friend to say,

"I was only teasing you, Sasha. We are all Ukrainian and Tatari. You, especially. Despite you being a Christian, you are more of a Tatar than I am."

"Da," Sasha replied, nodding.

"But, of course, unlike me, Sasha is not just a simple man who knows how to work with his hands. He is a genius!" Mustafa added.

"That's not true," Sasha insisted modestly, "I know electronics and can program things. It's not a special talent."

"Don't let him fool you!" Mustafa insisted.

"You work as a programmer?" I asked.

"Yes," He replied.

"For a local company?"

He shook his head and said,

"I work for myself."

"Freelancing?" I asked.

He nodded.

"Lots of work for foreign companies. Some big names. Mostly for little companies that need small jobs done."

"And, his brilliant criminal mind also comes into play!" Mustafa proudly pointed out, "He also works as a troll for an infamous Russian IT company."

Sasha shrugged his shoulders.

"It's my cover," he admitted. "The pay is good and they hired me because I know English."

Mustafa was busy nodding his head and laughing under his breath.

"They hired him, yes." He said. "He works for the Internet Research Company,"

I recognized the name immediately.

"Isn't that..." I began to ask, but Mustafa cut me off.

"Exactly," He said, "A partisan warrior working part-time for Prigozhin! A Wagner Group troll who gets paid to write stupid comments, in English, in Western news media."

"I hate some of the crap I write." Sasha insisted.

Mustafa nodded, and said,

"But, it saved our asses more than once. The FSB would have arrested us long ago if he were not on Prigozhin's payroll. They were hot on our trail after we blew up a military recruiting station. But, then, they found out who he works for, and assumed no Wagner Group guy would do that. So, they moved on to investigate other people."

"Da..." Sasha agreed. "That is why I do it. Aside from the pay, of course."

"You're fluent in English?" I asked.

"Of course," he replied, in nearly perfect English.

I continued to speak in Russian out of courtesy to Mustafa, who didn't speak English.

"But, you also do software outsourcing work?"

He nodded, and said,

"Maybe I will go to Silicon Valley someday..."

"What about the sanctions?" I asked.

"What about them?" he asked in reply.

"Well, you are based in Crimea. And, Russian-held territories are cut off from the international banking system. How do you get paid?"

"Easy," he claimed, "nobody really knows where I am. I use VPNs. I pretend to live in Turkey. My PayPal is linked to a Turkish bank account in Istanbul. It's not easy to withdraw the money and I haven't withdrawn anything for over a year, but it's there. Like a forced savings account. When I need to, I'll take a trip to Turkey. Right now, I don't need the money. That asshole, Prigozhin, pays me enough to live on. I'm single and I don't need much."

"As I told you," Mustafa interjected, "a brilliant criminal mind at work!"

"Ah," Sasha dismissed him with a wave of his hand, "Shut up, already, Mustafa."

"He's just smart," I commented.

Sasha nodded, smiled, and pointed with his silver circuit drawing pen.

"There, you see?" he said, "did you hear that, Mustafa? Pay attention and learn from the Americans!"

Mustafa, smiling, but shaking his head, turned to me and said,

"I say criminal..." Then he feigned whispering something, making sure it was loud enough for the other man to hear. "Don't feed his ego. It's too big already!"

I turned back to Sasha.

"What caused you to join the partisans?" I asked.

"I brought him in." Mustafa blurted out before Sasha could reply.

"Yes, he did, because I hate Putin..." Sasha added.

"Come," Mustafa said, "You need to meet more people."

Giving Sasha a final look, he added,

"We'll see you at dinner."

Sasha, occupied with his electronic machinations, nodded, but said nothing more, as he looked down at his work.

We walked deeper into the dacha complex and came upon another man. This one was young and scrawny, sitting on one side of a long, weather-worn, wood table. He looked to be in his early 20s and sported an untended black beard, greased by pieces of rendered fat, along with bread crumbs. There was also a measure of vodka that wet part of the beard, and the man continued drinking vodka from an open bottle.

We were a short distance away from the outdoor fire pit, where the shashlik was roasting and it continued to smell delicious. Mustafa pointed to the young man.

"This is Muhammad, my nephew..." he said, shaking his head with dismay. "Who, unfortunately, drinks like a fucking Russian..."

The young man glanced up with a resentful look on his face.

"Why don't you say something good for a change?" The drunken young man asked.

"I hope that is not the fat of a pig," Mustafa commented, obviously irritated.

"Of course not!" the young man insisted. "It is halal fat of the cow. What do you take me for?"

"I take you for a drunkard, who might now know one from the other," Mustafa replied and then added, "My nephew says he is an Islamist, but he drinks against all the teachings of the Quran."

"You never have anything good to say..." the young man complained, dismissively waving an open palm. "Am I an old man like you? I need to live. And, by the way, I face Mecca every day and pray, three times a day. Do you? Of course, not. You don't even know where Mecca is! When was the last time you prayed? You cannot even remember, can you? And, yet, you lecture me about alcohol!"

"I don't need to constantly pray to prove my devotion to God," Mustafa replied. "Almighty Allah knows me and I worship him in my own way..."

"Formal prayer is required by the Quran, as you know." Muhammad pointed out. "Maybe, you are a Christian now? Have you converted?"

"What kind of stupid question is that?" Mustafa demanded.

"I can criticize you, also?" Muhammad replied. "Do you see?"

Mustafa said nothing but shook his head, frustrated, mumbling something under his breath that only he could hear. But, then, he spoke openly again.

"As you can see, my nephew is a disappointment," Mustafa said, "Thank Allah that his mother, rest her soul, is not alive to see this drunkenness. But, he has good qualities too. When he isn't drunk, he is a very good shot, for example. An excellent sniper. And, he has courage beyond that of most men. Believe it or not, he single-handedly attacked an entire group of Russian soldiers with nothing more than a Kalashnikov, killing all five. He was wounded himself, with injuries that would cripple most men. Yet, he returned to assist on another operation only a few weeks later."

Listening to his uncle praise his virtues as a soldier, the young Tatar man beamed with pride.

"That is why I drink." He claimed. "Because of the wounds. And, the pain..."

"You were an alcoholic long before that incident..." Mustafa pointed out.

"I would stop drinking now, if not for the pain..." Muhammad insisted. "So, this is the American?"

"Yes," Mustafa answered, "This is John Kovalenko."

"He doesn't look so impressive." Muhammad mused, saying it slowly, in case my Russian skills weren't good enough to understand him at full speed. He wanted me to hear his low opinion of me. "Why are you all making such a big deal out of him?"

"He will help us destroy the missile storehouse," Mustafa advised.

"We don't need him." the young man insisted, shaking his head. "We could easily do it ourselves."

"No, Muhammad," Mustafa corrected him. "You are wrong. The base is heavily defended. Surrounded by many kilometers of electronic sensors. We would be captured or killed if we tried. John spent years in the American Special Forces. He is an expert at high technology warfare…"

"You think this American is more blessed by Allah than we are?" Muhammad asked. "That he can do things that we cannot?"

"He has electronic countermeasures that can defeat the Russian detectors," Mustafa explained, "He has micro-drones that can clandestinely penetrate their bases from several kilometers away."

"Very impressive," Muhammad said, snidely. "But, I don't see the difference between Americans and Russians. If this American is so powerful, let him do whatever it is that he needs to do, himself…"

The comment merited a response, and I was on the verge of saying something, but my attention was momentarily diverted. A striking young woman – tall, slender, and dark-haired, appeared, emerging from the communal kitchen, which was nestled near the crackling fire pit. She approached us carrying a tray laden with glasses. Despite her delicate frame, her poise and adept handling of what had to be a heavy tray were remarkable.

She was a true Tatar beauty with subtly almond-shaped blue eyes that stood out in contrast to long, black silky hair that flowed over her shoulders. Her olive-toned skin was unblemished. The high cheekbones, ruby-red lips, and aquiline nose made her the portrait of perfection. Every feature harmonized with the next and she captivated me immediately. My heart might have been hardened by war, but her soft gaze melted it.

It didn't take her long to notice I was staring at her. Women have a way with such things. She averted her eyes, only to swiftly return them with a playful smile, meeting my gaze directly. This fleeting interaction lasted not more than a few seconds. The smile was gone almost as soon as it came. But, she continued to approach our table, her demeanor shifting to stoicism. Her expression was now a poker face concealing inner thoughts.

"Kompot?" she asked, putting down the tray. "Help yourselves."

"Thank you," I said, with an idiot's smile on my face, transfixed by her beauty.

"Kompot" is a homemade fruit beverage prepared by simmering fruit in water until the essence is extracted. The process reduces the fruit to a bland pulp. Its essence is transferred to the water. The drink is reminiscent of juice, particularly when sweetened with sugar. But, as tasty as it was, the kompot was obviously not what caught my attention or that of others. Because I was not the only one who saw her smile, which was fatefully unfortunate.

"She is very beautiful, yes?" Mustafa commented.

"Kok eye zavut?" I asked a Russian language question, which translates to "What is her name?"

"It's none of your business!" Muhammad snapped angrily.

But, Mustafa ignored him.

"She is called Yasmina," Mustafa answered, "Granddaughter of our deceased leader, Igor Fedorov and our current leader, his wife, Svetlana Fedorova."

"And, she is a devout Muslim!" Muhammad interjected loudly, speaking directly at me. "Which means she is not interested in you!"

With a look of burning rage, he fixed his eyes on me as if I had committed a grave sin. My mere inquiry as to the girl's name had provoked him. That slight trace of a smile, which had briefly graced her lips, had infuriated him. There was nothing I could do to change the fleeting moment of connection, nor did I have any desire to do so. Looking back, I doubt there was anything I could have done to appease his jealousy, short of immediately leaving Crimea.

In some bizarre way, however, I empathized. The girl obviously captivated him as she did me. We were both trapped by her beauty. I wasn't drunk or irrational, as he was, but I was smitten nonetheless. That said, I was not yet willing to admit it even to myself. I didn't yet understand the depth of my attraction to the girl. However, I readily understood his infatuation. That small gift of a smile had transformed Muhammad from a skeptic, unenthusiastic about both western culture and me, in particular, into a bitter adversary.

"What kind of talk is that, Muhammad?" Mustafa chided him.

"Yasmina is required to marry a Muslim man." Muhammad insisted. "That is Sharia law!"

I recognized, right away, that this resentment might jeopardize my mission and that it would be best to nip it in the bud. It seemed prudent to downplay the incident.

"I asked her name, nothing more," I said.

"Anyone can see what you want," he insisted. "It is in your eyes. Your intentions go beyond getting a name."

"John Kovalenko is our guest, Muhammad!" Mustafa reproached him. "You must treat him with respect."

"Why should I?" Muhammad blasted back. "He is a smug American, who travels the world, like other decadent westerners, seeking to play games with the women of poorer nations!"

"First of all, let us get one thing clear," I retorted, "My purpose here is to blow up a Russian missile warehouse. That's my only purpose. I am not here looking for a woman. I'm sworn to fight for the Ukrainian Foreign Legion and that's what I'm going to do. Accomplishing my mission is what you see in my eyes. The only thing. I assure you. There is nothing more. The rest is your imagination."

"You are a very bad liar!" he exclaimed. "It is obvious that you want her."

"Stop this nonsense, Muhammad," Mustafa interjected. "Yasmina is a grown woman. If she chooses to befriend this man, the choice is up to her, not you."

"No, it is not up to her!" Muhammad insisted, "And, it is not up to me, you, or this decadent American. It is up to the Almighty Allah. He forbids it!"

"So, in addition to being a drunkard, you are also a Prophet now? Who speaks for Allah?" Mustafa asked, dismissively.

"I speak for Sharia law, which is clear," Muhammad answered immediately.

"Does Allah forbid people from smiling or asking a name?" I asked.

"He forbids marriage between non-Muslim men and Muslim women!" Muhammad exclaimed. "So, keep your eyes off of her!"

"We are not living in Arabia," Mustafa replied. "We are a secular people. This man is our guest and he is not a polytheist, an idolater, or an atheist. He is a Christian, one of the people of the Book..."

Mustafa was making an assumption that, to be honest, was not entirely true. For most of my life, I have not considered myself a Christian. I am more of an agnostic. I believe, sometimes, that there is a God, but I've seen too much injustice to think that, even if He does exist, that He particularly cares what happens to us, individually. I've seen my best friends die in front of my eyes. Why would God allow that to happen? And, why would He let the Russians kill so many innocent people? Still, I appreciated Mustafa's attempt to defend me.

"There is no explicit prohibition in the Quran that says a Muslim woman cannot marry a man of the Book." Mustafa contended.

"The Sunnah and Hadith forbid it!" Muhammad argued.

"Interpretations by men who came after the Prophet." Mustafa stated, dismissively, "Some hadith imply that the Holy Prophet, himself, lusted after the wife of his son! Do you also believe that? We each must read the Quran, and reach our understanding of it, knowing the people involved. We Tatari are a modern people. And, soon, Ukraine will be inside the European Union. Will we join Europe by returning to the dark ages?"

"Why should we join with infidels in Europe?" Muhammad asked. "Idolaters, no better than Moskali, allies of the Great Satan. Supporters of homosexuality and sin. Insulting Almighty Allah with their twisted laws and culture. No, we don't need Europe. We need only ourselves. Our task is to bring about a worldwide Caliphate!"

To be perfectly honest, I've never read the Quran, the Sunnah, or the Hadith. I probably never will. Nor do I really care what they say. I did not understand anything they were discussing. I knew only that Mustafa's arguments and explanations were getting him exactly nowhere. That was probably because no logical argument would ever soothe his troubled nephew's injured pride.

His anger didn't arise out of true religious offense, but from unrequited affection for Yasmina. She had no interest in him. In fact, as I would later learn, she despised him. My presence reminded him of that. It didn't mean that Yasmina wanted to be with me. But, it did tell him, in no uncertain terms, that she didn't want to be with him. For that reason, Mustafa's attempt at giving a civics lesson fell flat. It only served to increase Muhammad's envy, anger, and frustration. It made him think more about his inadequacy.

"You are keeping company with the wrong people!" Mustafa exclaimed in frustration. "That Imam is one of them. Stop parroting his words. You are making me embarrassed that you are my sister's son. If she were still here, she would set you straight!"

"If she were here, she would agree with me!" the young man countered. "It should embarrass YOU to keep company with infidels!"

Mustafa was quickly losing his patience.

"Such loyalty to the Faith by a p'yanitsa!" he replied sarcastically.

The word "p'yanitsa" has no direct English equivalent. Such a person is not only addicted to alcohol, like an alcoholic, but is always drunk and out of control of himself at all times. The remark simply slid off his nephew's alcohol-fueled Teflon coating, as the young man paid no attention.

"Let there be no doubt that the Caliphate will be restored!" his nephew proclaimed, repeating the words his local preacher had been saying daily. "Sharia will return to the land. And, in Almighty Allah's holy name, all will be bound to the Quran, the Hadith, and the Sura. Infidels and evildoers, alike, will be punished. It is only a matter of time!"

Mustafa responded to his nephew's proclamations with a derisive snort.

"You and your so-called 'Islamist' friends speak a lot about this supposed Caliphate," he replied, his tone laced with skepticism, "But, where is your 'Caliph'? When he arrives, let me know. But, until then, we fight for Ukraine's right to exist. Our ultimate goal is and always will be to join the free nations of the world. That means joining the EU."

The conversation had reached a stalemate, with neither of them willing to concede. Muhammad, his anger and intoxication clear, abruptly stood up and grasped his bottle of vodka. He took another swig and stormed away. The tension was palpable as he exited, leaving an uncomfortable silence in his wake.

Mustafa's voice became low and apologetic.

"I apologize for my nephew's terrible behavior," he said, his eyes conveying a mix of embarrassment and concern. "He is drunk."

I tried to reassure him with a calm and understanding response.

"Don't worry," I replied, "I don't take it personally."

But, Mustafa felt he needed to say more.

"He was not always like this," Mustafa explained. "He drinks more and more these days. And, he is also under the influence of an Islamist Imam."

"Mostly, I think, he is simply fixated on that girl..." I said, smiling.

"You may be correct." Mustafa agreed. "He has admired Yasmina from afar for many years. But, she has never had any interest, and I doubt that she ever will. Not, at least, until he reforms himself. You can see how beautiful she has become, can you not?"

"I'm not blind," I admitted. There was no use in lying about it.

"She is a practical girl," Mustafa added, "and has no use for men addicted to the bottle. And, of course, no time for fools who dream about Caliphates. She is only 21 but possesses the mind of a much older woman. She does not smile often or easily."

So, there it was. Mustafa had also noticed the smile. Was it that obvious? It lasted no more than a second, yet it seemed that everyone had seen it.

"How did she come to be a partisan?" I asked.

He shrugged his shoulders.

"Her grandmother didn't want her to be," He said, "She tried everything she could to stop it from happening."

"Her grandmother is Svetlana, the same woman you said is the leader of this partisan cell?"

"Yes," he replied.

"She doesn't want her involved?" I asked.

He shook his head.

"No," he explained. "Too dangerous."

"But, not for her?" I asked.

"Of course," he replied, "Svetlana doesn't care whether she lives or dies anymore, but she cares about Yasmina."

"How is it, then, that Yasmina became a partisan?" I asked.

"It is a long story," he said, shaking his head in dismay.

"The girl has suffered much..." Mustafa continued. "She was born in Russia, where her father and mother lived for several years. But, her father was drafted into the Russian army and sent to Chechnya. He died, and her mother died of grief shortly afterward. She was brought to Crimea by her grandmother when she was still a baby. And, now, Yasmina is very much like her grandmother was as a young woman. Very stubborn, for example..."

"But, my question was how did she become a partisan if her grandmother didn't want her to?" I asked.

"Her grandfather, grandmother, and I...we did everything we could do to hide the fact that we were partisans," He said, "But, as I told you, Yasmina is stubborn. She's also smart. She discovered we were fighting the Orcs and insisted on becoming a partisan fighter. Eventually, we had no choice but to accept her."

While Ukrainians often use the pejoratives "Moskali" or "Rashisti" (meaning Russian fascists) to refer to Russia's leadership, they creatively call common Russian soldiers, lower-ranking officers at the front line, and lower-level occupation forces "Orcs." This nickname is derived from J.R.R. Tolkien's "The Lord of the Rings," where Orcs are a genetically altered, degenerate species created by the dark lord Sauron.

I couldn't help but wonder if such a delicate flower, regardless of how dedicated she might be, had actually seen combat against those Orcs.

"She's been on a mission, then?" I asked.

He nodded and said,

"Yes. More than one."

"Hand-to-hand combat?" I asked.

He nodded again.

"She is a fierce fighter for a woman." He noted.

"I wouldn't have imagined that," I replied. "She looks so delicate..."

"She IS delicate," he agreed, "but also a fierce fighter!"

That made no sense. The two features couldn't exist together in one person. Not in my mind, anyway. But, I didn't want to argue. I simply wanted more information.

"Tell me about Svetlana..." I said.

"Well, let's see," Mustafa said, "Svetlana Fedorova is the widow of Igor, our deceased leader. When Igor died, our group would have died too, but she kept it alive, even while she grieved. We follow her as we once followed her husband. Some refuse to admit it. My nephew, for example. But, it is true."

"Interesting..." I mumbled.

"You will meet her any minute now." He said with enthusiasm.

"Anything more you can tell me before I meet her?" I asked.

"Well," he asked, and then thought of something, "Here is something...Igor, like Sasha, was a half-Russian."

Mustafa detected my surprise from my expression.

"Surprising, yes?" Mustafa said, "Didn't you notice? The name Fedorov is Russian. Igor's father was an apparatchik in the old Soviet Union. Secretly, he embraced Islam when he married Yasmina's great-grandmother. That's Sharia law, as my nephew pointed out earlier. In those days, it was followed more closely than today. So, he had to become Muslim. Yasmina's blue eyes come from her Slavic heritage."

"Hmm," I said, "maybe, the combination is what makes her so beautiful..."

After I uttered those words, I was immediately sorry. Mustafa looked at me carefully, sizing me up.

"I think you *are* interested in our lovely Yasmina..." he mused.

I shook my head.

"No, no," I insisted. "I'm only curious. I can see, though, that she's very attractive. I was just wondering about the reason. It's purely academic interest..."

But, the old man was too canny to let my pitiful attempt at denial fool him.

"I see," he said, suspiciously, "Well, let me tell you, if you want to marry Yasmina, you must first get permission from her grandmother, as she has no male guardian."

I put up my open hands and shook my head.

"I'm here to complete a mission. Nothing more."

My desperation to convince him came from the desire to convince myself. It was technically true. I certainly wasn't considering marrying anyone I hardly knew. I also couldn't afford romance under the circumstances. Furthermore, I had a job to do. The way these traditional Tatars equated romance immediately with marriage differed greatly from the way Americans see things. Marrying her was out of the question in my mind at the time.

I admit there was a contradiction inside me. I had come to war partly because I was depressed at the fact that I had no wife or children. But, I'd been a bachelor for 42 years. I liked the freedom. I didn't consciously want it to change. A temporary love affair was one thing. But, marriage? That was quite another. But, even a temporary fling would interfere with my mission.

Yet, the desire continued to build. In some respects, Muhammad was right. My fascination with the girl began the moment I saw her, even before she'd smiled at me. But, now, I was hooked. No amount of denial, self-coaxing, or self-hypnosis would help. I was as deeply infatuated with Yasmina as he was. I was simply less honest about it. I refused to admit it even to myself. Her image consumed my thoughts. I couldn't get her out of my mind.

The fact that I hadn't been with a woman for months might have played a part. Maybe, I should have heeded General Rutanov's suggestion about the River Palace whorehouse. If I'd gotten that out of my system, it would have been easier to resist temptation. But, that opportunity was closed and I think it wouldn't have helped anyway. Physical desire was part of it, but my infatuation went deeper than lust alone.

These thoughts ended abruptly with the appearance of an elderly woman, who emerged from the same kitchen that Yasmina had just come out of. She also walked toward us balancing a heavy tray, but this one was laden with chebureki, a renowned fried meat turnover, created by the Crimean Tatars, and now enjoyed all over Ukraine. The fragrant smell, a combination of minced meat, onions, and spices and the scent filled the air.

I began to realize how much trouble was being taken on my behalf. This fine dinner was being painstakingly prepared, with appetizers and more to come. The occasion was far more significant to them than to me. This was more than a mere meal—it was a joyous celebration—a warm embrace of Western culture and assistance, which I represented to them. But, more to the point, it was my first glimpse of Svetlana Yurievna Fedorova.

She was tall and elderly, standing about 5'8", or just shy of 173 cm, just a little bit shorter than her 5'9" or 175 cm tall granddaughter. Her kindly brown eyes peered through wire-rimmed glasses, set in a wrinkled face marked by deep furrows between thick dark eyebrows, with a few flecks of gray. Those wrinkles told a story. They had been formed from years of worry and hardship. Her gray hair was neatly styled in a bun. Though acting as a server, she approached us with an unmistakable air of authority.

When she was reaching the table, she set down the platter and took her seat at its head. She held no official position of power within the group—save perhaps that of "universal grandmother"—but her demeanor spoke volumes about her de facto authority. In Tatar culture, men eagerly remind you that women are "just women." Matters of war are traditionally a male domain. But, Svetlana effortlessly assumed her role. As I would later discover, her status stemmed not merely from being the widow of their fallen leader, but from her own charisma. As with General Rutanov, her presence was enough to command respect. She was born for the job.

She looked me over, for a moment, and spoke, introducing herself.

"I am Sveta," she said, simply, using the informal version of her name.

"My name is John," I replied, offering my hand across the corner of the table.

She looked, for a moment, at my hand, but didn't take it right away. She simply stared at it like a curiosity. Reaching out without reciprocation felt awkward. But, then, she suddenly took my hand in her own and shook it enthusiastically.

"It is the custom, in America, for men and women to shake hands," Mustafa offered his wisdom.

"Yes," she said. "I know..."

"You must excuse me, John," Svetlana said, "For us, handshakes are normally between men."

"I'm sorry for making you feel uncomfortable..." I said.

"No!" Svetlana insisted. "It is I who should be sorry..."

"In America," I confessed, "we like to downplay the differences between the sexes. In the last 50 years or so, everybody has started shaking hands, regardless of sex."

"That is interesting," Svetlana said, "Here, we celebrate the differences between the sexes. But, both concepts are equally valid. I was simply taken by surprise. Shaking hands is a good custom. I like it. There are many things I like about America. I also like English. My granddaughter speaks it. I was never able to learn because, I think, I started too old. But, I am surprised you speak such good Russian. They told me that few Americans can. You also have a Ukrainian surname, which interests me."

"My ancestors, on my father's side, were Ukrainian." I explained. "They immigrated to America in the late 19th century, fleeing the Russian Tsar."

"Many Tatari also fled the Tsars," she commented. "Only the foolish ones, who loved this land more than they loved themselves, stayed. We are their descendants, and as such, we continue to be fools, living in this land under Moskali rule."

She smiled at her own words, which amused her, turning to Mustafa, and pointing him toward the fire pit.

"You must check on the shashlik, Mustafa..." she advised. "It should be ready by now."

He looked at me for a moment, smiled, patted me on the back and left the table, trotting off to his new assignment. She began speaking again, but now our discussion had become purposefully private.

"I am told you are a mighty warrior."

"Who told you that?" I replied.

"Our contact people inside the Ukrainian armed forces," she stated.

"I prefer to think of myself as a man fighting for principles."

"But, that makes you a warrior, does it not?" she concluded.

"Yes, I suppose so."

"We are also warriors," she said.

I nodded.

"That's why I've come to you," I said. "to get your help..."

"We will help, of course," she confirmed. "It was arranged before you arrived."

"Good," I said.

There was a moment of silence, and then she continued talking.

"But, I have some questions..." She said.

"Ask me whatever you want," I responded.

"Why do you fight in a war that is not your own?" She asked.

I paused briefly, carefully considering my response. Despite my fluency in Russian, I am not a native speaker, and it can be challenging to express myself precisely on sensitive topics. This being my first encounter with the partisan leader, I was particularly keen on carefully choosing my words.

"Because Russia must be defeated," I answered. "Putin's government is a new type of tyranny. A national government entirely based on mafia principles, coupled with fascism. It is a cancer. It'll consume every bit of decency in the world if it's allowed to metastasize."

"That is an idealistic exaggeration," she stated, "Putin is a common dictator who enriches himself and his friends at the expense of his people. Nothing more. All dictators are criminals. But, I agree that the Moskali are particularly bad. Still, compared to America, Russia is very weak. It cannot seriously threaten you. So, why do you even care?"

"It has the largest stockpile of nuclear bombs in the world," I said.

"And, if it were to use those weapons, the result would be its own destruction." she countered.

"Good point." I admitted, "But, if Putin absorbs Ukraine, he will add its human talent and physical resources to make Russia much more powerful. The new Empire will pose a very serious threat to my country."

"Perhaps…" She agreed, and moved on to something else, "Did you know that 'Atesh' is a Tatari word?"

I shook my head. I knew the partisans called themselves the "Atesh". But, that was all.

"It means fire," she said.

I nodded,

"That's interesting," I commented.

"We are the fire that burns the Moskali bear." She proclaimed. "Our goal is to make it whimper in pain as it runs back to Moscow. They stole this land from our ancestors, long ago, and have sought to exterminate us ever since. But, we are determined to free ourselves. We will be a nation within Ukraine. We will be free of the Rusiski occupation."

"Rusiski" is a common pejorative used by Ukrainians to refer to Russians. It means Russian fascists.

"Mustafa tells me your husband was half-Russian…"

"His father was a member of the Communist party," She replied, "but Igor was Tatari. He was born Tatari, and died Tatari. Not because of genes, although his mother was full-blooded Tatari, but because he chose to be what he was. Do you know the solemn oath Igor took?"

I shook my head.

"It is the same oath every partisan takes, no matter that his father or mother happened to possess Russian genes. Each of us pledges our lives and worldly goods to an unending war upon the Moskali."

"They have done terrible things, intentionally targeting civilians," I pointed out.

"You point out only the most recent evil deeds," She agreed, "But, we make war against them, not because they're evil, but because they make war against us. This war has continued for hundreds of years, long before Putin. Their goal is to wipe us out."

"I've studied a bit about Crimean history," I said, "What Russia has done to the Tartars is terrible."

"They don't fear Allah Almighty, unfortunately," She replied. "But, they do fear America. They fear you very much."

"For now…" I cautioned.

But, she continued, unwilling to leave the question of why I had fought for Ukraine until it was answered to her satisfaction.

"And, because your enemies fear you, your nation is peaceful and prosperous," she continued, "The Moskali don't dare to attack you. Yet, you chose to fight for our land, a nation filled with hardship and suffering. Why?"

"War is just something I know how to do," I explained. "It's what I trained for. My skills are useful to Ukraine. Fighting for Ukraine was the right thing at the right time."

"What about your wife? Children?"

"I don't have any." I conceded.

"You are certainly old enough." She countered.

"Yes," I replied. "But things didn't work out that way, at least not yet. I don't want to sound egotistical, but I believe destiny moves me. It calls me, compels me, and gives me a reason for being."

"You're a holy warrior, then?" she asked.

"Not holy," I said. "Just a warrior."

"What if you have no children and are killed?" She asked. "Your line will end."

"Maybe," I explained, "I won't go willingly to my death, but death will take me someday, whether I am willing or not. I could hide, but it would find me anyway. Yet, if I am not meant to die, I won't die. When the day comes, it won't matter where I am or what I do. That is what I believe."

I had explained my philosophy before, but never with as much conviction as I felt then. It must have made some impression on her because she stayed silent for a moment. After that moment, she nodded and continued speaking.

"I think I understand you," she said. "My husband believed as you do."

"So, I'm not so strange after all, and I..."

She interrupted me.

"But, he is dead now."

There was another short instance of silence.

"I'm sorry," I said, finally.

She stood up from the table and smiled.

"There is no need for sympathy," she said. "I am proud of my husband and the way he died. He was a great man and a martyr, a hero of his people."

"I understand," I replied.

"You surprise me, John, and I like you," she said, with complete directness. "Tonight, we will eat, drink, and be merry. None, save Almighty Allah, himself, knows what tomorrow will bring. You are welcome here!"

"Thank you."

The old woman rose and turned abruptly, walking back to the kitchen, having said what she came to say. Meanwhile, Mustafa arrived shortly thereafter, carrying a huge plate, piled high with roasted meat.

"She is impressive, is she not?" He said.

I nodded, "Yes, she is."

"The meat is cooked to perfection!" Mustafa insisted, spearing a few pieces and depositing them in my plate without asking. "Try!"

Then, he set the plate down, on the table, and sat down next to me, taking a few pieces for himself, biting in and savoring the taste. I took my fork, speared a piece of meat and tasted it. It was delicately spiced with garlic, pepper, possibly ginger, and some other ingredients I couldn't identify. Subtly different from the shashlik that Mustafa had made in the cave, and very different from what I had enjoyed in other parts of Ukraine. He was right. It was delicious.

"You like?" Mustafa asked, eagerly.

I nodded.

"Eat more!" he insisted.

I hesitated.

"I will eat more," I said, "but I'll wait for the others."

"Ah," he stated, dismissively, "There is plenty for everyone..."

Meanwhile, the old Tatar woman came out of her kitchen, again, this time grabbing a large brass bell hanging just outside. Holding the bell in her weathered hand, she rang it loud and clear. The clanging cut through the bone-dry air, a signal to everyone that the meal was about to begin. Organized meals were important occasions, not to be missed. They were rare moments of order, enjoyment, and camaraderie.

She rang it again and again, harder and louder, each time, to make sure it was heard. In obedience to the bell, people arrived, one by one, taking places at the long, well-worn dining table. Sasha arrived first. He sat down across from Mustafa. Following him were two partisans I had not met. Finally, Mustafa's alcoholic nephew, Muhammad staggered in, bottle in hand. In all, about 13 people arrived for the meal.

I didn't know it at the time, but this gathering was very rare and unusual. Few partisans stayed at the rest complex at any one time, because having too many there, too often, might attract unwanted attention. But, many of the partisans believed my arrival signaled the direct involvement of the government of the United States of America. It wasn't true, of course. I was nothing more than a volunteer working for the Ukrainian military, without any formal connection to my government.

Yet, for them, I represented hope for active assistance from the great western democracy known as America. Hope, even when misplaced, is a valuable military asset without which victories are impossible. Nations that lose hope don't last long. With hope, anything is possible. Hopeful people can win wars against all odds. My arrival had ignited a spark of hope among the partisans. As a wise leader, even though she knew exactly who I was and what I represented, Svetlana Fedorova was happy to allow this hope to grow.

The aroma of freshly roasted shashlik and fried chebureki, among other Crimean Tatar delicacies, continued to dominate the air. The tall graceful elderly woman moved from table to table like a mother feeding many children, even as her even taller, and very beautiful granddaughter, Yasmina, assisted her, helping with every task. They traveled back and forth from the kitchen, carrying plates piled high. As Yasmina passed me, she once again met my gaze with a smile and this time, even though it was still fleeting, it was even longer than before.

There were plenty of refreshments. Mostly pitchers filled with kompot of different flavors, made from various fruits, were strategically placed around the table. Alcohol was not officially served or sanctioned, but Muhammad, sitting several seats away from me, clung to a new bottle of vodka. Tatar customs are far more liberal about many things, including alcohol, than Islamic people elsewhere in the world. Consumption of beer and wine is common. Muhammad's alcoholism was frowned upon, but because he had proven himself to be a fierce fighter, it was tolerated. No one, save his uncle, ever criticized him.

"Try the chebureki, my American friend," Mustafa urged, as the plate was handed, from person to person, around the table. "They're always delicious, and Sveta's are better than most."

I took a bite.

"What do you think?" Mustafa asked, eagerly.

"Delicious!" I exclaimed, and it was.

"I told you!" Mustafa said, proudly. "Do you have anything so delicious in America? Tell the others, when you return, about our meat pies!"

"Did I tell you that I used to sell fried chebureki in the central market in Novorossiysk?" Sasha began, as he started to eat a meat pie.

"That is one story you never told me," Mustafa commented. "You said you were a smuggler."

"I was." Sasha insisted.

Mustafa laughed.

"What kind of smuggler fries meat pies on the side?"

"Are you so old that your memory is sclerotic, Mustafa?" Sasha said, with a smile. "You don't remember the 1990s?"

"I remember," said Mustafa.

"Then, you remember the bread lines and the ration tickets?"

"Of course."

Sasha had turned very serious in remembering the hardships of the past. He redirected his attention toward me, assuming, I suppose, that I knew nothing about the bad times after the fall of the Soviet Union. He was mostly right. I knew something about those days, the rampant hyperinflation people suffered, and the lack of basic necessities, but not a lot.

"It was a terrible time," he explained, "right after the Soviet Union collapsed. The Communist system was bad, but it was the system, and when it collapsed, everything fell apart. There was no money. The ruble devalued to nearly zero. There was no food. Only ration tickets. It was difficult, sometimes impossible, to find a job. And, I had just graduated from a University..."

He turned back to Mustafa.

"You probably also don't know that I have a Master's degree in electrical engineering, do you?"

Mustafa shook his head.

"I knew you had some kind of fancy degree with that big brain of yours..." he replied.

Sasha turned back and continued his autobiography.

"I searched everywhere. The only job I could find was frying meat pies. It had some perks. I got to take home what we couldn't sell. Maybe, it saved us from starving? Who knows?"

He returned his attention to Mustafa.

"So, yes, I was frying pies in the central market..."

Then, back to me,

"My boss was always bribing the food inspectors," he explained. "They'd have closed us down otherwise. We had cockroaches and we violated every health code. They should have closed us down, but he paid them. I realized then that you could bribe any public official. Well, smuggling was a lot more profitable than frying pies. So, I and a couple of my friends started to bring in cheap goods from Ukraine to Russia and from Russia to Ukraine, without paying the tax. Wherever it was cheaper, which was usually Ukraine, we bought stuff. Wherever things were more expensive, usually because of the tax, we sold stuff."

"Did you make much money?" I asked.

"We made a huge amount of money!" Sasha confirmed.

"But, you stopped..." I noted.

"I did."

"Why?"

"Partly because, unlike what Mustafa likes to say, I don't like being a criminal. But, also, because the inspectors got too greedy. They started to demand such big bribes that our profits disappeared. Thankfully, I got lucky."

"How so?" I asked.

"I stumbled upon a discarded notebook PC in the trash of a mini-oligarch who owned a small chain of convenience stores," he recounted. "Back then, personal computers were a rarity. I salvaged the device, disassembled it, and discovered it was really just a simple issue – a broken power input. All it took was a bit of soldering. I fixed it. That was the turning point. I downloaded lots of pirated books on modern programming languages and web design, and taught myself everything I needed to know. And, I transformed myself from a smuggler into an IT specialist. The rest, as they say, is history."

"Rags to riches..." Mustafa interjected with a smile. "I've heard the latter part many times, but the meat pie salesman part is a first!"

"That's because you never paid attention," Sasha retorted.

Sasha's narrative gave me a valuable insight into the struggle of individuals at the fall of the former Soviet Union. The level of desperation must have been extreme. He said that he made lots of money smuggling. But, if smuggling was so lucrative, why did he need to scavenge through an oligarch's trash? Either his account was embellished, or his perception differed dramatically from mine. There was no point in pursuing the matter. He was sharing sensitive subjects with me. I wasn't going to ruin things by challenging him on inconsistencies.

Privately, I wondered about the desperation. Apparently, the desire and need for money outweighed everything, including the humiliation that would have come from being arrested. That was true not only for the smugglers, like Sasha, but also for the corrupt officials. Any of them could have been prosecuted. That, to me, would have been humiliation. Honor besmirched. Dignity destroyed. But, for them, it apparently didn't matter much. Then, again, I suppose, the prosecutors and judges were also corrupt. If they did get caught, they could just buy their way out. At any rate, it was an emotionally driven story and I felt compelled to acknowledge it.

"You've been on a truly incredible journey," I remarked, as diplomatically as I could. "And, you turned adversity into opportunity by being smart!"

His face lit up, very pleased with the way I had just described things and, by extension, with me.

"Yes, and a lot of other people have amazing stories too," he said, proudly. "Some even more clever than mine. Those were difficult years, unless you had your wits about you. But, if you did, you could survive."

"I don't have any amazing stories," Mustafa confessed, "I also suffered through the bread lines and the ration tickets, of course. And, the Weights & Measures Institute, my employer, went bankrupt, but I found work elsewhere."

"Eh, it's not true," Sasha waved his hand dismissively, "He has a lot of stories to tell. Just not the ones about being desperate for work…"

"Maybe," Mustafa agreed, a trademark smile forming amid the craggy lines of his wizened old face, but Sasha interrupted him.

"According to Mustafa," He now imitated the voice of his much older friend, "a man who knows how to fix a toilet will never starve…"

Mustafa smiled at that.

"I could not have said it better myself." He agreed, nodding wholeheartedly, "And, I know how to fix them, better than most!"

"He's very proud of his plumbing," Sasha said with a smile. "In the afterlife, Mustafa will fix toilets for the dead. I am sure of it!"

"If heaven is in need of a plumber, Allah be praised, I will be ready!" Mustafa said, slyly. "But, I can tell you about when I served as a Soviet helicopter pilot…"

"Not again…" Sasha pleaded. "Spare our American friend, please!"

"Mustafa and I worked for the Weight & Measures Institute, before and after it was privatized." a woman's voice interrupted, from behind.

I looked around and saw Svetlana Fedorova again. She took her seat at the head of the table, one seat away from me.

"Igor, Sveta, and I, we all worked there," Mustafa said with a sigh, "But, it was a long time ago…"

"So, you've both been in Crimea a very long time," I said, "I thought the Tatars were exiled to Uzbekistan and places like that…".

"Yes," Mustafa agreed, "but many families began to return during the 1980s, with Gorbachev and Perestroika. My family returned even before that, in 1975. Sveta's family came a year later. She met Igor very quickly, but she can tell you more about…"

"To this day, the Moskali believe that Igor was unquestionably loyal." Svetlana confided, "Of course, they did not know him. His father was a Soviet apparatchik, but he chose to be a secret Muslim and part of the Tatari people. The Moskali government doesn't know how Igor died, or that he took six Russian soldiers to their graves with him. But, enough of that. It is time!"

She stood, suddenly, walked over to the bell again, and began ringing it to get everyone's attention. The chatter slowly died down. Finally, there was silence.

"Fighters for freedom," she said, loudly, "We endure, in the name of Allah, Almighty, to fight the Moskali scourge. Many of us, including my husband, Igor, have been martyred. They watch us now, from heaven, above. A few days ago, we celebrated the end of Ramadan, during which we remembered the sacrifices of our martyrs. And, now, we celebrate again, for a stranger has come into our midst. He is from a far-off but powerful land. He comes with a purpose. Like us, he is pledged to fight for the rightful government of Crimea. He is charged with a mission, as we are. Warriors, will we lend this man our assistance?"

There was an outcry of support. Loud cheers. Clapping. Cups clanging against the table. Then, after a moment of excitement, she held up an open palm. The clapping and cheering began to die down and she continued.

"The Moskali believe they frighten us," she continued, "but do we fear them?"

"No!" came the uniform cry from the table.

"Indeed, the Prophet, himself, was a warrior," she said. "And Allah called upon him to fight, just as He calls upon us now. Like the Prophet, we shall be kind, helpful and spare no effort to assist our friends. But, to our enemies…to the Moskali occupiers, what shall we do?"

"Burn them!" Came the uniform cry, "Fire!"

Cheers and claps came from the table, and when it died down again, she continued.

"They have tried to destroy us for many years," she said with intensity. "But, I say we will prevail and destroy them in the end. This American will help us! Give thanks to Allah, Almighty, who gives us this food and drink, and whose divine intervention has brought him here!"

In response, the clapping and the cheering resumed, louder than before.

The partisans were fighting a desperate guerrilla war in the shadows. By day, they might be IT specialists, salesmen, doctors, bakers or serve in many other professions. But, underneath the compliant exterior, they were ready to kill. More toasts and announcements were made by various other people but, then, the festive mood was interrupted.

"Let us not be fools!" Muhammad exclaimed, loudly, attracting everyone's attention. "Do none wonder why this man comes, supposedly to fight our battles for us? He who has no roots in our soil? We are Tatari and Muslims! We fight for our land and our people. But, what does he fight for? Why is he here? We must ask ourselves this!"

I could see that Svetlana was about to shut him up. But, it was incumbent upon me to stand and address the challenge. Before she had the chance to silence him. I stood, steady and calm, meeting his hostile gaze with a determination.

"I'm here to fight tyranny by the side of the Tatari people," I said, "It doesn't matter what soil the fight is upon. It is the same fight. A fight for freedom and justice! If I can lend a hand to those fighting for it, then that's where I want to be. That is why I am here."

The other partisans listened intently, their eyes darting between Muhammad and me. As Muhammad stared back, his gaze hardened. While some people become cheerful when drunk, alcohol served to unleash Muhammad's darker side. It brought forth a more aggressive and malicious version of himself. And, he wasn't very nice to begin with. But, years of heavy drinking had honed his ability to articulate clearly even while intoxicated. My calm yet pointed response clearly agitated him. He had expected—and perhaps hoped for—a different reaction altogether.

"Fancy words!" He barked, "But, let no one forget that he is an infidel, a nonbeliever! No matter how smooth his words are, he does not understand our fight, or how it intertwines with our faith..."

"I respect all faiths, including yours," I replied, my voice steady. "In fact, there are many Christian Ukrainians who support your fight too. You fight by their side and they by yours. Is this not so? A man's values are defined by the actions he takes. That is why I have come. To take action. For Ukraine!"

The atmosphere had become tense. Some partisans exchanged glances and whispers. That's when Sasha joined the conversation.

"You are misled, Muhammad." He said. "Our fight is not about faith. It is about identity. Am I not a freedom fighter? Am I not a partisan? Are my deeds forgotten? Yet, I have been baptized as a Christian. We are a nation, not a religion, Muhammad. John Kovalenko has already risked his life just by coming here. And, he will risk it again when, with our help, we destroy that missile storage bunker. He's already fought the Moskali up north, and he will fight them here. He fights for Ukraine, and for the Tatari. It is one cause and one fight. That is enough for me!"

His words made a strong impression on everyone, and I heard murmurs of approval spreading all around. But, Muhammad wasn't done.

"Maybe, Sasha, it is enough for you," Muhammad replied. "You are a Christian and I admit that we have fought together like brothers nonetheless. But, this man is not even a Ukrainian. Not a Muslim. Not a Tatar. Just an adventurer, nothing more. He stumbled upon our fight and wants to bring his foreign influence into it. Are these the people who will replace the Moskali? Americans? People who marry men to other men. Those who encourage homosexuality and sin? Those who follow the Great Satan?"

Another partisan interjected, "It's not true. Many Americans say they don't support such things. Besides, once we've defeated the Moskali, we can reject any of their ideas that contradict our Faith..."

"Can we?" Muhammad challenged. "Really? Do you think that? By then, mercenaries, like this one, will control everything. He has nothing to offer us!"

"That's a lie!" I snapped, my anger rising. "I'm no mercenary. Fighting for Ukraine has not earned me money. It's cost me money. I've purchased most of my own equipment out of pocket. I came here because I believe in freedom."

Muhammad quickly countered, his voice laced with contempt.

"Yet you speak the language of the Moskali, and not a word of Tatari!" He jabbed a finger accusingly. "That says it all, right there. You are a tourist with a gun!"

"Enough, Muhammad!" Svetlana finally cut in. "You're embarrassing everyone. This man is our guest."

But, attention was fixed, now, on the banter between him and me.

"It is true that I don't speak Tatari," I said, sincerely, trying to defuse the situation, "I've never had an opportunity to learn. But, I respect the Tatari and even your personal commitment to the cause, despite all you have said, today. All I ask is that you respect mine. We need unity, not division. Otherwise, we will never achieve our goals."

Muhammad laughed dismissively.

"Ha!" he scoffed, "What goals do we have in common?"

"Destroying the Russian missile storage warehouse, for one," I replied.

"That is YOUR goal," he retorted. "The Moskali don't use missiles against Crimea. All your so-called mission will accomplish for us is to invite retaliation! Every Russian soldier will be hunting us. It will no longer be possible to hold large gatherings like this one."

I had to concede, to myself, that his observation had some validity. The Russians would undoubtedly realize that my operation had local assistance and they'd intensify their pursuit of the partisans. But, there were ways around that, and the overall benefit justified the cost. If need be, the partisans could be relocated out of Crimea.

Thankfully, the unpleasant exchange wasn't going to continue much longer. The others were losing patience with him. Tatar custom includes being gracious to guests, and most of them were fed up with his behavior.

"You speak like a coward, Muhammad!" Sasha exclaimed, "Are you now afraid of the Moskali?"

Before he could respond, however, his uncle Mustafa, who had earlier criticized his nephew, came to his defense.

"My nephew is no coward," he rebuked Sasha. "He is simply drunk and speaks nonsense due to the devil's brew! The Prophet warned against alcohol. It brings foolishness. Sit down, Muhammad, and be quiet!"

"I won't be quiet!" Muhammad snapped, "You are all misled. I say what needs to be said!"

"Your uncle is right," I said, dismissively, "You are drunk and there's no basis for anything you've said. You claim to fight for your religious beliefs and say I don't understand, but then you claim that attacking a Russian warehouse is too risky because, afterward, you will be hunted and won't be able to attend fancy dinners! Which is it, then? Do you want to fight the Russians, or run away?"

"I want to fight them without mercenaries like you!" came the quick answer.

In some ways, the man amazed me. He spoke eloquently, in the face of drunkenness, but was filled with anger and resentment, none of which had anything to do with the issues he raised. His arguments were conflicting and, as a result, they were easy to refute. But, he wasn't finished yet. He was about to discredit himself completely.

"Fine." I replied. "You fight in whatever way you choose. But, everyone else knows I can help."

"You think you're better than we are," he complained. "You think that, because you are an American and speak English, you can steal our women!"

I shook my head with a smile.

"It's back to that, again, is it?" I said. "This fight is bigger than your personal jealousies, Muhammad. Put aside that pettiness and work for the greater good."

Mustafa rose abruptly, not waiting for Muhammad's response. He lifted his glass of kompot high, his voice ringing out with determination.

"To the destruction of the Moskali missiles!" he proclaimed.

A chorus of cheers erupted from the partisans. I raised my glass, clinking it against Mustafa's and as many others as I could reach. We all drank deeply—all except Muhammad.

"We stand with you, John Kovalenko!" Mustafa declared, hoisting his glass once more and taking another long swig.

In a show of solidarity, the other partisans began a rhythmic chant:

"Kovalenko! Kovalenko! Kovalenko!"

Muhammad's reacted badly to the chant. He hurled his glass to the floor, shattering it, and stormed away from the table. Yasmina, who had been observing from just outside the communal kitchen doorway, rushed in to clean up the mess. The chanting faded away and I turned to face Mustafa.

"Thank you for your support," I said sincerely, happy that Muhammad was gone.

Mustafa lowered his voice and spoke directly.

"I ask, again, for your forgiveness. Please ignore my nephew when he is drunk."

I nodded.

But Svetlana interjected quietly.

"He cannot be ignored, Mustafa," She insisted, "He has contributed much in the past. But his words are outrageous and he has insulted an honored guest. Keep a close eye on him..."

"He is merely drunk," Mustafa said. "By tomorrow, he won't remember what he said tonight."

Svetlana shook her head.

"Perhaps," she said, concerned, "but I think this goes deeper. He is dangerously unstable. Even if he had such misgivings, they should have been expressed privately."

Mustafa shook his head.

"No," Mustafa replied, "he is just drunk. He doesn't know what he's saying."

"If it continues," she pointed out, "something will have to be done..."

Then she turned to me and added,

"Keep your door locked tonight."

"Of course," I replied, with a short laugh. "I always do."

The group immediately forgot the unpleasant moments and they returned to the serious business of enjoying dinner. The meal ended on a delicious note with a dessert of baklava, but the atmosphere and merriment continued for a while longer. Eventually, the people filtered out and retired to their cabins, and I did the same.

My bungalow was a simple place, just like all the others. The bed was small and narrow, but it wasn't uncomfortable. I'd slept much worse, but I still couldn't go to sleep. Too many things were on my mind. After a long bout of staring at the ceiling, I stopped trying, and left the cabin to get a breath of fresh air. The night was chilly, and the sky was crystal clear. There was nearly a full moon and the stars were shining bright. The moonlight alone was more than enough to see by. Just outside the dacha complex, I found a tiny stream that ran parallel to the dirt road. I walked towards it, and when I was almost at its banks, I came upon a roughly semicircular set of boulders on top of an intensely green grassy area, separated from the thin forest that surrounded it.

It seemed like a perfect place to sit, contemplate and, perhaps, make some plans. I found myself a seat on one of the large boulders and, from there, I stared at and listened to the water as it rushed by, for a while. It calmed me and helped me feel less anxious. I begin to consider my next move. We still needed to scout out the area near the Russian base. While I was enmeshed in thought, a cloaked figure approached.

5

The dark figure steadily came closer. The face was hidden beneath a hood, making it difficult to discern any distinct features. I sat on my boulder, watching this enigmatic presence silently draw closer to me with each passing moment. The air thickened with unspoken questions and potential danger. Silence hung heavy. I weighed my options.

Friend or foe? A fellow partisan or a Russian operative? The proximity to our base suggested the former, but nothing could be taken for granted. My hand inched closer to the concealed pistol at the bottom on my leg, even as I maintained a facade of being unconcerned. Whatever was about to unfold, the next few seconds would be crucial. The figure was almost upon me.

Suddenly, with a flick of her hand, the mysterious figure removed the hood, revealing her identity. To my surprise, Yasmina Fedorova stood before me, striking blue eyes sparkling in the moonlight, although they appeared slightly gray in the pale glow. My hand, poised to grab the concealed 9mm from its holster on my leg, relaxed and returned to my side.

Truthfully, she was the last person I expected to encounter in this remote area, far from the dacha complex's center. Her presence added a new layer of complexity. I knew our meeting would be anything but ordinary. We locked eyes for a moment. Then, almost in unison, we exchanged smiles.

"Zdravstvujte," she said, greeting me with the formal "hello" of Russian. Then, she reverted to English.

"Can I sit down?" she asked in English.

"Of course," I replied.

"It is correct, is it not?" she asked.

"What?" I asked.

"How I said that?" she asked.

"Yes. Perfect. How did you learn to speak such good English?"

"I took my lessons seriously." She replied.

"Well, that's good," I commented.

"And, I watch many American movies in the original language," she added.

I nodded in acknowledgment.

"That's probably an excellent way of learning..." I commented. "So, what brings you out tonight?"

"You do," she replied, honestly. "To be honest, I followed you."

Her candor impressed me. Few women would admit such a thing so openly.

"Really?" I asked, surprised. "Why?"

She hesitated. "Because, well..."

I was at a loss for words.

"Do you mind?" She continued.

I shook my head.

"Of course not, not at all," I replied. "I'm glad to have the company."

She took a seat nearby, close enough for her delicate perfume to reach me. I'm not sure if it was deliberate or by accident, but the scent of her was intoxicating. During my time fighting in Kharkiv Oblast, I encountered fanciful rumors about Tatar women. It was said they could craft perfume from unique local flowers, infuse them with magic, and ensnare the hearts of men. Of course, this is ridiculous and is the produce of pure superstition. The truth is far simpler. Captivating beauty needs no supernatural aids. Yet, her enigmatic fragrance, whatever its source, served to enhance her already considerable allure.

"Tell me about Great Britain," she asked, her tone naive.

I suppressed a chuckle.

"Great Britain? America and the UK are separate countries. I'm from America, not England."

"Wow!" she exclaimed, her eyes widening.

"They're really very different," I emphasized, but a bit amused.

"Tell me about America, then..." she prompted, her voice brimming with childlike curiosity.

"Ah, well, where to begin? It's a big country..."

"Is it beautiful?" She asked.

"Some of it is," I answered. "It has both beauty and ugliness. It depends on where you are. What state, what part of the state? Some people like cities. Some like mountains. Others like the sea. There's something for everyone. Mountains, prairies, oceans, beaches, rivers, lakes...it all depends on what you define as beautiful."

"What state are you from?"

"I was born on Long Island, in New York State," I explained. "Its name is descriptive, actually. It's a very long island, situated just outside New York City."

"New York City?" she interrupted dreamily, "Wow!"

"Some people like it," I said. "But, I don't"

"I can only dream about it," She said.

"I can understand why." I replied, "People think New York is glamorous. But, I joined the army at a fairly young age, and I'm not even sure where I'm from anymore. The government started to move me all over the country, and even outside the country, from one army base to another. I haven't been back to Long Island in many years."

"But, what about your parents?" she asked. "Don't you visit them?"

"I did," I replied, "but they passed away last year."

"My mother and father are also dead." she confided. "They lived in Moscow. But, my father died when I wasn't even a year old. Then, my mother died. I don't remember them. I was raised by my grandmother in Crimea. What is New York like?"

"Well, the climate is different," I replied. "It's colder and wetter. Actually, a lot like Kyiv. It's on the Atlantic Ocean, though. We had beaches. It's too cold to use them most of the year. But, the biggest difference is size and the density – the New York metropolitan area is fairly small, but it has a population of around 35 million."

Her eyes widened. "That's nearly as many people as in all of Ukraine!"

I nodded.

"That's true. But, that's part of what I don't like about New York. Too many people. Feeling like a sardine in a can. I like smaller cities and rural areas better, but a lot of people feel otherwise."

"Do Americans live in big separated houses, with green lawns and white picket fences, like in the movies?" she asked, innocently.

"I don't know about the white picket fences," I answered, "but most people live in the suburbs. That's what you're seeing in the movies. Suburbs mostly have detached single-family homes on small plots of land. It's typical on Long Island, for example. In New York City, itself, and other big cities, most people live in apartments. The suburbs have more people than the cities, though."

She nodded.

"Unless you live in a village, everyone in Ukraine lives in an apartment..." She stated.

"You want to see America?" I asked.

"It's my dream!" she admitted, "I want a house like in the movies. A big one. I want to live where there is no war and, definitely, no Russians..."

I smiled, and replied,

"There are actually quite a few Russians in New York City, at least in one section of the city known as Brighton Beach, but they're mostly the good ones, who would kick Putin's butt if they could."

Yasmina's desires were not much different from those of most American girls. She longed for a peaceful life, the freedom to choose her partner, and the option to raise children if she wished. These seem like modest aspirations, yet in Putin's Russia, such basic rights were far from guaranteed.

I would later discover that beneath the innocent exterior, Yasmina carried a concealed pistol and knife, just as I did. Some might argue this set her apart from the average American girl her age. They are typically engrossed in their friends, TikTok and Instagram, whereas she was engrossed in the business of being a rebel soldier. But, I would argue that this difference is merely circumstantial. Had Yasmina grown up in America, she likely would have shared social media obsession. Instead, she was raised in a war-torn nation where nothing could be taken for granted. Many American girls find the world served to them on a silver platter, but every bit of happiness Yasmina would ever experience would be hard-earned and fiercely defended.

"You should, uh..." I started, but then stopped.

"Tell me," she insisted, "what were you going to say?"

I glanced at her, her eyes big and curious, intensely focused on every word. I was flattered that she was so intensely interested in everything I had to say and, perhaps, that encouraged me to say too much. Looking back, perhaps, I should have given more thought to my words, before uttering them. If I had, perhaps, everything might have turned out differently. Instead, I blurted out an impulsive statement.

"You should let me show you America," I said enthusiastically. "I could take you there..."

My words hung in the air. Innermost thoughts laid bare. There was no taking them back. Truthfully, I didn't want to. I was well aware that getting involved with a local woman, especially this one, would complicate things. Yet, as I sat beside her, I found myself intoxicated without a drop of alcohol. Perhaps it was her perfume, or perhaps it was simply her presence.

The expression on her face revealed that she appreciated the offer, regardless of whether she intended to accept it. Putting her into my life was surely going to complicate my mission but, at that moment, it seemed a price worth paying. I was smitten with her the way that a young schoolboy fixates on his first crush. She was literally the girl of my dreams but found in the strangest of places. I wanted to wake up next to her for the rest of my life.

But, she seemed surprised.

"Are you teasing me?" she asked.

I shook my head in the negative.

"I don't know about the logistics," I said, "We're in Russian-controlled territory. But, maybe, I could buy you a ticket to Istanbul. Then, meet there and fly to New York together. We'd figure it out."

She smiled deeply and touched me lightly on the shoulder. Our eyes met and locked. There was unspoken longing in my eyes. Did she feel the same way? I didn't know. I still don't know. But, if I venture to guess, I'd say that she probably felt the same way I did. It was a longing that almost ached. A feeling of deep desire. A yearning to unite. I wanted to kiss her more than anything, but I didn't even try, because it didn't seem right, given that we had just met. Instead, we kept talking.

"Tell me more..." She said, her eyes sparkling with curiosity.

I smiled, and reached out, playfully tucking a stray strand of her hair that had begun dangling in front of her eye, behind her ear. It was the greatest liberty I took with her that evening.

"You deserve to see it for yourself."

Yasmina blushed, averting her eyes. Then, she met my gaze again, the deep blue of her eyes shining with emotion. For a moment, the world seemed to fade away, and it felt like we were the only two people in the world. We kept talking for more than an hour. But, suddenly, Yasmina glanced at the little watch on her wrist and realized it was getting late. Her expression changed.

"I don't know where the time went. My grandmother will wonder where I am."

"You're right, it's late," I said reluctantly. "Can we meet again, tomorrow night, same time, and continue our conversation?"

She nodded.

"If you promise to tell me about all the other places you have been..." She said with a smile.

With great reluctance, we finally parted. I agreed to wait at least a half hour before returning to avoid any suspicion. We had done nothing more than talk endlessly, but some people might imagine other things. So, for her sake, it was important that people believed she had simply taken an evening stroll.

Over the next three days, I met Mustafa by day, and we scouted the terrain meticulously, in preparation for our upcoming mission. But, by night, I secretly met Yasmina and we talked for hours. I told her about the places I'd been – the bustling streets of New York, the ancient ruins of Rome, the serene beaches of Hawaii, the cities of Paris, Berlin, London, Buenos Aires and more. She seemed to have an endless desire to hear more. So, I shared war stories, about my experiences in Iraq and Afghanistan. That seemed to fascinate her. It was delightful to watch as her eyes grew wide at particularly poignant moments. But, it was not all one-sided. She did less talking, but she told me about Crimea, her life and her family.

On the fourth night, it happened. We were sitting next to one another, and I was telling her more travel stories about the faraway, exciting places she had never seen. Mid-story, I found myself lost in her eyes, words failing me. Her lips beckoned, and my desire for her clouded my senses. Her lips seemed ready for kissing, even if their owner didn't know it yet. Caught in the moment, and forgetting all else, I acted on impulse, gently wrapping my arm around her shoulders and drawing her close. Finally, our lips met.

There was a slight resistance, but it was weak, unsure and didn't last long. The uncertainty disappeared as she accepted my invitation. Our lips parted for a moment with both of us breathing hard. I kissed her again. But, then, she looked downward and away, trying to catch her breath. It almost seemed like she was afraid to look at me. But, I felt her heartbeat race. My heart was racing too.

"You're so beautiful," I said, with total sincerity.

That was enough to prompt a look and a soft smile.

"Is this the way it happens?" She asked, looking away again, "Between men and women..."

"As far as I know, yes..." I replied, wondering, for a moment, why she had even asked such a question.

"Maybe, it is too fast?" she said, looking away again.

"We can go slower, if you want," I replied, between heavy breaths, "The pace is up to you. But, we're alive at this moment. Tomorrow we could be dead, and the moment can be lost forever..."

That seemed to affect her greatly. She looked back at me, her nervousness obvious, shaking her head in the negative.

"Fate would never let that happen..."

"Maybe not," I said. "But, fate plays tricks on people like us."

Our eyes locked, and then she glanced downward again, seemingly unsure, shaking her head gently, confused and uncertain.

"We are not married and you are not a Muslim..." She commented finally, looking up again.

It was hard to talk after kissing her and feeling her tender body next to mine. We were too close and I found it hard to think. The scent and feel of her was too intoxicating. I wanted her. I think she felt the same way, even though she might not have even known it at the time. So, I ignored her uncertainty and drew her closer, kissing her gently, again. And, this time, there was not even the slightest hint of resistance. We kissed deeper. She started to passionately return my kisses, turning her body fully toward me, so that we could face directly toward each other. We embraced, and our bodies slowly slid down from the boulder, together. Soon we were lying on the grass and passion overtook us.

Logic and reason has a place in determining what people do. Those two skills separates people from animals. But neither logic nor reason are up for the challenge of primal moments. We were both hungry animals, desperately needing nourishment in each other's arms. The rhythm could no longer be denied as we moved together as one, forgetting everything around us. Our clothing slipped off and that is when I learned, for the first time, that she kept a hidden pistol and a knife. But, I had no time to think about such things, let alone ask questions.

We were lovers, dancing to the tune of our hearts. As we danced, moving rhythmically inward and outward, eventually I arrived at the crowning instant of ultimate joy. Capturing the essence of that ancient dance, she reacted in a primal way as my instant of joy became hers as well. As quickly as it arrived for both of us, the supreme ecstasy was over in an instant, and we lay next to each other, exhausted but satisfied.

I lay in the grass, silently recovering. Then, I raised myself onto my elbow, leaned over, cupped her pretty face in one free hand, and kissed her again.

"I love you," I told her.

The words were as true as any mouth had ever uttered. I had not simply satisfied my physical needs at her expense. I was madly in love with her. Not only that, but I've been with many women in my life but had never felt such intensity before. I wanted her by my side forever. There was no one I wanted to be with and nowhere else I wanted to be. As I looked at her soft eyes, I knew I would give everything for her, even life itself.

Feeling the way I did, it was very distressing to see tears begin to heavily flow from her eyes like a rushing river. It was simply unbearable. There is no greater sorrow than watching the woman you love cry. It was very hard to understand. She had seemed happier than ever, satisfied, just as I was. But, the happiness and satisfaction seemed gone. In its place was a deep-set feeling of guilt that seemed to weigh on her. I was happier than I had been in years, but she was deeply troubled.

"What's wrong?" I asked.

"I am ashamed," she said, as the tears continued.

I took her face in my hand again and kissed her again, thinking that, somehow, doing that would solve the problem, but it didn't.

"There's nothing to be ashamed of." I insisted.

"Not for you," she said, "because you are a man. But, I am... nothing."

"You are the most perfect thing I have ever known in this world," I answered.

There was a moment of silence before she spoke again.

"No." She said, "I am a whore..."

I shook my head.

"Don't you understand that I love you?" I asked, confused.

"How many other women have you loved?" she asked, through her tears.

I hesitated. I didn't want to lie to her. After all, I was 42 years old. She was not the only woman I'd ever been with. But, I now suspected, in spite of her 21 years, this was the first time she had been with a man.

"A few," I replied.

"Many?" she asked.

"A few," I repeated.

"And, it is the same for you with all women, is it not?" She asked as the tears flowed like a mountain stream during a major snow melt.

I shook my head.

"No," I answered. "It's not. You're very special. I can't even put it into words. You make me so happy."

"Why?"

"Because I love you," I said.

"Why didn't you love the other women?" she asked.

"I don't know." I confessed.

"Maybe, you thought you loved them at the time?"

"No," I replied, shaking my head. "I wanted them, but never loved them."

"Why not?"

"I don't know," I said, "I've never felt this way before."

"I also feel that our relationship is special," she conceded, the words coming out, almost like a sigh. "But, how can I know?"

"Trust me. I love you," I assure you, "You can feel it. I can feel it too."

She placed her hand over her heart and spoke.

"I feel that there is no other man like you, John Kovalenko. That you are very special..."

Despite her positive words, which I thought ought to get us clear of the tears, the river hadn't slowed down. The water volume seemed to be rising, rather than falling. It wasn't what I expected.

"You don't believe I love you?" I asked.

She shrugged subtly.

"I'm not lying." I insisted.

"It is not that I don't believe you, John Kovalenko." She said, "I love you too. Even more. Tonight, there was an instant of pain... but after that, I went to heaven."

"Then, there you are!" I pointed out. "I love you. You love me. What else can there be?"

"There is no heaven on earth." She retorted.

"We make our own heaven and ignore the rest of the Earth," I said.

She smiled through the tears.

"You are funny..." she said, shaking her head. "It is so easy for you because you don't understand."

"What do I not understand?" I asked.

"That everything can't be solved by love," She explained. "By loving you the way I did this night, I sinned against Allah Almighty. An unforgivable sin..."

"That's ridiculous." I countered.

"Only married women may do this," she said.

"Your people spent 70 years in the secular Soviet Union," I protested, "How can you still think that way?"

"Many believe in the old ways. My family does..."

"Well, okay," I argued, "We're automatically married now, biblically speaking, so we're both in the clear..."

"Not according to the Quran," she said, between her tears. "A formal contract is required."

I shook my head in temporary frustration. Then, I shrugged my shoulders.

"Then, let's have a formal contract," I said, finally, "We'll go to a Minister or an Imam, whatever. We have to marry, anyway, for me to bring you to the USA. Just stop crying already..."

She began to smile, through the tears, at my words, but shook her head.

"It is impossible..." she said.

"I told you... I'm willing and ready if you are..." I insisted.

"No one knows you are here," She pointed out, "And, for you to be successful, it has to stay that way. You want to go to jail?"

"Surely, the partisans have people they can trust..." I pointed out.

"You are not a Muslim," She said. "No normal Imam would marry us. It isn't permitted."

"Not permitted?" I asked. "By whom?"

A memory of the heated debate between Mustafa and Muhammad came flooding back into my mind. I remembered some talk about pronouncements on the subject by Muslim holy men.

"Tradition, religious law, by everyone," She replied, "We would be shunned."

"Mustafa disagrees..." I pointed out.

"Mustafa speaks only for himself," She said, "I know my people..."

"So, we get married in a government office," I said.

"By a dirty, stinking Moskali judge?" She asked.

"No," I insisted, "First, we go to Ukrainian controlled territory, or to America."

She shook her head in frustration.

"You don't understand." She repeated.

"In America, or even in mainland Ukraine, what you're saying doesn't matter anymore," I replied. "Nobody cares what religion you are. It only matters who you love..."

I saw, to my relief, that her tears were finally beginning to dry up. She smiled more broadly than before and she even reached out and placed her hand on the side of my face.

"You would really take me...to America?" she asked, meekly.

I nodded and said,

"Yes. Didn't I tell you I love you? You think I'm a liar?"

"It's a dream..." She sighed, smiling through a few more tears, "You are a sweet man...but, really, you still don't understand..."

"What's left that I don't understand?" I asked. "Mustafa told me that Tatar women come in all sizes and shapes. Some wear veils and long dresses. Others wear jeans. Some are religious. Some are not. But, you are all very independent. You all have the right to make your own decisions. You wore a long dress today, but you didn't wear a veil. That was your decision, was it not?"

"Yes." She agreed.

"And, your grandmother didn't wear a veil, either, did she?"

"No." She confessed.

"So, there you have it." I said.

"It is said that there were once mountain Tatari who were Christians," She pointed out, supporting my argument against her own, "But, not many. My grandmother says we are all Tatari, united by a common language, a common love of our motherland, and a common history..."

"Doesn't that say it all?" I asked, "Your grandmother is wise. Listen to her."

She smiled and almost seemed on the verge of a laugh.

"But, you are not even Tatari..." She said, finally.

"I'm fighting side by side with your people, am I not?" I insisted. "I'm risking life and limb, standing shoulder to shoulder with your people. You know that. And, so does everyone else."

"Yes..." She agreed.

"That gives me brownie points..." I insisted.

"Brownie points?" She asked.

"It's not important," I replied, "It means things that argue in my favor."

I could almost detect the beginnings of a quiet laugh, but she suppressed it. Instead, she put her hand on my cheek again. She was smiling now. The tide of tears was going out.

"It is true." she agreed.

Since I was making some headway, I decided to take a leap of faith. I knew nothing about the culture or customs of the Crimean Tatars, but if there is one thing I've learned in many adventures in different parts of the world, it's that people aren't so different from one another, regardless of their ethnic or religious background.

"By the customs and traditions of the Tatar people, fighting by your side, I become one of you. I am a Tatari!"

"And, you are impossible!" she exclaimed, finally, smiling broadly now.

"An acquired skill, I assure you!" I said. "But, really, we'll find a way to get you out of here, and then we'll get married."

"Even in America," She mused, "I don't think any Imam would marry us. You are still not a Muslim."

"I guess we'll see about that," I replied, "But, we can always get married in a church or a court of law, or even with a Jewish rabbi! Who cares? If I have to, I'll become a Muslim. Because I don't really care about religion."

"No," she insisted, "you can't. Not unless you believe..."

"Who's to say I believe, or I don't believe?" I replied.

"You don't even know what you are supposed to believe!" She said with a laugh.

"Whatever I need to believe, I believe," I said. "And, you can take that to the bank, as we like to say in America."

She continued smiling, even as she shook her head in feigned frustration. The conversation, it seemed, was going along lines that were making her happier. Then, she stared at me for an extended moment, the vast improvement in her mood evident on her face.

"You are a very strange man, John Kovalenko." She said, finally.

"Why?" I asked.

"You just are." She replied, as her last tears dried up.

"You can call me John, by the way, without the Kovalenko," I suggested. "We really ought to be on a first-name basis. Don't you agree?"

She giggled and nodded her head.

"Yes, John..." she said, continuing to smile.

I reached out and wiped away a few remaining tears from her cheeks.

"So, we're okay now?" I asked.

She nodded and stood up, pulling her underwear back on, before checking on her pistol and her knife, putting everything back into proper order. In a matter of moments, she was fully dressed and, using a small pocket mirror, she wiped away the tear-smeared mascara and reapplied her makeup. Within minutes, she stood perfectly composed. No one who hadn't been there would suspect anything had happened.

"I must return, quickly, now," she said, anxiously. "Otherwise, people may ask questions..."

"Will we meet tomorrow night?" I asked.

She furtively looked around, as if searching for someone who might see or hear her. It was ridiculous, of course, because if there had been anyone nearby, what they had already seen and heard would be far more serious than anything she was about to say. But, confirming we were still alone, she nodded.

Just before she was about to leave, I grabbed her again, held her close, and kissed her again.

"I'll be waiting here for you, as usual," I said, still holding her.

The feel of her tender body, so close to mine, made me want her again. She was young, vibrant, and exciting. I was ready for another round of lovemaking, but I was able to control myself better this time. So, instead of making love to her again, I released her. She smiled, turned, and began to walk away, back toward the main area of the dacha complex. Every so often, she turned back to look at me until, finally, she was too far away. I watched her, mesmerized by the graceful movement of her hourglass figure. She slowly dissolved into the surrounding darkness and was gone.

I felt better than I had in a long time. The nervous tension was entirely gone. I was calm and relaxed. It wasn't just the sex. That had been fantastic. But, it was also the emotional bonding. Before meeting Yasmina, I wouldn't have imagined that I could still fall, head over heels, in love with someone. I knew now that I still could. It made me feel like a schoolboy, but as I reflected on the depth of my newfound love for the girl, I began to feel anxious.

I didn't like Muhammad and everything he said was out of animosity and jealousy. But, he was right about one thing. A successful attack on the Russian missile warehouse would likely expose the local partisans to more danger than they had ever faced before. That included Yasmina. It hadn't bothered me previously because, I figured, they were partisans, and accepted such risks by joining the movement, just as I accepted the risk of being a soldier.

Now, it bothered me a great deal. The Russians would disregard whatever little semblance to rules that they followed in pursuit of the perpetrators. The thought of Yasmina getting caught was painful. If she were identified as a partisan, the regime wouldn't only arrest her. It would torture her for information, and eventually, kill her. That was the Russian way. It was how they did business.

I had promised to wait before returning to the rest complex grounds. While I was waiting, I began thinking more and more about the war. Why was it even important? The Russians had been trying to erase Ukraine's national identity for 500 years, as far back as the early Tsars. Was that my business? That my ancestors came from Ukraine had nothing to do with what was happening now. I was an American, born and bred. But, I had made it my business by volunteering. I believed in freedom.

Yet, as an American, I had no obligation to this war except for the one I had created for myself. No draft could compel me. I didn't have to risk my life destroying Russian missile warehouses. I didn't even need to be in Crimea. What if I left for Istanbul? What if I gave Yasmina enough cash to buy a ticket, so she could join me? We could fly to New York together, leaving the war far behind. I could wake up beside her every day, inhaling her intoxicating scent, gazing at her lovely face morning and night.

Yet, even as these thoughts formed, I realized how treacherous they were. Though I am an American, I had sworn an oath to defend Ukraine. The ideas now floating in my mind were contemptible. Would I respect someone who thought such things? A man who capriciously abandoned his duty, had no honor, and ran off with a young pretty girl at a moment's notice simply because he wanted to? Such thoughts were worthy of contempt.

Betraying my vow would leave the Russian missile stockpile intact, free to be used for its intended purpose, and the Putin regime's tactics were clear. Terrorism was their stock-in-trade. The missiles would undoubtedly be used to attack innocent Ukrainian civilians in churches, museums, and shopping centers. This was their method of warfare, verging on outright terrorism. Blatantly violating decency and international war conventions. Their primary strategy was to wage a war of intimidation, aiming to erode the resolve of Ukraine's defenders through relentless civilian targeting.

How many innocent lives would be lost due to my selfishness? Would Yasmina want a man who broke his oath? Her grandfather had died a martyr. He was a hero to his people. Her grandmother continued the fight despite losing her husband. Yasmina was a dedicated partisan, willingly risking her life for the cause. Yet here I was, an American soldier, who had taken a solemn oath, ready to disregard that oath, thinking only of myself.

Yes, I wanted to ensure her safety. I wanted her to bear my children. I wanted her to wake up next to me every morning. But these dreams couldn't come at the expense of duty and honor. We had obligations to carry out, promises to keep, oaths to honor. Only after fulfilling them could we rightfully pursue our personal aspirations.

6

In the early morning of the next day, under the cover of darkness, Mustafa and I cautiously approached the Russian airbase for the first time. It was the riskiest of our scouting expeditions, but also the most important. The base was near the sea, but on all three sides that did not meet the shore, it was surrounded by empty steppe lands. Brownish grass spread out in all directions, and there was little cover. We did manage to find a hiding place for the tiny Jigoli car behind a cluster of low bushes about 5 kilometers away from the edge of the base. We masked it with a greenish-brown tarp so that it was hard to distinguish it from surrounding grass.

Equipped with special cloaks from Kyiv that dampened the heat signatures emitted from our bodies, we embarked under the cover of darkness, with the help of night vision goggles. Thankfully, I was in possession of Russian army protocols. The Ukrainian intelligence service had obtained these from defectors and had provided them to me. It gave us an advantage. I knew where most of their infrared observation cameras were likely placed. But, I needed to remain vigilant. I might still miss a few.

The heat-dampening so-called "invisibility cloaks" were our greatest asset because they caused us to appear as little more than fleeting shadows or digital artifacts on a video monitoring screen. If we moved with precision, we could slip past their surveillance measures undetected. Every step had to be calculated. Every movement deliberate. But, I was confident that the Russians wouldn't know.

The plan was to stay beyond the range of any laser sensors to avoid tripping them. This outing was for the purpose of observation, not attack. Armed with high-resolution night-vision binoculars, I wanted to gather the necessary intelligence with minimal risk. The combination of optical and digital magnification clarified even the small details. As I peered through the binoculars, I whispered to Mustafa, who took notes.

"At least two dozen armed soldiers at the entrance, all well-equipped, each carrying an automatic rifle and encased in body armor."

He donned his pair of binoculars to look for himself.

"Bad..." he said.

I continued,

"... Three tanks, four attack helicopters, and several heavy machine gun emplacements near the entrance gate..."

He continued to take down what he observed, himself, and what I commented on. By now, it was already clear that our mission was going to be far more challenging than expected. The target, which had been viewed as exquisitely vulnerable, was fortified beyond expectations. Previous satellite imagery had shown extensive damage from a Ukrainian Air Force missile strike in late summer 2022. It depicted scorched land, ruined equipment, destroyed aircraft, and a damaged runway. However, the Russians had been busy. Even though the area continued to look, on the surface, as if it were still badly damaged, they had actually repaired most of it.

Contrary to the portrayal, in the western press, implying that the Russian army is completely inept, they're actually resilient adversaries who learn from their mistakes. All the more valuable Russian aircraft had been moved to bases deep inside Russia, outside Ukrainian reach. But, the base was not abandoned. They had added significant anti-missile and anti-drone defenses that were not immediately clear on satellite imagery. And, it was now repurposed. It was no longer a platform for storing aircraft for battles inside mainland Ukraine, but it was now a major forward supply depot. Countless aircraft still came and went, landing, being outfitted with bombs and missiles, but rarely staying long enough for the Ukrainians to target them.

The base had essentially been transformed into a fortified warehouse. We couldn't see them from our vantage point, but the storage units were dug deep underground and hardened with the extensive use of concrete. They were even safe even against attack highly accurate, but relatively small warheads carried by American ATACMS missiles, which can carry a maximum warhead weight of about 500 kg. Of course, at the time, Ukraine didn't have such missiles yet. They were certainly safe against the type of anti-ship missiles Ukraine had launched against the base in 2022.

The satellite footage showed charred foliage. Hidden, and not so easily seen, however, were the protective concrete domes, which were carefully painted to blend into the landscape. The domes concealed newly constructed underground bunkers protected by multiple layers of dirt and concrete. They were designed to withstand virtually any possible missile barrage, save nuclear. I didn't know how deep the tunnels went, but from the look of things, even the biggest American bunker-buster bomb couldn't take them out. Of course, Ukraine didn't have bunker-busters anyway. The point is simply that, unlike exposed aircraft protected by light hangars, these reinforced underground facilities were impervious to conventional attack.

Only a covert ground attack could succeed. That was why General Rutanov had sent me. But, even with a ground attack, our prospects for success now looked grim. From intelligence reports, sourced from the same disgruntled Russian servicemen who had supplied the camera protocols, we knew that there were hundreds of cruise and ballistic missiles housed here. They had to be destroyed. The hardened bunkers would be defenseless from the inside. The key was to get inside.

If my drones could enter the main bunkers via a window or door, they could do the job. They just needed to land on some targeted warheads. As I had pointed out, to Mustafa, back at the sunflower fields, the plan was to initiate a chain reaction that would destroy the entire facility from within. To facilitate that, we had to carefully examine the enemy base, capture detailed infrared digital photographs, and document all possible vulnerabilities for later analysis. We were also noting the level of helicopter and other air activity.

Enhancing the binoculars' magnification, I noticed a troubling sight. There were several anti-drone radiation dishes tactically scattered across the base. When activated, these electronic warfare devices could generate an interference field, enveloping the entire area, disrupting drone circuitry and cutting off any control I might exert from the outside. Even the drone's inertial navigation systems, and many of its sensitive circuits, might be rendered useless by the intense radiation that could come out of such dishes.

The Russian defense created an invisible shield preventing heavily electronics- dependent devices, like drones, from penetrating. I had to put those dishes out of commission. Otherwise, it was entirely likely that my drones would simply fall to the ground, useless. They'd be collected after that, and the secrets of our tiny fireflies would be laid bare to Russian engineers. They'd be quickly reverse-engineered and, in a few months, Ukrainian battalions would face micro-drones. That had to be avoided at all costs, even if it meant terminating the mission.

To neutralize the dishes, we would have to act very quickly, almost simultaneously conducting both the neutralization and the attack itself. The job had to be done quickly and decisively, before the Russians had any chance to deploy their superior numbers to stop us. And, naturally, we would also need sufficient time to swiftly retreat, after putting them out of commission, so that we could safely flee the area. As things stood, I didn't have the manpower to pull it off.

"What about these drone defenses?" Mustafa asked, recognizing the issue without my even mentioning it.

"They'll have to be crippled," I replied.

He shook his head.

"It's impossible," Mustafa stated what he thought to be the obvious.

"Not if we had more men," I said, confidently, as I kept my gaze fixed in the binoculars.

As I continued to survey the base, recollections of past success came to mind. We had done it before. In Iraq. Iran. Afghanistan. Other places. I couldn't share the details with Mustafa. I trusted him completely now. But, he didn't have US government top secret clearance. Those operations were strictly classified, having taken place within the sovereign territories of countries we had officially withdrawn from, or in some cases, never admitted to entering. We just needed more manpower. That was the only thing that mattered.

"With more fighters, we could do it," I declared.

"If that is your opinion, it is mine also," Mustafa responded. "Finding more men is no simple matter, however."

Recruiting additional fighters was the key to success. We needed at least double our human resources. As I pondered the alternatives, two Su-24 jets roared overhead, a stark reminder of Russian air superiority. Mustafa pointed at the retreating aircraft.

"If we had Stingers, we could bring them down," he lamented.

I nodded. At that altitude, it would have been easy. Placing a reassuring hand on his shoulder, I spoke again,

"We don't have Stingers. They're too hard to get into Crimea. But if we gather more men, we'll make a much bigger impact by destroying that missile bunker."

He smiled, and nodded. We continued to observe the enemy for a while longer. Eventually, we exhausted all possible observations. It was time to leave, and we made our way back to the car a few kilometers away. Our scouting mission raised serious questions. In spite of my past experience with overcoming such odds, I had lingering doubts. I tried not to show my uncertainty but, generally speaking, I spoke frankly about the challenges we faced.

"One thing is for sure," I said, "we won't be able to complete this mission with the resources we have now..."

Mustafa understood and, after thinking for a moment, a thought came to him.

"I might know where we can get more men," Mustafa suggested.

"Where?" I responded immediately.

"There is a leader named Ismail," He said, "He once worked closely with Igor, Svetlana's husband. They coordinated raids. He has a group of fighters in the capital. Svetlana might be able to convince him to help..."

His words were music to my ears. I knew nothing about Ismail or his resistance cell. But, if he represented more manpower, reliable men who could be recruited to our cause, I was desperate to have him.

7

At first light, we visited Svetlana Fedorov in the rustic wooden summer cabin she and Yasmina called home. I had never seen their apartment in the city, but if it was even remotely like the cabin, it helped me better understand why Yasmina would want to go to America. The door creaked open when we knocked, revealing a run-down interior.

Virtually all the tiny houses in the "rest complex" were old, worn, and in terrible repair. This one was no exception. They were used only during the summer and studiously ignored the rest of the year. It had been that way for decades, before and after the fall of the former Soviet Union. It was the same way all over Ukraine. Other than the fact that this complex happened to double as headquarters for local resistance fighters, it was like every other typical company-owned rest complex from Soviet times.

The room was dimly lit by the few rays of sunlight that made it through the cracks in the draped windows. The scent of old wood and dampness hung in the air, mingling with the aroma of freshly brewed tea. The worn-out furniture, remnants of the Soviet Union, reminders of a day and age now long past, stood against a background of peeling wallpaper. A tired Persian rug covered the rough wooden floor. The once-vibrant colors of the carpet were faded with use and age. Two narrow single beds sat in the corner, perpendicular to one another.

As former Director of the now-defunct Soviet "Institute," Svetlana's husband had a cabin a cut above the rest—slightly larger and better situated than most others. It occupied a prime spot right in the center of the complex, conveniently close to the kitchen and communal toilets.

Despite its privileged status, however, the cabin was far from luxurious. Even in its heyday, it had always been a dilapidated structure. Back then, not knowing any better, few if anyone noticed or cared. For decades, the family used it as a summer retreat, spending every late spring and summer there. It was the only one building in the entire complex that had a somewhat different design. Though still modest in size, it was noticeably larger than its neighbors, a silent testament to its owner's former position of importance.

There were now four of us: Mustafa, Yasmina, Svetlana, and me, and we were gathered around the only table in the house—a weathered wooden piece placed near the window. Yasmina had taken it upon herself to serve tea. Svetlana, usually seen with her hair in a tight bun, had let it down in the comfort of her own home. Her silver mane cascaded over 68-year-old shoulders, a surprising sight. I found myself marveling at how a woman her age could maintain such luxurious long hair, even if it had lost all its color.

The setting created a stark contrast to our usual interactions. As we sat there, sipping tea and surrounded by the rustic charm of the cabin, the gravity of our situation seemed momentarily suspended. Seeing her with her hair down for the first time, I began to realize that, once upon a time, Svetlana had been a beautiful woman, just like her granddaughter. And, like all true blooded Ukrainian women, she had no intention of letting anyone forget that, least of all Mustafa, who had known her in the bloom of her youth.

As Yasmina served tea, Mustafa began the conversation.

"John and I have finished scouting the airbase."

"Excellent!" she responded. "I hope you have good news."

"Actually," he continued, "we have a problem…"

"What kind of problem?" she asked.

"We need more men."

She looked at him, saying nothing, for a moment.

"What did you see?" She finally asked.

"There are more defenses than expected," I interjected, "It has an electronic anti-drone system that we'll need to destroy before my drones can be released onto the base. We can still succeed, but we must destroy the field projectors before they can activate. There's quite a few of them. We simply don't have enough men to do that, launch the drones properly, and make our escape."

"We have what we have," she replied. "I can't conjure people from thin air. It is not easy to recruit people into the resistance. Everyone hates the

Moskali, of course, but few are willing to put their lives at risk. You speak only of men. I am not a man, but I can help..."

I struggled to imagine how a 68-year-old woman, with no military experience, could possibly help me with this. She was unquestionably a good speaker, and a leader, but I was in need of tough fighters. I also wanted to keep Yasmina far from danger. If her grandmother joined, Yasmina might come too. That was out of the question. It was too dangerous.

"I was thinking that we could bring in Ismail and his group," Mustafa suggested. "Their fighters would more than double our numbers."

"What makes you think he would be interested in that?" she countered.

"He worked closely with Igor,,," Mustafa mused. "He owes you favors..."

"That was years ago," Svetlana insisted, "Any favors he might have once owed me have been repaid long ago. He has his own plans and also his own funding sources. You know he gets his main support from the Turks? He rarely coordinates with the Ukrainian government."

Her words hung in the air, and the implications were sinking in. Mustafa had raised my hopes, but it seemed increasingly clear that I would have to call off the attack. The thought of returning to Kyiv empty-handed weighed heavily on me. The failure wouldn't just be a personal disappointment. It would be embarrassing and disheartening. And, worst of all, if the missiles were not destroyed, many innocent Ukrainians would die.

There was so much at stake. It wasn't just about my reputation. It was about the missed opportunity to make a real difference in the war. The possible retreat loomed large, casting a shadow over my carefully laid plans. It would be a depressing end to a mission I had hoped would make a big difference.

"What do you suggest?" I asked.

"I will talk to him if you wish," she said. "Maybe, there is something we can give him, in trade, but I doubt it. Who knows? Maybe, he has turned crazy, and will say 'yes' just to screw the Moskali. If I were him, I would say no."

Svetlana had shattered my confidence. But, the old lady wasn't finished yet...

"There is also an important private matter we need to discuss." She said directly to me, glancing at Mustafa and Yasmina.

The two of them sensed the message she was sending. They shared a glance with each other and quickly retreated outside, closing the door behind them. The room felt hushed, and the walls themselves felt like they were closing in on me. When the others were out of earshot, she began to speak.

"My granddaughter keeps talking about you constantly." she said, finally, "Never before has any man constantly been on her mind. John says this and John would do that. I cannot help but wonder why?"

Anxiety at being discovered and, perhaps, a bit of confusion as to how to respond, must have flickered across my face. It took a moment for me to think of something to say.

"Maybe, you should ask her, not me…" I offered.

"I have asked her," she said, "several times. I never get a straight answer. Instead, she tries to change the subject."

"I don't know what I can add to the discussion, then…" I commented.

"Sometimes, the best way is simply to ask an open, clear question…" She mused. "Do you agree?"

"Yes, of course," I replied.

"Then, I have a question," She said.

My heart missed a beat as I worried about what she would ask me. Did she know about our torrid love affair? Did she suspect I had taken her granddaughter's virginity? Yasmina would never have told her. She had already admitted that Yasmina kept changing the subject when she tried to talk to her about me. Still, I felt as nervous as a schoolboy whose secret naughtiness was just discovered by the teacher.

Taking a deep breath, Svetlana leaned forward, into the table, her eyes locked onto mine, and the worst possible scenario seemed to take shape.

"What is going on between you and Yasmina?" she asked, calmly. "You two have been…intimate?"

Despite her warning, the question was so open and direct that it still caught me by surprise. I leaned back in my chair, without answering right away, trying to process the situation and think of something that would sound acceptable, without actually lying. But, what could I say? What would buy me the time I needed for a clever response?

"I…why would you ask me that?" I muttered, unable to come up with anything better.

My fumbling attempt to avoid answering gave the canny old lady the answer she was looking for. I suddenly feared that my inability to control my urges was now going to irreparably jeopardize my mission. I needed the old woman's help. Yet, my relationship with Yasmina might sabotage everything. In the eyes of a conservative Muslim, our relationship was pure heresy. Had I destroyed any hope of getting help from her? Had my rash behavior single-handedly undermined Ukraine's defense against Russia?

Instead of the expected outburst, however, she smiled knowingly and touched my hand.

"Love must find its own path," she said. "I'd much prefer it if you were Muslim and a Tatar, but honestly, I don't care much for Islamic law, anyway. I'm not particularly observant. You and Yasmina are beautiful young people. Why shouldn't you be in love?"

Relief washed over me.

"How did you know?" I asked.

"I am old," She replied, "But I am not blind yet. I can see what is in Yasmina's eyes and in yours, especially when you are together. I see that she loves you. I hear it from her mouth, though she doesn't speak the words. Her heart is filled with hopes, dreams, and fancies. But, I worry...I am not sure you two have thought this out completely. What if she becomes pregnant? It would be a humiliation to have a child out of wedlock. And, how do I know that you are truly serious about my granddaughter? Will there be a future between you?"

The old lady's words helped me recognize the depth of Yasmina's affection for me, as well as mine for her and the consequences. The questions were important and correct, even though it was a sensitive subject. But, I felt uncomfortable. More than that, I didn't want to make mistakes in how I responded. I looked down for a moment, thoughts racing, as I carefully considered her words. Then, I suddenly knew what I wanted to say, and I looked up again.

"I care deeply about Yasmina," I said, my voice tinged with determination, "I can assure you that nothing will happen without being planned. I love her as much as she loves me. Of course, I could die tomorrow. But, that makes today so much more important. As long as I breathe, I promise you I will love Yasmina. I take our relationship very seriously. We have already agreed to marry, subject to your permission, of course. I'll take her to the United States with me..."

"No Imam in Crimea will marry you..." She cautioned.

I nodded.

"That's the reason we haven't married already," I replied.

Her eyes softened, and her grip on my hand tightened slightly.

"Life is a fleeting moment," She said. "Only Allah Almighty knows what tomorrow will bring. Yasmina is young and fragile. If you die tomorrow, she will be devastated. But, women have lost the men they love for thousands of years, to war and other hazards. Such losses are painful, but they don't break the woman. But, if you live, yet abandon her, it would shatter her so completely that she would never recover. I hope you understand this, and that you keep your word."

"I will cherish Yasmina as long as I live," I replied, sincerely.

With the old woman's wise words and my pledge to love Yasmina forever, I felt a new sense of purpose and responsibility. I wouldn't break that vow. I loved her. I would marry her as soon as I could. Even if it meant that I had to become a Muslim and claim to believe in things I didn't believe in.

But, to marry her now was impossible. It would require too many new and unknown people and put us all in jeopardy. Svetlana knew this better than anyone. I wished I could open my mind to her, to show her how sincere I was. But, the best I could do was to meet her gaze with a firm nod and confident words. That had to be enough, for now.

"I will do everything in my power to protect Yasmina," I said, finally, and decided to disclose my latest plan, "We'll marry in Ukrainian controlled territory. I'll buy her tickets to Istanbul and, then, from there, she'll fly to Warsaw. I'll meet her in Warsaw and we'll travel to Kyiv. We'll get married in Kyiv. When my contract with Ukraine expires, we'll go to America together. As long as I breathe, I won't let her down. I swear it."

She released my hand and there was a glimmer of reassurance in her eyes. I think I convinced her.

"I am happy that she is dear to you," she said. "Because she is dear to me also."

A moment of silence enveloped the little bungalow, as the weight of our conversation hung over us. Finally, she stood up, and a new fire seemed to light up her eyes.

"Now, we must focus on the mission." She said determinedly. "I'll try my best to convince Ismail. He hates the Moskali as much as we do, but helping you with the missile warehouse may not be in the best interest of his group. We will see…"

"Let him know he'll be paid well for his assistance…" I noted.

She nodded.

"OK, I will." She replied.

Svetlana Fedorova had agreed to all my requests, leaving nothing more to ask of her. Experience has taught me that once someone accepts a challenging proposal, it's best to stop talking. Additional words risk jeopardizing a favorable decision. Yet, countless questions swirled in my mind, and my curiosity about Yasmina's situation was insatiable.

There seemed to be an odd, but incredibly close interaction between Tatars and Russians even though the Tatars, supposedly, hate Russians and Russians have contempt for Tatars. In spite of the claim that Islam allows a Muslim woman to marry only a Muslim man, the number of mixed marriages between Tatar women and both Russian and Ukrainian men, is very high. So, I asked her what was on my mind.

"You hate Russians, but your husband was half-Russian?"

"His spirit was 100% Tatari." She replied.

"I see…" I said, although I really didn't 'see' anything.

"You must understand our history before you can understand us…" she commented.

"I would like to," I agreed, "I've read about how Stalin unjustly exiled your people from Crimea."

She nodded, and replied quickly,

"Yes, Stalin was one man, but he was also—how can I say it? A mentality. He was actually Georgian, but it doesn't matter. His mind was that of a Moskal, just as my husband's mind was Tatar. The difference is not passed on by the genes. It is a product of how you think. Moskali dream imperial dreams. They want to conquer and dominate. Putin is a Moskal. So was Stalin. Moskali demand the subjugation of other people, including Crimean

Tatars, but also their own Slavic brothers, the Ukrainians. Only power matters. It has been this way for at least 700 years..."

"Do you hate Putin?" I asked.

"Yes," she replied. "Of course, I hate him. He is KGB. The most evil of all Moskali. An example of everything bad."

As she continued, her voice became tinged with sorrow.

"You are from America," she said, "So, you don't know what it is like to be violently uprooted from your home, torn away from everything you know. You don't know what it feels like when a dictator, whether Stalin or Putin, sits on the throne and tries to exterminate your People. It is not about genes. It is about culture and mindset. We fight for the survival of our culture and traditions. Stalin uprooted my people, forcing us to leave a life filled with joy. He shattered the fabric of our existence. Putin is the same. But, we won't let it happen again. Not as long as we breathe..."

"You sound like a Jewish person talking about Nazis, and saying 'Never Again'..." I commented.

She nodded and spoke immediately,

"It is exactly like that." she agreed.

So far, she still hadn't answered my original question. But, she closed her eyes for a moment, as if summoning the strength to do so.

"I wasn't born yet, but my grandmother told me the story, and I feel that I lived it. It is a memory seared into my soul. I know every detail..."

She paused to gather her thoughts, seemingly bearing the weight of a painfully heavy burden. I almost felt guilty for asking, and forcing her to talk about such a difficult subject.

"Before the Russians came, this peninsula was a paradise." She explained. "Tatar Khans ruled from the legendary town of Bahcesaray, a city built of pure marble, which became known as the "Garden Palace." From there to the southern plains of Ukraine, our nation was independent and strong. We protected Crimea and southern Ukraine from the Moskali, who were busy conquering everything else to the north and east. But, in the late 1700s, while your country fought a war of independence, our country, the Crimean Khanate, was ruthlessly invaded by the Imperial Russian army. We begged for help from the Turkish Sultan, but he didn't come. He was busy fighting a war with Iran. We were outnumbered and outgunned and Russia prevailed. They subjugated our land."

A tear dripped from her eye, but she continued.

"Russia operated under the feudal system. Peasants were the slaves of the noblemen. Islamic law does not permit this. Our peasants were free and independent. But, the Moskali nobility forcibly seized land belonging to Tatari peasants. They tried to treat us with the same disrespect with which they treated their own serfs. They wanted us to become their slaves. It was intolerable.

"The Moskali continued to steal land. When we resisted being slaves, they imported waves of their own Slavic serfs to take our place. Both the Moskali nobility and their serfs showed no respect for our religion or our culture. Armed men rampaged throughout the land, killing people and destroying things for no reason. For example, Tatari mullahs had always climbed the minarets of our mosques at midday to announce noon prayers, but the Moskali began shooting at them when they did that, and many died. We tried to fight back, but we were massacred.

"Many believed that the Turkish Sultan would save us. But, in 1792, he signed a peace treaty recognizing Russian control over Crimea. Hundreds of thousands of our people abandoned this beautiful land, refugees who went mainly to Ottoman-controlled territories in Turkey and the Balkans."

She stopped for a moment, trying to control her emotions, a few tears falling down her cheeks, which she quickly wiped away. Listening to her telling the tale of her people's suffering made it seem like she had been there and experienced everything she spoke about. But that was not the case. It was a historical memory seared into her soul, so real to her and others like her that she would willingly fight and die in recognition of it. She continued telling her tale;

"A few Tatari remained, but the waves of Slavic serfs steadily overwhelmed the holdouts. Our people became a minority in our own homeland. And, then, to make matters worse, in 1944, even before World War II ended, Stalin and the Soviet government, continuing the policies of the Russian Tsar, accused us of being Nazi collaborators. We were condemned as traitors. Forcibly removed from our homes. Our men were fighting and dying in battles against the Nazis but the police came to take us away. They gave my family 10 minutes to gather our belongings! My grandmother and my mother, who was only 12 years old, were forced into railroad cars."

The story, with all its emotional depth, was fascinating. I leaned forward slightly to listen carefully. The depth of her pain in recalling the struggle of her people made it clear that some Tatars were emotionally reliving such stories, though they had been born many years after the described events occurred.

"Imagine being forced into a cramped train car with no food," She said, sadly, "No water either. No proper sanitation. Forced to travel where cattle had just been transported. The trains were filled with the stink of dung and, later, from human excrement as well. Families were torn apart, often sent to different destinations, thousands of kilometers apart. Dreams were shattered. Hopes extinguished. That was the work of the Moskali. The same fascism that caused the invasion of this peninsula in 2014, and the full-scale invasion of in 2022."

She stopped for a moment, wiping away another tear.

"Supposedly," She continued, "they abolished serfdom long ago, yet everyone in Russia is still a slave. Even related Slavic people, like the Ukrainians, are treated like dirt. Their own soldiers, Russians themselves, are treated as cannon fodder. They use them, in human wave attacks, and lose enormous numbers, but the Moskali rulers don't care how many serfs die. Their serfs are too stupid to do anything but drink vodka and obey orders."

"Many Tatari died during the deportation, according to what I have read," I commented.

She nodded and continued the story,

"Yes. My mother's teenage brother died. He demanded to be allowed off the train, at a stop, to use the station toilet. The guards refused. He called them swine and they shot him in the head on the spot. They dumped his lifeless body off the train in the middle of nowhere. My grandmother reported the crime in Kazakhstan and demanded justice, but there was no justice. Not one guard was ever prosecuted. He was just a teenage boy…"

Terror and sorrow seemed to intertwine with words, and she no longer seemed like the confident leader I knew. Her eyes were watering, and her hands trembled as she continued.

"Twenty percent of us died before arrival at the destinations. Those who survived were dropped off in places like Kazakhstan, Uzbekistan, and various other locations. But, the terror didn't end. The government poisoned the minds of the local population, using every tool of propaganda they had. They branded us traitors. We were shunned in workplaces and attacked on the streets. Few would hire us in the jobs we were trained for. We struggled to survive. Within a year, 40% of the Tatari who left Crimea were dead. It was a genocide, which the Moskali are very good at."

I had read about the Tatar exile, but reading is an academic exercise, and, for the first time, I understood the suffering. Svetlana was too young to have experienced it firsthand, but the stories that she now repeated were a part of her being. It was almost as if she had been there. Almost as if they were her own memories. But, they were not. They were the collective memories of her people. Each word was filled with sadness and pride.

She continued to speak;

"During the war, my father fought for what he thought was our country. He was seriously wounded. He survived and wanted to return home, but by late 1945, instead of allowing him to return to Crimea, the Moskali government was forcibly sending demobilized Tatar soldiers to Kazakhstan. That is where his parents, as well as my mother and my grandmother, were living. I don't know much about the time between 1945 and 1955, because I wasn't born yet, but I know that my mother and father met in Kazakhstan and married.

"Unlike ethnic Russians, wounded Tatar veterans were not given much financial support. Despite a limp and a permanent disability from the war, he was forced to work with his hands, tirelessly, in the harsh Kazak sun. It was the only job he could get, and his love for my mother and determination to provide a future for us kept him going for a while. But, Central Asia is not our homeland. Crimean people are very susceptible to diseases that are common there. He passed away a few years after I was born. And, when that happened, things became worse for us."

The room felt physically weighed down by the horrifying history, and the crimes against humanity that had been committed by the Russians against the Crimean Tatars. The stories she now told were not distant memories – they were integral parts of her being. Her very identity was so deeply intertwined with the stories that she felt she had experienced the whole miserable thing herself. I could now better understand why the Tatars hated Russia and why they were willing to risk their lives in support of the rebellion.

"I am sorry for what your people went through," I said softly, trying to convey my compassion.

Svetlana smiled, but beneath her attempt at stoicism, more tears were forming, and a few slipped down her cheek. She quickly wiped them away.

"Thank you," she replied. "It is important to remember our past and share our story, as painful as it is. That is how we preserve who we are. We are simply fighting for justice and for the right to reclaim our lives. As long as Qirim remains under Moscow's control, it will never be a true home for us. It must become part of Ukraine again, even if that means some of us die in the process."

I nodded.

"I understand," I said, sincerely. "The bravery of the Tatars is impressive."

"Enough of this," she suddenly said, ending the discussion. "Some things cannot be changed. We can only change the future. That is why I will go to Ak Mecit and speak to Ismail."

"Thank you," I said.

8

As I said, earlier on, Ak Mecit is the Tatar name for the City of Simferopol. Svetlana, like many fighting partisans, preferred to call things by their Tatar, or "true" names. It wasn't very far away, longer in time than distance. It takes about an hour and a half by car to drive from Yevpatoriya to Simferopol, although the two cities are only 75 kilometers apart, mainly because the roads are so bad. She didn't intend to stay overnight. But, by nightfall, she had not yet returned. We hadn't heard a word. That wasn't entirely surprising. With the enemy surrounding us, and all lines of communication controlled by them, it was inherently difficult to send confidential information from one person to another.

Telephone calls, especially on a mobile phone, can be tapped. Modern internet-based instant messengers, voice-over-IP services, and email are better because they can be encrypted, but the messages can still be intercepted. Even if the enemy can't read a message, the mere fact that you are sending encrypted messages back and forth, can raise an alarm. For that reason, personal couriers are still heavily used despite the rise of computers and smartphones.

I was inside my cabin, just having fallen asleep, when a loud knock on the door jolted me awake. A surge of adrenaline filtered through me from head to toe, and I quickly rose and opened the door. It was Mustafa, standing there, in front of the door. He looked more haggard and exhausted than I felt.

"My friend," he said, "I know it is late, but Svetlana has returned and Ismail, the leader of partisans in Ak Mecit. whom we spoke about, is here with her. They ask you to come."

Ismail had accompanied Svetlana back to our camp. That seemed like a big deal in itself. It made sense only if he was ready to commit his men, which was something I had almost given up on, after Svetlana's skepticism.

Obviously, he wanted to meet me and size me up before making a final commitment. If the shoe were on the other foot, I would do no less. No responsible commander would risk men's lives without taking the measure of the man asking for help. A smile curled my lips. This was best news I could have ever hoped for. I had come close to writing off the mission, but my spirits were now lifted.

"I take it that he's ready to commit his men?" I asked as I put my shoes on as fast as I could.

Mustafa leaned on the door frame, with a sigh.

"I'm not sure," he said.

"Money won't be a problem..." I replied, as I incorrectly assumed that Ismail was looking for a cash payment in exchange for his services. "I'm authorized to commit whatever money and resources are needed. He and his men will be well compensated..."

"I don't think that is the issue," Mustafa said, stoically.

"What's the issue?" I asked.

Mustafa shrugged and said "Luchshe uslyshat' eto iz pervykh ruk". Roughly translated, this means:

"Better to hear it from the horse's mouth."

I followed him out, and we walked, together, through the dark camp toward its center where they were waiting for me. The cool dry air of the Crimean spring and, perhaps, the fact that things seemed to be going my way, made me feel energized. The night was crisp and refreshing. The crescent moon was several days past the full phase, and didn't provide much light, but its soft glow still cast an enchanting aura over everything. The difference between the mildness of Crimea, with its clear skies, and the cold wetness of northern Ukraine made it clear why Crimea is coveted by Russians, Ukrainians, and Tatars alike.

Moments later, we arrived at the same large table at which we had eaten the formal welcoming dinner, many days before. Everything looked the same except that the partisans were gone. It was too dangerous to keep so many people at the rest complex for too long especially when most had no connection to the former Institute that owned the place. Gathering too many, too often, might raise questions.

There were six of us. Svetlana, Sasha Melnyk and this new person, Ismail Yusofov, sitting at the table. Yasmina was serving tea. Ismail watched me carefully as I entered, and stood up, respectfully, to greet me. Standing, he seemed like a sturdy oak tree in a forest of saplings, but it wasn't because of his height. He was a mere 5'9" (175 cm.). Just an inch taller than Svetlana and no taller than Yasmina. But, his shoulders seemed as broad as mountain peaks, and there was no fat on his body. His hazel eyes seemed to pierce through the darkness, twinkling in the reflected light of the fire. His chiseled features – high cheekbones and a square jaw – added to a fiercely determined look. He had short, brown hair and a neatly trimmed beard, both of which were speckled with gray. His rough skin was heavily wrinkled by long exposure to the Crimean sun.

"Here they are!" Svetlana said, with a smile, when she saw us. "Come...come!"

She gestured towards Ismail. The two had been talking to each other in the native Crimean Tatar tongue. Only about 20% of Crimean Tatars still speak it, but a far higher percentage of partisans do. For them, speaking the native tongue is part of their rebellion against Russian rule. She switched to Russian when I arrived, to make sure I could understand, and began by introducing me.

"This is John Kovalenko," she said, "The American I told you about."

Ismail extended his hand and shook mine firmly.

"I am Ismail," he introduced himself and sat back down.

"Nice to meet you," I replied, as I and Mustafa both took a seat at the table.

Sinking into the chair brought relief to my weary body, aching from the extended reconnaissance near the Russian airbase. Only adrenaline kept me alert. Sleep beckoned, but the need for additional manpower was more pressing. Ismail's potential aid fueled a spark of excitement that kept my fatigue at bay. The man took a long sip of tea but wasted no time in getting to the point.

"The Moskali have imprisoned my people," Ismail declared, his words echoing like a battle cry. "My older brother is among them."

"Why? He's a politician, not a warrior," Sasha interjected. "He always seemed to side with them anyway..."

Ismail bristled. "He was NEVER on their side! He simply urged pragmatism."

"Generous interpretation..." Sasha retorted, undeterred.

I winced, recognizing the poor timing of Sasha's provocation. Getting Ismail agitated and angry was the last thing I needed, I desperately required his assistance. Yet I had no way to silence Sasha.

"I don't care how it seemed to you!" Ismail snapped. "We've had differences in opinion, but my brother has always been a patriot."

Sasha rolled his eyes, but thankfully the gesture was not seen by the other man. He had already turned his attention back to me.

"The Russians arrested my brother because he finally spoke out against them," Ismail stated. "He was one of our more pragmatic politicians. But, a few weeks ago, almost all our leaders got arrested and put in prison. In three days, they will be transferred to the Lefortovo prison in Moscow."

"A notorious place," Mustafa whispered in my ear, "No one ever escapes..."

"What did he say against Russia?" I asked.

"He spoke out against the pressured enlistment of our young men," he replied. "When the war began, they sent only professional contract soldiers. But, now, they're dragging young men to war. They claim the draft is limited to people with military experience. But, many Tatari, even below the age of 18, have been pressured to join the Russian army. The contracts they are forced to sign say they're volunteers but, in truth, no one wants to fight and die in Putin's war."

"I see..." I said, not knowing what else to say.

"If nothing is done," he continued, "we may never see them again. We must act immediately before they're transferred to Moscow!"

"Where are they being held?" Mustafa asked.

"In a special facility, newly built for political prisoners, on the territory of Detention Center No. 1, in Simferopol. There are 181 people, including our Tatari politicians. Also prisoners from other parts of occupied Ukraine."

"How do you propose to get them out, without getting killed?" Sasha asked, skeptically.

"That is the problem," Ismail admitted, with an uncertain look on his face. "We are guerrillas. We know how to strike hard where the enemy least expects. But, attacking a prison is not like planting a bomb on a railway track, or inside the engine compartment of a traitor's car. We are not familiar with attacking a fortified place, in a city like Simferopol, where there are huge numbers of Russian troops. How can my seven men defeat hundreds of Russian reinforcements?"

Sasha shook his head in disbelief.

"They can't," He stated, scornfully, "Unless they want to die. What do you expect us to do about it?"

"I want you to help me," Ismail replied.

Sasha seemed taken aback.

"You expect us to commit suicide with you?" he asked, in forceful and undisguised contempt for Ismail's request. "Even if we manage to live through the attempt, we would only join your brother in rotting, for the rest of our lives, in a Moskali jail."

"You are wrong," Ismail insisted. "Similar assaults have been successful in the past. And, with fewer men than I have. I've read about it!"

Sasha suppressed laughter.

"You've read about it?" He said, scornfully. "In a novel?"

"No." Ismail insisted. "In American books on military procedure, given to us by the Turks."

Sasha shook his head.

"American military books?" he blurted out, and laughed. "But, you can't even read English!"

That's when Ismail added something.

"Not just books..." he said. "This American is a Special Forces soldier. He is trained in such things. He can help us..."

Ismail was looking directly at me now, and I felt uncomfortable. I began to regret sending Svetlana to seek his help. This wasn't what I wanted. It wasn't what I planned. It was now clear how she had convinced him to return with her. She had promised him I would help him with his brother's imprisonment in exchange for his help in the planned attack on the Russian airbase. But, getting involved, whatever the merits might be, would divert time, attention, and necessary resources. I was inside Crimea to destroy Russian missile bunkers. That was the mission. Not freeing Tatar political prisoners. Orchestrating a prison break was a distraction that would consume precious time and equipment.

Ismail began speaking directly to me.

"Svetlana says you served for 20 years in the American Special Forces..." he said, with hope lighting up his eyes.

"Well, that's somewhat true," I confessed. "20 years in the US Army. About 18 in a Special Forces unit."

"The bottom line is that you have the training..." he concluded.

"I'm not sure that I do," I replied.

"But, she says you came here to attack a heavily defended Russian air base." He pointed out.

"True," I conceded.

"That is much more difficult than a prison." He insisted.

"Maybe," I admitted.

"She says you intend to do this in a matter of days, but need more men..."

"That's correct," I replied.

None of it was a secret to anyone present. Everyone knew why I was in Crimea. They also all knew I had asked Sveta to contact Ismail to get more men. But, the motivation that had dragged me from well-deserved sleep, was ebbing. My object was to enlist *his* help, NOT for him to enlist mine!

"All the generals in Kyiv seem to have full confidence in you." He concluded. "They must know details of your record. Given that, I also have confidence in you. You have successfully attacked heavily fortified facilities using small numbers of men, many times in the past?"

I took a deep breath.

It was true. I had been a part of many such missions. We always achieved a successful result. But, the enemies I faced had never been as sophisticated as the Russian army.

I nodded but qualified my answer.

"Mostly in the Middle East and Afghanistan..."

"It doesn't matter where the enemy is located, does it?" he asked.

"No," I admitted, truthfully. "But, it does matter who the enemy is, and how sophisticated they are in deploying countermeasures."

"You must believe that the Moskali are the type of enemy that such attacks can succeed against. If not, you wouldn't be planning to raid their airbase." He proclaimed, "Help me now, and in return, I will help you…"

It was a reasonable deal, but disconcerting to have the tables turned on me in this way. It was all coming out of left field. Unexpected and, to be frank, unwanted. I knew nothing about the facility holding his brother and the other prisoners. I didn't have time to study it the way I should when planning a raid. It felt like I was being strong-armed into participating. If I helped him, I would probably lose rare and irreplaceable technical equipment in the process. But if I refused, I could kiss any hope of receiving his help a sweet goodbye!

"I'm not sure what to say," I admitted.

Ismail misinterpreted my statement, taking it not for indecision, but as an expression of humble gratitude for his praise. His subsequent words assumed my agreement to assist him, though I had not actually consented to do so.

"They won't see our strike coming!" he exclaimed, enthusiastically. "The guards are notorious for their drinking. They'll all be intoxicated. The real threat is reinforcements."

His analysis was likely correct. I had seen Russians operate, time and time again, in Kharkiv, Bakhmut, and elsewhere. Their greatest weakness was always habitual drunkenness. It greatly undermined their effectiveness. However, dealing with reinforcements would be a challenge. In Bakhmut, no matter how many we killed (and we killed tens of thousands) more always kept coming. Russian officers, up and down the chain of command, have no concern for the lives of their men. Russian soldiers are just cannon fodder.

In this case, however, things were different. Stopping the Russians from overwhelming us with numbers simply meant that we had to stop the guards from calling reinforcements. That was impossible on a wide-open battlefield. But, a defined area, like a jail, is very different. Wires could be cut, electronic devices could inundate the area with interference, and both cell phone and mobile data use could be blocked. If done correctly, the guards could be isolated for a considerable period of time.

Svetlana finally injected herself into the conversation, repeating the terms of the offer Ismail had made just a short time before. Unlike Ismail, who seemed to assume my eagerness to help him, she accurately saw the hesitation on my part.

"If you assist Ismail in rescuing these political prisoners, his men will support your mission against the missile storage warehouse." She pointed out again, knowing my desperation for men. "That's correct, isn't it, Ismail?"

"That is what I said," he replied confidently. "Help me free my brother and you can count on me now and in the future."

It was a worthwhile proposition, but I felt like I was being pushed into something without proper consideration. I needed time.

"It's strange, isn't it, that the Russians just suddenly decided to arrest so many Crimean Tatar politicians, all at the same time?" I asked, hoping to buy time to weigh my options. "It seems doubtful that all of them suddenly began opposing Moscow's mobilization initiative…"

"They weren't all just arrested." Ismail explained, "Many were arrested long ago. And, others left for mainland Ukraine. My brother, and those he closely works with, thought they could play by Moscow rules. For a long time, the strategy worked. They thought they were being pragmatic and that they could help the Tatari people. My brother believed that by quietly urging the Russian government to treat us fairly, he could accomplish what we could not. But, the war in Ukraine has been going badly for Russia. They're desperate to fill the ranks of the army. When my brother opposed mobilization, they charged him with disrespecting the military. That's a crime now, and a convenient excuse to arrest whomever they wish."

"It's a huge risk…" I pointed out, "Attacking a prison like the one you describe, inside a city like Simferopol, gives us no place to run if we get caught."

"That is why we need you," Ismail insisted, "So, we won't get caught! But, we must rescue them."

"What about your own mission, John Kovalenko?" Sasha asked. "Destroying the missile storage area is vital to Ukraine. Saving Ismail's brother from the results of his own foolishness is not. If you agree to attack the prison, you will be distracted, at the very least."

I was thinking the same, but was happy he was the one to say it, rather than me. That's when Mustafa chimed in.

"Perhaps, there is a way to do both," he suggested.

I nodded, thoughtfully, conceding to myself that I had little choice but to help Ismail to have a chance of succeeding in my own mission.

"I understand the importance of freeing the Tatar leadership," I stated, "But we cannot free these prisoners or destroy Russia's missile bunkers without a very well-thought-out plan."

Mustafa nodded.

"Yes," he said. "But, can both operations be carried out successfully?"

"Ismail seems to be very familiar with the prison's location and the layout will be fundamentally the same as it was when the Ukrainians controlled it," I pointed out, "We do need intel about their security protocols…"

"We already have that." Ismail said eagerly, "A member of the prison's clerical staff is a sympathizer. She gave us complete specifications in exchange for a small payment."

"Well, that's a start." I said, encouraged, "We need a quick entry and exit strategy. We need to block their communications, to stop them calling for reinforcements. But, we can't keep that coverage going for very long."

"There might be heavy resistance…" Sasha pointed out, anxiously.

"It's possible," I said. "The priority is on neutralizing the first line of guards before they realize what's happening."

"Based on your experience," Svetlana asked, "is there a good probability of success? Can we successfully attack this prison and free the prisoners with minimal or no losses?"

I sighed. It was a very difficult question.

"We're talking about a military operation," I explained, honestly. "It's not a guerrilla attack, where you sabotage things while no one watches. The more men we have, the higher the probability of success. But, open confrontation always means an elevated chance of serious injuries and deaths."

"I understand," Svetlana confirmed.

"We've got five fighting men plus me, available here, in the Yevpatoriya region, right?"

Mustafa nodded.

"How many men do you have?" I asked Ismail.

"Seven plus myself," he replied.

"A total of 14 men…" I said, "How many guards?"

"They're understaffed," Ismail replied. "Many guards are mobilized and serving in the army now. About 19 are still guarding the prison. Not all will be on duty at the same time."

"They work in eight-hour shifts?" I asked.

"More or less, yes." the man replied.

"Three shifts per day?"

"Yes."

"Okay," I noted, thoughtfully, "that means we'll be facing only 6 or 7 guards. And, the only way they can get reinforcements is to call for them."

The man nodded.

"We can stop them from calling, at least temporarily," I noted, "What about the rest of Detention Center No. 1?"

"Another 6 to 7 guards at most," he answered.

"So, our strike force of 14 potentially faces the same number of defenders," I concluded aloud. "And, we'll have the element of surprise and the potential to be very organized. They'll be facing chaos and uncertainty. If they can't contact each other or call outside the prison, they'll be in complete disarray."

"You think it can be done successfully, then, with minimal losses, then?" Svetlana asked.

"Based on the information Ismail has given me so far, yes." I opined. "But, cutting them off from communication with each other and the outside world is critical. Otherwise, they call for reinforcements, and our chance of success falls to zero. We'll need to cut the physical phone and internet wires, and use electronic warfare to block their cell phone connectivity."

"Excellent!" Ismail exclaimed.

"But, let's say we free the prisoners...what do we do with them afterward?" I asked.

I stopped there to assess the reaction.

"You are right," Ismail said, as if I was expressing an opinion rather than asking a simple question. "We can only free the Tatari prisoners. We don't have the time or resources for more."

"How many Tatar prisoners are there?" I asked.

"Twelve." the man replied.

I shook my head.

"That's a lot of people…" I said. "I don't know about your resources in Simferopol, but it's one thing to free them and another to hide them for months at a time, in a city that's filled with Russian surveillance cameras."

"You would be surprised," Ismail replied.

I shook my head.

"Unpleasantly surprised, perhaps," I retorted. "The face of every political prisoner is well known. Facial recognition programs will ID them almost immediately."

"Which is why we won't try to hide them," Svetlana interjected. "Not for more than a day or two. We have more resources than you think. We can send 12 people to Ukrainian-controlled territory using the underground railroad."

She said it in Russian, but once translated, it sounded like something out of the American Civil War.

"The what?" I asked.

"A network of people," she explained, "About 1,000 sympathizers are embedded inside the Russian army. They help us from time to time. And, even many Moskali officers can be paid to look the other way…"

"A thousand sympathizers?" I asked, astounded.

"The Moskali involuntarily conscript many young Tatari and other minorities, and claim they're volunteers." She explained. "They want casualties far from the power center where angry people can overthrow them. The result is our eyes and ears inside the Russian army. Many are ready to shoot their commanders when and if the opportunity arises."

"Interesting…" I said, thinking about the implications.

Putting armaments in the hands of people who hate you is usually not a good idea. The Russians might be able to control those people to a point, threatening to shoot them, for example, for the slightest disobedience. But, they would turn on them, and use those guns against Russia the moment they got the chance. Out of desperation, the Russian army was creating a fifth column, inside itself, just waiting to rebel.

"Svetlana, we have never tried to get twelve people out at the same time!" Sasha complained.

"We could put them in safe houses, temporarily," Mustafa suggested, "Feed them into the network, two or three at a time…"

"Only at great risk…" Sasha warned.

Then, Svetlana spoke in a calming voice,

"Everything we do involves great risk, Sasha," she stated firmly. "There are many things we can do, But, what we cannot do is allow the Moskali to silence and imprison the voice of the Tatari people. I am correct, am I not, John?"

I was momentarily at a loss for words. Who was I, as a foreigner, to opine on the voice of the Tatar people? I saw things from my point of view. Not from theirs. I had given my opinion about our prospects for success, but I felt like I was being sucked in. This proposed rescue posed a significant risk to my goal of destroying the missile warehouse. If I had no choice but to help make a side operation a success, I would do my best, but I didn't want to give opinions on political questions.

Nevertheless, it is obvious that abandoning the entire local Tatar political wing to the clutches of a Russian prison was out of the question. Ismail's brother was important to Ismail. But, his fate alone was not the point. The point was the survival of the Tatars. The partisans could not allow their political leadership to wither away and rot in a Russian jail.

"Yes, I agree." I finally replied, putting myself in the fray, neck deep.

"Good!" she said. "Once we free them, we'll join forces, and destroy that missile warehouse,"

Ismail nodded his agreement, and she turned her attention back to him.

"The decision is made." she asserted. "We stand by you and fight by your side. Our combined forces will free the prisoners. John Kovalenko, who possesses the experience necessary to make it a success, will lead the team."

Her declaration caught me off guard. While my participation in freeing the prisoners seemed a logical step, her assumption that I had agreed to lead the entire operation was flawed and presumptuous. But, to achieve my objective, I needed Ismail's assistance. And to secure his help, I had to reciprocate. Cooperation, it seemed, was the path forward.

Ismail, however, was the one who actively objected. He shook his head.

"This is my fight, my responsibility. My men look to me for leadership, and I cannot relinquish command."

Svetlana frowned and leaned back slightly.

"You are a great warrior," she said with sincerity, "respected by all. But, you must consider the larger picture. Our American ally has many years of experience with this type of operation. He knows the special equipment he has brought with him and its limitations. We must ensure the most effective and efficient operation, which can only happen if he leads it."

Ismail turned toward me, as if I had personally demanded command authority and spoke;

"You are still an outsider. My reservations don't come from personal desire or ambition. My people may not readily follow your commands..."

Svetlana leaned forward and began speaking without giving me a chance to say anything, her gaze fixed upon Ismail.

"They will do what you order them to do." She insisted. "If you order them to obey Colonel Kovalenko, that is what they will do."

I shook my head.

"I don't remember ever volunteering at all," I finally blurted out, bluntly, "Let alone asking for command..."

It was the truth, but it seemed to shock everyone. Perhaps, my Russian language skills were not as good as I thought they were. Ismail, Svetlana, and everyone else assumed that I not only had agreed to participate but intended to lead the mission.

"You don't want to help us, then?" Ismail said, angrily, his tone underlain with worry.

"I didn't say that..." I replied.

He knew as well as I did that I needed his help as much as he needed mine. My harsh-sounding objection was made out of frustration and annoyance. So, I backtracked and said,

"This operation demands precision and quick decisions. I can offer my guidance. But, you must make the ultimate decisions. Follow the plan I set out, and the decisions I make as we execute it, but retain command in the eyes of your men. But, you must do exactly as I say..."

The room was thick with tension as everyone awaited Ismail's decision. He paused, torn between his ego and practical considerations. After a long moment, he let out a deep sigh as understanding finally settled over him.

"I accept your proposal," Ismail conceded, meeting my gaze, eye to eye. "I will instruct my men to obey your commands. You will make the decisions, but I will be with you and will back you up if needed. I, too, will obey your commands."

"Ismail, you have made the right choice." Svetlana said, "This will inspire everyone and fuel our fight. Together, we will free those who have been imprisoned unjustly, including your brother, and it will mark a new chapter of cooperation."

I was impressed. She was presumptuous and far too ready to substitute her choices for mine. However, she was also superb at giving speeches, motivating men, making necessary decisions, and in generally getting things done. It was clear that neither I nor Ismail had taken command. She might not be physically present when the rescue occurred, but Svetlana had taken command. She wielded authority like a seasoned general.

"After this mission is completed, we will devote our combined resources to destroy the missile warehouse." She announced.

But, Sasha remained skeptical.

"If any of us are still alive, afterward..." he added, sarcastically.

I didn't like being coerced into a mission. But, participating in freeing the Tatars meant I would get more men. We had a binding promise from Ismail that, just one day earlier, seemed almost impossible. It meant that I could soon attack the Russian airbase safely and successfully. Now it was crucial to make sure that the attempt to rescue the prisoners was successful. If not, we might not even survive, let alone combine our forces for a second mission.

9

Simferopol is an ancient city at the heart of the Crimean Peninsula. It is the administrative center and largest city. According to modern historians, the city was founded in the 6th century BC, by ancient Scythians. Ancient Greek and Roman historians, however, told a different tale. They claimed that the area around Simferopol was the origin of the Amazon people, a legendary ancient race of female warriors whose capital was in the ancient city of Taurica. Part of the modern city of Simferopol is built on top of Taurica's ruins. Traces of the ancient Amazon capital no longer remain. But, according to the Romans, Taurica's ruins could be visited by anyone who chose to go to the area.

Simferopol's Tatar name, Ak Mescit, translates literally to "White Mosque." The name refers to an ancient mosque built from white stone, which stood at the city center during the age of the Crimean Khanate. Over the course of 27 centuries, the city has been ruled by many empires. The most recent is the Russian Federation.

Time was pressingly short, and our group arrived in the city after an hour and a half drive, a day after I met Ismail. We gathered, together with the local partisans, inside a small, somewhat run-down old Soviet-style apartment. Mustafa, his nephew, Muhammad, Sasha, two other men from our group, and seven unknown partisans from Ismail's group, were there. Both Svetlana and Yasmina desperately wanted to come, but Ismail refused. His opposition was not based on any preconceived notion about the role of women, as you might suspect. It was pure practicality.

We were preparing to launch a fierce attack on a heavily fortified complex. Yasmina and her grandmother were both intelligent and capable women. However, it was unrealistic to expect them to hold their own against well-trained burly men in hand-to-hand combat. I saw potential roles for them as backup snipers, but I didn't press the matter. I was relieved because it meant that Yasmina would stay out of danger, safe and sound.

A detailed map of Simferopol was displayed on a large screen TV, mounted to the wall at the front of the room. Ismail was standing in front of it, pointing to specific areas.

"This is Elevatornyi Street," he said, as everyone nodded their understanding.

He traced the path he wanted them to follow, his finger gliding along the map.

"We're going to follow this route, through here. Now, here is where the detention center is located...and here, just behind the old building, this is where political prisoners are kept. And, now, I am going to turn this information session to our guest from America, John Kovalenko, an American soldier with expertise in Special Forces operations. He will be fighting by our side..."

There was a murmur of approval and seeming excitement rippling at this announcement. Encouraged by the positive reaction, Ismail continued.

"Colonel Kovalenko will assist me in leading the attack and he will explain the rest to you. Once we are in the field, you must follow his orders just as you would mine."

He motioned to me and I walked over to the map, pointing to the relevant points as I spoke to the group.

"Our approach will be under cover of darkness, from the east, here, except Rustem's group, who will approach from the west," I said, clicking forward on the computer's remote, which removed the map of the city and replaced it with a diagram of the correctional facility itself. "Everyone will wear a bulletproof vest for personal protection."

I stopped for a second to make sure I had everyone's attention and, once reassured that I did, I continued:

"You'll be with me, Mustafa..." I said, pointing to a place on the map projection, "and we split up here." I pointed to another spot not far from the first.

"You will plant a radio wave interference emitter, as close as possible to the northeastern side of the facility," I continued, "I will plant the other one, here, very close to the entrance. Once both generators are placed, I'll activate remotely. While active, they'll block all mobile phone and data signals. We also need to cut all the physical wires leading into the building, here and here, and I'll do that. They'll be cut off and isolated. Unable to call for reinforcements."

I pointed to the place where the wires all converged, near the entry door, but was rudely interrupted.

"What is this?" Muhammad blurted out, preventing me from moving on to the next part of the plan. "I didn't sign up for this!"

"What is what?" I asked.

Muhammad continued, turning to address Ismail.

"I joined the partisan movement because it was Tatar and Muslim." He stated. "I didn't sign up to work for Americans. Why is he being allowed to control this mission?"

"I remain the leader." Ismail immediately responded. "He is assisting me."

"He is the one telling us what to do…" Muhammad objected.

"He is a trained soldier with 20 years of experience in Special Forces," Ismail replied. "His knowledge and experience assures our success."

Muhammad was not yet aware of my intimacy with Yasmina, but he hated me with a passion and was a constant source of irritation. This now marked the second time he was openly ridiculing and opposing me. But, I felt powerless to act decisively because I feared alienating the others. I took a deep breath and remained calm and composed, ignoring his disdain and willful lack of respect.

Anger simmered beneath the surface, but I suppressed it. This was far too important to let my personal feelings cloud my judgment. If we failed, the prisoners would remain prisoners and we might end up captured or killed. In that event, my mission to destroy the Russian missile bunkers would also be a failure.

"I understand that you have concerns, Muhammad," I said, keeping my voice steady. "But we don't have the luxury of doubting each other now. Let's work together for the common good."

Muhammad crossed his arms over his chest, his dark eyes narrowing.

"We were fighting a successful guerrilla war long before you came," he replied. "I know this place better than anyone. I was imprisoned here for a while. If anyone, other than Ismail, should be leading this attack, it is me. I refuse to follow a plan that will get us all killed!"

"How would you know that the plan is going to get you killed when you haven't even finished hearing about it?" I asked.

I could feel the tension building in the room. The other partisans seemed to grow restless and uneasy at the sudden clash. It seemed wise to defuse the situation.

"Muhammad, I respect your experience with this place," I said, finally, choosing my words carefully. "But, right now, we need to work together."

His eyes bore into mine, the resentment clear. He was having none of it.

"Why should a Muslim cooperate with an infidel?" he blurted out. "What common ground can we possibly have?"

Yasmina's unspoken name hung in the air. Love had dealt its own set of cards. We were both in love with the same woman. But, she was in love with me, not him. He didn't know that yet, of course, but he hated me anyway, because he already viewed me as his potential rival. The resentment was like a cancerous malignancy, constantly growing.

"Right now," I said firmly, but continuing to keep my anger in check, "we must set aside personal feelings for the greater good. Our people, the people of Ukraine, they need us..."

For a moment, it almost seemed like a flicker of understanding passed through his eyes. But then, his face hardened again and the walls of anger and resentment were back up.

"*Our* people?" he said, sarcastically. "You are NOT one of our people? You never were, you are not now, and never will be!"

"I'm talking about Ukraine," I explained. "My ancestors came from Ukraine, just like yours."

He scoffed at that and was about to say something more, but a resounding and authoritative voice loudly interrupted him.

"Enough!" Ismail exclaimed. "Continue the briefing, John Kovalenko."

But, Muhammad refused to stop.

"No!" he exclaimed, turning away from me, and speaking to the others. "Did he serve in the American Special Forces? Maybe. Who cares? If Iblis, himself, came to tell us he would help us, would be work with him? Iblis is powerful, is he not? But, we wouldn't. We would reject him. The same with this man..."

I was trying very hard to stay under control. But, Iblis is the Islamic name for Satan and that went too far. I was about to lash back. However, before I could, Ismail interjected forcefully. That was a very good thing. As an outsider, my words would have had very little impact.

"I told you, that's enough!" he repeated more sternly than before, staring angrily, straight at Muhammad. "It means shut your mouth! If I hear another word out of you, I'll take you down and lock you up. You will have no place among us on this mission. I am in command. Whether you like it or not, John Kovalenko is second in command. This is my decision. Not yours. You WILL obey his commands. If you don't, you suffer the consequences. Do you understand me now?"

Ismail's stature transcended rank. As a respected elder who'd been an adult when Muhammad was born, he wielded moral authority. Muhammad had long admired Ismail's military acumen and reputation. He had been in awe of the man even as a teenager. His deference stemmed not just from being outnumbered, but from a deep-seated emotional inability to oppose such a revered figure for long.

"I always do my part," Muhammad grumbled in response, backing down, "but mark my words, you will regret listening to this man. No infidel should to give orders to a Muslim!"

"Are you deaf?" Ismail asked, again, in an even harder tone, stepping toward Muhammad, clearly about to act on his threat. "Did you not hear what I just said?"

"I heard you," Muhammad muttered, unhappily.

"Then shut your mouth!" Ismail ordered in no uncertain terms, and the angry young man said no more.

It was clear by now that he would continue to be a problem going forward. Trying to reason with him was pointless. Logic, reason, common sense, and even ultimate success or failure, didn't seem to matter. It wasn't about differences in religion or a genuine question about my knowledge, experience, or skill. It was all about Yasmina.

From that point, I decided that he wouldn't be a part of my mission to destroy the missile bunkers. But, it was too late to get rid of him now. I tried to keep my focus on the plan to free the prisoners. Fortunately, Muhammad did shut his mouth. I meticulously outlined my plan, detailing each person's role, and the group listened carefully. Everyone seemed to understand their roles. Best of all, they seemed convinced that we would succeed. Despite Muhammad's earlier intransigence, I had gained the trust and respect of the other partisans.

10

That night in Simferopol, the streetlamps weren't working. This wasn't unusual. Public services often fail in both Ukraine and Russia, just as they did in Soviet times. Despite decades of change, the reliability of utilities like water and electricity remains poor. "Repairs" seem to happen constantly, but one problem just replaces another. Nothing ever gets fixed for good.

The moon, dim and partly hidden by clouds, gave little light to the empty streets. As we moved through the shadows, I was thankful for the darkness. It came from both nature and the ongoing incompetence of post-Soviet utility companies. While on leave, I'd often been frustrated by these system failures. But now, I welcomed systemic failure. The darker, the better. It worked to our advantage.

Our group split into two teams. One team got out of their vehicle at the intersection of Elevatornyi Lane and Elevatornyi Street. The other arrived separately at the corner of Geroiv Stalingrada and Elevatornyi Lane, just to the west. Yes, you read that right. Simferopol really does have multiple nearby roads named Elevatornyi, and the big prison is located there. One is called a street, another a lane, and so on. It's confusing, but that's typical for the former Soviet Union.

I sent the teams in different directions to avoid drawing attention. The plan was simple: converge on the prison, storm it, get in quickly, free the prisoners, and get out even faster.

As always before a major operation, I felt both excited and uncertain. The prison was intimidating—a huge complex with ancient, decaying, but massive walls. It stretched from our position on Elevatornyi Lane all the way northeast to the train tracks leading downtown.

Climbing those high walls would have been too difficult. I had no intention of trying. Our approach was simpler and faster: we'd go right through the front door!

My AK-74 rifle was at my side. I patted it, and felt reassured. The AK-74 was designed by Kalishnikov, the same Soviet weapons expert who created the more famous AK-47. It is a lesser known example of his art, but it is a much better rifle. I was confident that it would serve us well. Meanwhile, as usual, I also had the Sig Sauer P365XL, safely hidden inside a holster strapped to my lower leg, just in case of emergency, but I preferred not to fire either gun.

My plan was to avoid injuring or killing guards if it could be avoided. But, injury and death was a risk, not only for the enemy, but for us as well. The two radio interference generators would render every cell phone inside the prison grounds useless. That meant that our own phones would be useless also. So, I carried an old short-distance walkie-talkie on my belt. The range was limited to about one kilometer, but that was more than enough.

Mobile phones operate on radio waves with frequencies within the range of 900 MHz to 1.8 GHz. Mobile data services, such as 4G and 5G operate between 1.8 GHz and 4.7 GHz. The electronic jammers were set to jam frequencies between 800 MHz to 5 GHz. Short distance walkie-talkies use frequencies in the Ultra High Frequency (UHF) band, in the range of 462-467 MHz. They'd remain unaffected.

"Go! Now!" I whispered to Mustafa.

He vanished into the darkness, knowing exactly what was expected of him. He needed to carry a small box, containing a radio frequency interference generator, to the location I had chosen for it. For an older man, Mustafa's energy level and agility were extraordinary. He was the most reliable fighter I had, despite his age, and that was why I assigned such an important task to him.

I headed towards the entrance, momentarily finding cover behind a rundown wall. Navigating in the darkness by infrared goggles, I carefully positioned my radio frequency interference generator. It was only a matter of time before Mustafa placed his. When I cut the physical landlines for the phones and internet, I would use a remote to activate both generators. We would need to act quickly after that.

We had full plans for the facility, sent electronically by the Ukrainians, via Telegram Messenger, an off-the-shelf messaging app the Russian government had once tried to ban but was now commonly used by Russian operatives is all areas controlled by them. Before the Russian invasion in 2014, Ukraine had also used Detention Center #1 as a prison and Ukrainian intelligence kept track of everything the Russians did there, including changes to the building's structure. They might miss a few things but, generally, they knew everything about the facility. I knew exactly where to go. The physical communications lines entered the buildings near the front door at a metal box, which housed incoming phone and optical fiber lines as well as electric wires. I had to reach that box and cut the lines. Not a big deal.

I felt the silent vibration of my walkie-talkie, and picked up the handset..

"Done." Mustafa announced quietly.

I pressed the response button.

"Good." I whispered back. "Stay on call."

I returned the walkie-talkie to its hook.

Arriving at metal box, I took out a small pair of wire cutters and snipped the phone and fiber optic cables and flipped the switch on my remote, activating the radio frequency interference generators. They snapped into action, creating an invisible barrier that blocked all cell phone call and mobile based internet traffic. The prison was cut off from the outside world.

In the darkness, in spite of my night vision goggles, I almost cut another set of wires by mistake, but stopped myself in the nick of time. I realized at the last possible moment that I had almost cut the electric lines, thanks to the difficulty in seeing and discerning size differences of cool objects under infrared vision. For one thing, I was not interested in electrocuting myself and, for another, we needed the lights on, not out. It was important to the plan. Having saved myself, just in the nick of time, from a catastrophic error, I unhooked my walkie-talkie again, and sent a message to all team leaders.

"Operation Midnight Storm is a GO!" I exclaimed in Russian. "I repeat. Operation Midnight Storm is a GO!"

I was the closest to the front door, but knew they wouldn't be far behind. So, I didn't wait. I quickly picked the lock on the outside door, and stepped inside the building through the unlocked door, finding myself inside a sort of empty waiting room. A host of plain looking, old empty chairs lined the poorly maintained walls. There was a window, in front of me, that could be slid open, during opening hours, in response to an outside inquiry. Something like a doctor's office. A large doorway, with a heavy lock, stood a little way to the right of the window. I ignored the window and went for the door.

The inner door's lock was far superior to the one on the building's exterior entrance. It resembled a lock that might be built into a miniature vault door, serving as the true barrier to entry. It guarded the actual threshold to the jail's inner sanctum, unlike the outer door that merely led to a waiting room and clerical staffed areas. Picking such a sophisticated lock would have been too difficult and time-consuming.

A silencer was tightly screwed onto the end of my AK-74, but shooting out the door lock still made a huge racket that almost seemed like an exploding grenade. I kicked the door open. Two guards sat at a small table across the room. They were drinking vodka, shot glasses still in hand, apparently trying to watch an American movie which had been dubbed into Russian. It was being streamed in from an internet pirate channel, on one of their phones.

I had cut off their Wi-Fi and the radio jamming devices were blocking 4G and 5G data streams, but streaming video operates redundantly, with data streams slightly ahead of the picture formation. The picture on their phone began breaking up at about the same time as I kicked in the door. One guard, a blonde, fair skinned, overweight, giant of a man, was busy shaking the phone, trying to get the picture back. He didn't realize his communications channel had been severed.

Their state of utter intoxication delayed their response time, but it didn't take more than a few seconds for them to realize that I was covering their every move with a deadly AK-74. The other guard was both slimmer and smaller. He was dark haired, with swarthy skin and somewhat almond shaped eyes, looking like he was part Kazakh or some other central Asian nationality. In spite of the fact that I was pointing my rifle at them, it seemed like he was about to reach for his gun.

"Stop!" I warned in Russian, my voice cold as ice.

I preferred not to kill him, but I would it if I had to.

"You go for that gun and you're dead!" I warned.

His hand stopped moving, and he slowly withdrew his arm back to his side.

They were visibly drunk, and the vodka bottle was nearly empty, a testament to the notorious drinking habits of the average Russian. As a nationality, they usually consume far more alcohol than Americans. Still, because most of them start in childhood, their brains become accustomed to operating at high levels of alcohol. Although their motor functions and reflexes were impaired, they suffered no immediate loss of basic faculties. With my AK-74 pointed squarely at them, they were well aware that any misstep could prove fatal.

"Hands up, NOW!" I barked in Russian.

The guards' eyes widened and they obeyed. All four hands went skyward—they had no desire to die.

"Who are you?" one guard asked, his voice quivering.

"Not your business to know," I replied curtly.

Seconds later, the rest of my team arrived, clad in bulletproof vests, masks and black latex gloves, just like me. I didn't know all their names. Half were from the resistance cell in Simferopol and I'd just met them. I could roughly identify the individuals from Yevpatoriya even with their faces covered. An unlikely bunch—ragtag former smugglers, plumbers, IT experts, poets and so on—forged into fighters by the tumultuous times. I also recognized Muhammad and Ismail. I saw Sasha and one of Ismail's men take charge of the two guards

"Secure the weapons and search them to see if they have more," I ordered in Russian, "Tie their hands behind their backs. Tightly. We'll bring them with us."

The video surveillance camera in the corner of the room, fixed just below the ceiling, was obvious. One shot from my silenced rifle took it out. Pieces of the device scattered over the floor.

My attention returned to the guards, who had now been stripped of weapons.

"Where are the keys?" I demanded.

The fat guard trembled and sweated. His pants were already wet and there was a small pool of liquid at his feet.

"The, the... desk..." He said.

I checked it, and found a big key ring with many keys in the top drawer. Trying each key sequentially, on the next armored door, in front of us, I finally found the right one and opened it. Past that armored door was the inner prison. I signaled to the others. In a few seconds, everyone, including the guards we'd captured, were inside, heading through the hallway. The fat blonde haired guard seemed a little less drunk than his smaller companion. Maybe because he was bigger. Maybe, because he had peed out some of the alcohol already.

"Where are the Tatar prisoners?" I demanded.

"I don't know..." he said. "I was on leave until yesterday. I only work at the front desk. I swear!"

I pointed my rifle at his head and looked at the other guard.

"What about you?" I asked, coldly.

He shook his head, feigning ignorance.

"If neither of you knows anything, then you're of no use to me. You know what happens to people who are useless?"

"I, I..." he stuttered, and shook his head. "I know that they came a few days ago..."

"Who is in charge of the Tatar prisoners?" I asked.

"Not me..." he stuttered again.

"I see." I said, moving back, and raising my rifle to make them think I would shoot them. "So, you are both useless to me..."

They were terrified, looking at each other with worried eyes, the blonde fat one creating a new puddle of liquid below himself. I knew they were judging me according to their own standards. A wrong answer could mean death or torture. That would be the case had our roles been reversed. If I were their prisoner, neither would likely hesitate before wounding or killing me for the slightest bit of information. I did not disabuse them of the idea that I would do the same.

In truth, I wouldn't have killed or injured either of them. Not while they were in my custody and control. I don't kill or wound men who are disarmed and helpless. It violates the Geneva Convention and directly conflicts with the training I received. It is also a violation of the traditions and customs of war. On top of that, that type of vile behavior isn't in me. But, I knew they were judging me by their own low standards. So, they were genuinely frightened that their next breath might be their last.

"I'm waiting for an answer," I said, in the same icy tone.

Combined with my mask and their utter intoxication, I may have seemed like a demon from hell, or as close an approximation as any rotten-to-the-core Russian guard could imagine. But, there was no immediate response, so I added;

"I'm not a patient man..."

"Don't kill us!" the skinny guard said, finally. "I remember, now. They're on the 3rd floor, in cells 301 to 306."

"Smart boy..." I said, "Assuming you are not lying, you may yet live to a ripe old age and tell this story to your grandchildren. Otherwise..."

I gestured with my finger across my throat, mimicking a slashing motion.

A self-proclaimed "do-gooder" might argue that I was "emotionally torturing" the guards, even if I had no intention of carrying out the threats. Maybe, they would be right. However, I had no choice. Lives hung in the balance, not the least of which were our own. We didn't have an endless amount of time to search around to find who we were looking for. The radio jammers, for one thing, had only a limited battery life. I desperately needed accurate information fast. Unless these two wretched souls genuinely believed that their miserable lives were at stake, they wouldn't cooperate. They'd lie and stall, hoping to delay us.

They didn't deserve sympathy. They could hardly be viewed as innocent victims. Exceptions might exist, but as a group, they're abusers. Prisoners in Russian jails consistently report sadistic treatment and extortion. Guards routinely steal scarce sanitary items and any high-quality food provisions meant for inmates. Inmates are habitually left in unsanitary conditions, lacking basic necessities. Knowing this, I felt little sympathy for the guards. So, I continued playing my game with them.

"It had better be the truth," I said skeptically, once more.

"It is..." the lanky guard insisted. "I swear!"

"We'll see..." I stated, deliberately leaving him in a state of uncertainty.

With a gesture, I signaled our advance. Approaching the stairway cautiously, I entered it only to be met by a hail of bullets. An overlooked guard, wielding an automatic rifle, had opened fire. Fortunately, like his comrades, he was intoxicated. Most shots went wide, but one struck my flak jacket, and the impact slammed me against the wall in a flash of pain. I marveled at how much vodka it must have taken to impair the guard's aim so severely. It had to be a lot.

The guard's extreme inebriation likely saved my life, turning what would have been a deadly ambush into a clumsy, albeit dangerous, encounter. The attack paused, but I heard the ominous sound of an old cartridge being discarded, replaced by a new one. I fired back, managing to shatter another video camera but, other than that, the bullets merely struck concrete. My assailant remained safely hidden. I was in the wrong place at the wrong time. If I stayed put, another volley of bullets could find me by sheer chance and statistical probability. A single bullet to an unprotected head or neck could kill or cripple me. I stepped back, ready to retreat, when a loud whoosh interrupted.

It was the sound of a bullet being fired from a silenced rifle, and the lifeless body of the Russian guard tumbled forward and down the stairs, still clutching his own rifle. When he finally stopped at the bottom of the stairwell, I saw a neatly delivered wound in his forehead. Surprisingly, Muhammad had fired that shot. War makes strange bedfellows. I looked at him, smiled and nodded in gratitude, but there was no response. He didn't seem to have changed his mind about me, but at least he was smart enough to see that, for the moment, his fate was wrapped up in mine.

I didn't have the luxury to devote any more thought to him. Instead, I motioned for the team to follow me and we climbed up the stairs. When we finally reached the 3rd floor, we found another guard, supposedly in charge of the floor, sitting in a chair at a small desk, his eyes closed, sleeping in an alcohol-filled stupor. As usual, there was the empty bottle of vodka next to him.

Apparently, he had remained soundly asleep despite the shooting in the nearby stairwell. I fired a shot at another video camera. My rifle was equipped with a silencer and the impact on the camera, alone, did not wake up the sleeping guard. But, after some effort, we managed to wake him up from his nearly comatose state, and we took him prisoner.

"Where are the Tatari political prisoners?" I demanded.

He pointed down the hallway with a quivering hand. The dimly lit corridor was now filled with freedom fighters. Together, we slowly approached the tightly locked prison cells, the sound of our footsteps echoing through the otherwise silent hallway. The captured guards, now weaponless, faced an uncertain fate that rested in our discretion. They exchanged nervous glances with one another, wondering what would happen.

I noticed two additional video cameras strategically positioned to observe about ten prison cells from multiple angles. Using my silenced weapon, I fired two bullets into each camera, instantly destroying them. This precaution wasn't enough. Once we freed the political prisoners, there was a high likelihood of conversations between Ismail's group and the newly liberated individuals. Although everyone in our group wore masks, the audio from such conversations alone might reveal their identities. To address this concern, I pulled a small device from my pocket and scanned the immediate area for hidden microphones. Fortunately, the scan came back negative. The only microphones present were those integrated into the video cameras we had already disabled.

I confronted the guard we had found sleeping on the third floor, my voice steely. "Which cells hold Tatar politicians?"

He raised a shaky hand, pointing to a specific armored door.

"Open it, now!" I commanded.

We had disarmed this guard but, unlike the others, hadn't tied him up. His free hands searched for the keys. With trembling fingers, he fumbled before inserting a key into the first cell lock.

"Where are the rest of the Tatar political prisoners?" I pressed. Again, he pointed with a quivering hand, two more times.

All the Tatars, along with a few non-Tatar political prisoners from other parts of Ukraine, were being held in adjoining cells within the same area. We repeated this process on a total of three armored doors. As the doors creaked open, a foul odor assaulted our noses—a nauseating mix of mold, mildew, feces, and urine. Inside each cell was a broken toilet, shared by all the people in the cell, and all were overflowing with human waste.

The prisoners emerged from the dark cells, blinking in the light, their skin covered in welts from insect bites. The inhumane conditions matched the descriptions I'd read, but seeing it firsthand was shocking. In total, we had released all twelve Tatar politicians and ten additional political prisoners from Kherson who were housed with them.

I glanced at my watch. Hundreds more prisoners were enduring similar suffering, but our time was up. We'd been inside for nearly 30 minutes. The batteries in my two electronic warfare generators were running low. They were top-of-the-line silver batteries, but even they couldn't sustain the power needed to jam cell signals throughout the entire building for long.

We'd only captured three guards and killed one, leaving at least three more who could call for backup once our jammers failed.

Even if our jammers continued to work for a while, one of the free guards might leave the prison grounds to make a call elsewhere. That would bring hundreds of armed Russian troops, spelling our doom. Despite knowing many more prisoners deserved freedom, I couldn't risk it. We had to leave now.

There was a mix of emotions on the prisoners' faces — gratitude, disbelief, and excitement. Personally, I felt a sense of pride at getting them out. They seemed somewhat emaciated. Not quite as bad as the pictures of Nazi concentration camp survivors, but still, in dreadful shape. Most had only been in the prison system for a short time. I shuddered to think what they would look like after many months. Now, they were free but that freedom hung by a thread. We had to leave before it was too late!

A tall, dignified man limped towards one of the masked men on my team, whom I knew was Ismail. The taller man's voice quivered with emotion.

"Thank you, thank you. I had lost all hope." he said, grimacing in pain.

"You think I would leave my own brother with these filthy pidari!" Ismail spat, using a deeply derogatory term for Russians.

He inspected his brother's arms, which were marred by insect bites and cigarette burns. He looked at his brother's face. Two teeth were gone, leaving bloody gaps, his eye and jaw were bruised and swollen. His jaw was broken. He had been beaten and tortured.

"Who did this to you?" Ismail demanded.

The tall man pointed at the guard we'd found drunk on the third floor, lifting his arm with difficulty, pointing an accusing finger. The Russian scanned the corridor, looking for a way out. But he was trapped. Ismail turned to the guard, raising his weapon, and said,

"This is how you treat your prisoners?" he asked coldly.

"It wasn't me, I swear." the guard pleaded, shaking his head, quivering with fear.

Ismail raised his rifle, and it seemed like he was about to put a bullet in the man's head.

"He mistakes me for someone else..." the Russian guard insisted.

Ismail turned to his brother.

"Any chance that you're mistaken?" he asked.

The tall man shook his head. Ismail raised his rifle.

"No!" I yelled, rushing towards him.

But, before I could reach him, he'd already shot the man in the knee. The guard fell to the floor, shrieking. Fragments of bone, cartilage, and flesh were on the floor. I stopped short of stepping into some of it.

"What the hell?!" I protested, speaking loudly to be head over the howling guard. "You gave me your word you would follow my orders, and I gave orders to avoid unnecessary shooting!"

"It was necessary..." Ismail replied. "You see what he did to my brother?"

He turned to his brother and spoke to him directly.

"You know better now than to try to appease the Moskali, yes?" he asked.

The man remained silent, looking at the floor. Then, he looked up, said nothing, but nodded.

Ismail took that as a sign and his movements signaled his intent. He turned toward the guard, and I was sure he meant to shoot again—this time, likely a kill shot or several more to the torso. Before he could act, I grabbed his rifle and pushed it down. Quickly, I reached for my utility belt, extracting a small jar of powdered medical coagulant and bandages.

As I treated the guard's shattered kneecap, he continued to cry out in pain. Despite my dislike for him and our urgent need to leave, I knew that without treatment, he would likely bleed to death. The rules of the Geneva Convention and the customs of war, deeply ingrained in me during my training, were clear: as a prisoner of war in our custody, wounded by one of my men, he required medical attention.

There was no way around it, no mental gymnastics to justify leaving him to bleed out. Even though he was probably guilty of an uncountable number of crimes against prisoners in his custody, I could do nothing else. Even though we had freed the political prisoners and needed to escape quickly, I was compelled to act. The job would be rushed and imperfect, but I had to do something, even if it cost a precious minute or two.

"Why do you protect this scum?" Ismail growled. "He deserves to die!"

I gave Ismail a quick glance. He was still pointing his rifle at the captured guard, but he couldn't shoot him again, from that angle. Not without shooting me.

"He is unarmed." I explained, but that didn't seem to satisfy him.

"You saw what he did to my brother." He complained.

I avoided arguing with him. His point was obvious. Very biblical. Eye for an eye. Tooth for a tooth. But, it didn't comply with the requirements of the Geneva Convention. And, I wouldn't tolerate it on my watch, if I could prevent it. So, I ignored him and focused on my task. I injected a quick shot of anesthetic into the man's sciatic nerve. That, I knew, from basic medical training, would numb the lower leg, from just above the thigh, downward. Then, I powdered the wound with anticoagulant and painted it with povidone iodine. The anesthetic would relieve the pain for several hours. By then, it was likely that Russian troops would have arrived en masse, and he could be taken to the hospital. I finished bandaging him.

The guard just lay there, making little noise at that point, entering a state of shock. I looked at Ismail once more and shook my head.

"Don't do that again!" I exclaimed. "I made it clear from the beginning: no unnecessary shooting!"

He shrugged, his shoulders tense.

"As I said, it was necessary," Ismail finally said, lowering his rifle. "And, he deserves worse. I treated him better than he's ever treated a prisoner."

This was his turf. His people. His world. Not mine. And, while I disagreed with his actions, I understood his reasons. The guard was unarmed and under our control. Under the laws of war, we could not injure him, and I felt we had a duty to honor that commitment. But it was not my brother who had suffered torture at the man's hands.

There were exchanges going on between the prisoners and their liberators. Words of gratitude and curses for the Russians. Thankfully, no more bullets. But there was also no more time. Apart from the shattering of one guard's knee, and the unavoidable killing of the guard in the stairwell, everything had gone according to plan. But, the cloak provided by the jamming devices was shielding us from swarms of Russian reinforcements. It would end at any moment.

"We need to move, people!" I shouted in Russian as loud as I could.

The partisan team, including Ismail, who now kept his weapon lowered, started to follow my orders, but not fast enough for my taste.

"Let's go! Go, go, go!" I urged.

With Sasha's help, I opened one of the cell doors again. The guard with the shattered knee was silently in shock. With Sasha's help, I dragged him into the cell. Then, we forced the other guards in, too, and locked the door. They'd experience the same mold, mildew, cockroaches, fleas, feces and other horrors they inflicted upon others, at least for a while. Eventually, hordes of Russian reinforcements would swarm the building and free them.

We navigated the maze of corridors, heading back down the stairs, and rushed toward the door to the facility. I led the way, trying to avoid any remaining free guards. Eventually, we left the prison's dark belly, finding ourselves back on Elevatornyi Lane. The escapees, still clothed in the drab prison uniforms of their captivity, glanced at one another, unsure of what to do. My mind raced, thinking about the journey that lay ahead. My two radio wave jamming devices wouldn't last much longer.

I unhooked the walkie-talkie and called Mustafa.

"Meet us at the rendezvous point," I said.

"Okay," he replied instantly. "I just need a few seconds to pack up the radio jammer..."

"Negative!" I exclaimed. "Leave it. Repeat: don't disconnect the jamming device!"

"But they're very expensive..." he argued.

"Irrelevant," I replied.

"You will need them for the raid on the Russian airbase," he insisted.

He was right. I did need them. But, it was still irrelevant.

"I'll have to do without them," I said

I also would have liked to recover them, but any attempt to shut one off would mean an end to the jamming zone. Landlines and internet connections might remain cut and disabled, but any guard with a mobile phone could call out. They'd call for reinforcements. We would be killed or captured, and what now appeared to be a huge success would convert to a bitter failure. There was no choice but to abandon the equipment, even though it would sting.

"If the Russians get their hands on these things, they will reverse-engineer them," Mustafa continued to argue.

"They won't get them," I answered. "But, right now, we can't turn them off without reopening Russian communications. Just come back here."

There was a pause.

"On my way," he said, finally.

The generators had about 15 minutes of power remaining.

Abandoning valuable equipment bothered me. As Mustafa correctly recognized, each radio wave generator was expensive. The devices cost over $75,000 each. He was also right in saying that I needed them for the planned attack on the missile storage bunker. However, trying to recover the equipment, under these circumstances, was impossible. Success requires sacrifice. This time it simply meant sacrificing valuable equipment. Losing multi-million dollar planes, missiles, tanks, and other expensive hardware is inevitable in war. Hardware losses can be replaced. Human lives cannot. I had already anticipated the loss of the radio signal jammers and was prepared for it. Each jammer was rigged with a small charge of C-4 explosive. I would detonate the explosive, using my remote, the moment we were all safe. The Russians would be left with nothing but a mystery. There would be nothing to reverse-engineer.

When I arrived at the front entrance, Mustafa was already waiting. We headed toward the rendezvous point. The freed prisoners, accompanied by Ismail's partisans, were placed in several vans and taken to prearranged locations. On the way, the license plates would be changed in locations out of sight of the traffic cams. People would be redistributed into private automobiles, and taken to safe houses. Eventually, all the freed prisoners would be spirited away to Ukrainian controlled territory.

Everyone associated with our Yevpatoriya partisan cell climbed into one old broken down van. We left the vicinity as fast as we could and a few moments later, when we arrived at a planned location, far from Russia's camera lenses, we transferred into multiple private cars ourselves, heading toward our own safe houses. I looked at my watch. It was time. I fished the remote out of my pocket, and pressed a series of buttons. A signal was sent on a radio frequency that was not being jammed.

A second later, two loud explosions shook the air near the prison building. Simferopol is not a large city, and C4 can explode spectacularly. Looking out, toward the location of the prison, I could barely see it, but two small balls of fire were rising. The jamming devices were gone, along with most of the evidence that might identify us. The Russian occupation authorities would sift through whatever wreckage they found, but nothing would be left. They'd only have the statements of the guards and the knowledge that a group of mysterious fighters had freed the prisoners. If they ever did fit all the pieces of the puzzle together, it would be far too late.

11

I sat on a large, moss-covered boulder at the edge of the clearing where Yasmina and I first made love. Outwardly calm, my mind churned with worry. I longed to hold her again, but my watch showed 10:58 pm. Where was she?

We had planned this secret meeting before I left for Simferopol. I'd rushed back as soon as Russian patrols thinned out. Now, minutes passed in silence as she grew later and later. The cool evening breeze touched my skin, but Yasmina was nowhere in sight. Had something happened? Was she captured by Russians? It seemed unlikely, but other troubling scenarios filled my mind.

Our long separation had fueled my burning desire to reunite. I strained to hear or see any sign of her. The grassy field remained unnaturally still and quiet. I held my breath, desperate for a glimpse of her familiar form or the sound of her footsteps. Scanning the dark horizon for her silhouette proved futile.

Then, suddenly, I heard a rustle in the bushes and quickly turned around, instinctively reaching for my gun. But, I relaxed when I saw her face emerge from the shadows, long black hair flowing in the wind, big blue eyes shining in the moonlight, dressed in a dark jacket and a pair of slacks, a light scarf around her neck. Yasmina was radiant all the time and even in the darkness of night, she was a ray of sunshine as she ran towards me and threw herself into my arms. I hugged her tightly, feeling the warmth of her slender body, kissing her softly on the lips, on the forehead, and then, again, on the lips.

"I was so worried about you." I whispered into her ear. "Why are you so late?"

She pulled back slightly and looked into my eyes, then suddenly shook her head in frustration for a moment, before again nestling her face against my chest.

"I am so sorry, John. I had to lose him, first." She said, and then moved away slightly to softly gaze into my eyes.

"Who?" I asked, confused.

"Muhammad."

"What?"

"He's been watching my cabin door ever since he returned from Simferopol." She said,

I shook my head in frustration.

"That stupid fucker!" I exclaimed.

She nodded.

"Yes, he is." she continued, "He's been watching me like this for years. It's always creepy. I've always done my best to ignore him. I have never encouraged him. Usually, he just goes away. But, this time, he didn't. Ever since you arrived, he's gotten a lot worse. When I finally left the cabin, he followed me. He thinks I'm his, but I'm yours. Only yours…"

I shook my head, seething in anger.

"I'm going to kill that son of a bitch!" I exclaimed.

She gently put her delicate hand over my lips.

"No." she said, softly. "He is not worth it. I'm yours. Remember that…"

Her words made me feel better, but the turmoil lingered. The more I thought about Muhammad, the angrier I became. He was a constant thorn in my side. I tried to calm myself, remembering that in Simferopol, he might have saved my life by killing the Russian guard. Still, I was reluctant to feel grateful to such a scumbag.

My main worry was his aggression towards Yasmina. I feared he might eventually force himself on her, regardless of her wishes. Of course, the pistol and knife she concealed under her clothes might prove a fatal surprise for him. Since she'd never undressed in front of him, he would be unaware of her hidden weapons. While he might not survive an attempt to rape her, the possibility still troubled me.

Stalking women is unacceptable. Yasmina's choice of partner was hers alone. He had no right to object. A rational, intelligent man would move on and seek love elsewhere. But Muhammad was neither rational nor intelligent. I was convinced it was only a matter of time before he tried to harm Yasmina, me, or both of us.

"How did you manage to lose him?" I asked.

"He was trying to be discreet," she explained, "but I knew he was trailing after me. I couldn't escape right away. That's why I'm so late. He is incredibly persistent and he knows the area. But, eventually, I managed to lead him into an old abandoned barn, not too far away from the camp. He didn't see when I snuck out the back door. By the time he realized I was gone, I was deep in the underbrush and it was too late. I could still see him, because I knew where he was, but he couldn't hope to find me in the darkness. I waited and, eventually, I saw him give up and leave. He headed back to the camp. That's why it took me so long. But I'm here now…"

She kissed me and smiled.

Her cleverness, devotion and loyalty impressed me. I kissed her again.

"You are the single most exciting woman I've ever met." I said, with complete honesty. "I love you."

"I love you even more, John." She replied with a smile.

We kissed again, and held each other. I could feel each of her breaths and her heartbeat against my chest. And, we began to forget about the war, the ever present dangers, and about the Russian enemy. The only thing I could think about was her and the happiness she brought me. Our clothing began to peel off, piece by piece, and we lay down on the grass, making love with our pistols still strapped to our naked legs. The world exploded in one spectacular moment and after that I felt satisfied, free, and complete. I withdrew from her, lying back, watching the stars, dozing off for a moment. Then, she nudged me in the side, waking me up, and pointed to the wooded area in the distance.

There was movement among the trees. An unnatural rustling of leaves, inconsistent with the wind. It was subtle but unmistakable: someone was there, watching our intimate moment. A silhouette moved between the trees, stopping occasionally, hiding in shadows.

Anger, disgust, and a sense of violation surged through me. I wanted to confront the perverted peeping tom and squeeze the life out of him.

I quickly dressed, my pistol still strapped to my leg and knives in place. Unlike most partisans who hid their weapons, fearing Russian patrols, Yasmina and I always kept ours ready. Yasmina dressed hurriedly, driven more by fear than anger. She sensed my rage and understood my deadly thoughts. In hindsight, killing him would have been right, but I didn't know that back then.

Before Yasmina finished dressing, I was already moving to intercept the contemptible voyeur. She ran to catch up, forcing me to slow down. When she reached me, she gave me a tender kiss and spoke urgently.

"I love you, John," She implored, her eyes revealing her worry.

At that point, I think, we both already knew who it was.

"Please don't kill him," She implored, "His actions are unforgivable, but you cannot afford to lose Mustafa's support."

Her words penetrated the psychological haze, and reminded me that rash action might undermine everything I had worked so hard to build. And, of course, Muhammad could be lethal too. I had already seen that, with the bullet in the prison guard's head. But, at that time, he was armed with an AK-74. Caution was essential, but I was determined to punish him.

"Mustafa can't stand him…" I argued.

"He is Mustafa's sister's son…" She insisted.

I gave her a curt nod, grudgingly acknowledging that she might be right.

"I'll be back soon." I said, and began running toward the figure in the distance.

He'd caught sight of me charging him, and that sent him into a panicked flight. That's the way it is with cowards. I could not even imagine what was going on in his sick mind. He had been watching from far away as I made intimate love to the woman he said he loved. A woman he obsessively claimed to be his own. He must have been seething with hatred and envy. But, his perverted nature apparently compelled him to watch.

Had he possessed a gun, especially a rifle, which he was good at handling, I knew he wouldn't run. I would already be dead. That meant he was unarmed. It was typical of the partisans to be unarmed unless they were actively on a mission. He was young but alcoholism sapped his physical strength. I was older, but leaner, faster, stronger and far better trained. He would stand no chance against me in hand-to-hand combat. I was able to swiftly close the distance. With a tackle, I slammed him to the ground, raining punches until he was senseless. For a moment, he could do nothing more than blink up stupidly.

Then, I pressed the muzzle of my pistol menacingly against his forehead. He didn't know that I had unloaded it during the chase to prepare for just that moment. And, neither did Yasmina.

"Don't," a woman's pleading voice cried out.

She had finally caught up to us, and rushed to my side, her hand grasping my arm. It made the scene that much more believable.

"Don't kill him here. Not like this. Please..." She urged.

I glared at the pathetic wretch below me, every instinct telling me I really ought to put a bullet between his eyes, but knowing that my pistol wasn't loaded. I had already decided that Yasmina was right. Killing him might turn Mustafa against me and jeopardize my mission. That's why I had taken the cartridge out. An empty chamber ensured that I wouldn't lose control and kill him anyway, against my better judgment. Instead of shooting him, I punched him again, breaking his lip open.

"You fucking asshole!" I screamed. "You were watching? You fucker!"

Muhammad stared straight at me, and could clearly see the fury in my face. With my gun at his head and with him having no way of knowing it was unloaded, he had to be feeling a sense of impending doom. Yet, to my surprise, as his uncle had once said, he actually was not quite the coward that I assumed he was. He displayed more courage than I expected. He was facing death, but that didn't seem to matter. Not only that, but he was as defiant as ever.

"I love Yasmina," he said. "I've loved her for years. You are an infidel. You don't belong here. You have no right to her. Why don't you leave? Never come back. Leave, and let me have her! She's mine. You stole her from me!"

As I listened to his foolishness, I felt a mix of emotions...anger, disgust, and pity. I felt anger because he had secretly watched us make love, violating our most intimate moment, and because he had stalked Yasmina. I felt disgust, because he thought he could own her. He claimed Yasmina as his property, to such an extent that he had even called me a "thief!" He obviously saw her as a product to be bought and sold! But, I also felt pity, and that was the weakness that would cause me to make a terrible mistake.

In his own twisted way, I think he might have actually loved her. He was facing what must have looked to him like certain death and yet he still declared his love. On the other hand, perhaps, maybe, he was just insane.

My gun was still pointed directly at him. Had it been loaded, he would have already been dead. That much I am sure of. But, it wasn't. Looking back, hindsight being better than foresight, I wish I hadn't unloaded it. I wish I had pulled that trigger, regardless of the consequences it might have had. I could have found a suitable spot in the forest to bury his body quietly. No one would have been the wiser. I suspect that many partisans would have been happy he was gone. No one would miss him. Not even his uncle. However, I am a soldier, not a murderer. I have killed many men, but only in combat. I was too decent to do it.

"John, no..." Yasmina implored again, still thinking I was on the verge of putting a bullet in Muhammad's brain. "He is not worth it. He is a foolish, hate-filled man who doesn't know you. He will never have me. My heart is yours. He needs help, not harm. Let him go with his life..."

Sparing that miserable wretch's life was a fateful mistake, but it cannot be undone. The consequences have rippled forward since then. But, instead of putting a bullet in his head, I dug into his pocket and retrieved his cell phone, keeping the pistol squarely pointed at him as I did so. I handed it to him brusquely.

"Type in the password!" I barked.

"No!" He refused defiantly.

Leveling my pistol squarely at his face, I snarled,

"Type it in now, or you're dead!" I snarled.

"Please, Muhammad," Yasmina implored him, "Do as he asks. The password will do you no good if you are dead."

Still, the man hesitated.

"Type it in!" I ordered again. "Because if you don't, I'll redecorate these trees with pieces of your brain!"

He read the lethal look on my face. If there had been a bullet in that pistol, he would have surely been dead already. So, he ultimately began typing, and entered his password. That let me access the phone. I snatched it back, keeping him covered with the pistol in his face, as I checked the camera app. Sure enough, what I suspected was true. He hadn't simply watched us. He had also filmed us, probably to satisfy his prurient pleasure later on. It was an older model, but the phone's camera had night vision mode and there we were, magnified by the optical zoom lens. A closeup of Yasmina and I making love.

"You fucking son of a bitch!" I roared, adding more blows of my fists to his bloody face.

By the time I was finished, he was a mess and lay silent and senseless, giving me time to examine the treasure trove of sleazy photos and ultra-HD videos he had taken of us. Yasmina watched, painfully silent, as I sampled the pornographic content in which we were the unwitting stars.

"You still think he deserves to live?" I asked her, my voice menacing.

She nodded.

"Can't we just destroy the phone?" She asked.

"Alright." I opened the file manager and systematically began deleting all the videos and pictures one by one. But, that might not be enough. There were apps that let people recover files even after they were deleted. So, I dug into the settings of the phone and performed a full factory reset, typing the password I'd carefully memorized while he was typing it in. As the wiping process started, Muhammad tried to grab the phone back, perhaps hoping to stop it. But, as he moved, I grabbed his arm, twisted around, and kept him immobilized by applying a tight arm lock.

"Did you hear what Yasmina said?" I growled.

He didn't respond. I increased the tightness of the arm lock and the level of pain it was causing him.

"She said she doesn't love you." I said, "You don't own her and you can't claim her! You respect her decision and leave her be! Do you understand?"

My grip tightened, and the muzzle of my gun was also digging painfully into the softness under his jaw.

"No more following her. No more bothering her. No more of your bullshit! If you don't stop, I'll kill you, I swear it. I'll put you into the fucking ground."

Finally, I could see naked fear in his eyes. Lowering my voice, I continued,

"And, if you ever try to take videos of us again...I'll kill you. Do you understand me? Answer me, you miserable piece of shit!"

After a tense moment, he bobbed his head in a jerky nod.

"Y-yes... I understand."

"And, are you going to stop?" I barked, giving him a vicious shake.

There was another pause and then, finally,

"Yes... I, I, I will." he stammered.

"Swear it!" Yasmina chimed in. "Swear it in the name of Allah Almighty!"

"Y-yes," Muhammad stammered. "I swear it by Allah Almighty..."

Releasing him with a disgusted shove, I stood up, and he looked up at me, with his hand out.

"Give me my phone..."

I shook my head.

"Fuck you, you son of a bitch!" I exclaimed. "Not a chance. I'm destroying it, to make absolutely certain those photos and videos will never be recovered."

"But..." He started to protest.

"I said, no!" I barked, cutting him off. "Be thankful you're crawling away from this with your miserable life intact. Now get the fuck out of here before I change my mind and bury you where you stand."

Muhammad needed no further prompting. Scrambling upright, he turned and fled, not daring to look back. I watched his retreat until he disappeared from sight.

Turning to Yasmina, I pulled her into my embrace.

"If he ever goes near you again, I swear I'll put him down for good." I stated.

She nodded against my chest, shuddering slightly.

"He understood you." She said, "You made it clear."

His phone had finally reset while in my pocket. I tossed it onto the forest floor, reinserted the clip into my Sig Sauer 9 mm and fired a silenced bullet at it. The bullet landed on target, shattering the phone into multiple pieces. Raking the ground with my foot, I buried them under leaves and twigs. The images were gone for good.

"That does it, I think," I said, bending down to holster the pistol.

I couldn't shake a nagging sense, however, that the confrontation would do exactly nothing to change Muhammad's behavior. The more I thought about it, the more I realized that I had made a grievous error. A man like him was too far too gone to keep his word about anything, no matter what god he swears by. His obsessions ran too deep. He couldn't be trusted. It would never be possible to remove the idea that Yasmina was his possession. I had been a fool to let him walk away. I should have killed him and buried him in the woods when I had the chance. Because when his fear subsided, he would lick his wounds, and plot something else. He was now more dangerous than ever.

12

I awoke to the sound of someone frantically banging on my door. Rubbing the sand out of my eyes, I glanced at the clock. It was only 7 am, and I had barely slept four hours after having spent most of the night with Yasmina. She also couldn't have slept much. But, when I opened the door, there she was, wide awake, standing breathless and pale, in a simple peasant style dress and a headscarf, a very worried look on her face.

She grabbed my hand and pulled at it.

"Hurry!" She insisted, urgently. "Get dressed! They're coming!"

"Who's coming?" I countered.

"The Moskali police!" She replied.

"How do you know?" I asked.

"Sasha told us." she replied.

"Sasha?"

"He has the entire complex wired with surveillance." She explained. "It's all connected to some kind of artificial intelligence. I don't know exactly how it works. But, it detected a police vehicle coming toward us."

I hadn't realized until that moment how active Sasha was in designing systems that protected the partisans. All I knew was that he was a self-taught IT specialist. Usually, in the outsourcing world, that mostly meant programming websites. But, I'd seen him soldering wires, drawing circuits and putting together electronic parts. I should have realized that he was much more than that. Still, I wouldn't have believed that he could program an artificial intelligence bot. It required complex programming, including deep learning algorithms to train the bot, managing to link camera systems with facial and object recognition software, and so on. An AI capable of distinguishing between friend and foe, as she described it, was something that seemed good enough to make even the Pentagon proud.

The thoughts were drifting slowly through my half-awake mind but Yasmina was in a hurry, and I wasn't moving fast enough to satisfy her. She was increasingly nervous and impatient and she was correct in that.

"They're only about five minutes away!" she warned urgently. "Come on! You need to hide!"

I looked around, searching for a suitable hiding spot, but there was no good place to hide inside my cabin. It would take much longer than five minutes to reach the nearby forest. I had my favorite pistol and set of knives, as always, still strapped to my leg, concealed beneath loose pajamas. The partisans had a substantial stash of AK-74 automatic rifles and other small arms, hidden inside an underground chamber. I could access the firearms, but openly fighting it out with the local police was sheer folly. There was no way to win such a battle. We could only win by stealth and surprise.

Thankfully, Yasmina's late grandfather, Igor, the former leader of the partisan group, had anticipated this and had prepared secret hiding places.

"Come with me," Yasmina urged. "My grandmother is waiting. You can hide in the basement."

I swiftly changed and followed Yasmina out. She practically dragged me across the yard. Mustafa and the others scrambled to hide weapons and equipment.

Yasmina's grandfather, like his father before him, had been a Communist party member and Institute Director before the Soviet Union's fall. He'd hidden his contempt for the regime, but became more open as Crimean Tatars returned to the peninsula. When Russia seized Crimea in 2014, he used his contacts and skills to organize a local partisan cell, despite his age.

The "rest complex" once owned by the state controlled, subsequently privatized, now-bankrupt "Weights & Measures Institute", was converted into a covert base. He knew the authorities would ignore a run-down rural property from Soviet times. To outsiders, it seemed to serve its original purpose as a retreat for former employees' families. But, in truth, it had been converted into a resistance base. The Russian authorities were unaware of the meetings held there and of the weapons stored underground.

Indeed, if Russian police had ever arrived at the right moment, they might have discovered scores of rebels. But they never got that lucky. Today, only Svetlana, Mustafa, Yasmina, and Sasha were present. Everyone except

Sasha and I were former employees or family members. I would hide, and Sasha's presence could be easily explained.

We reached the Fedorova cabin in a matter of moments. Yasmina's grandmother had been watching for us and she immediately opened the door, and ushered us in.

"Maybe, they're just doing a routine check," she said, hopeful, but the worry that it was likely to be more than that was obvious on her face.

She leaned down, lifting the rug. Underneath, there was a door built into the wooden planking, and it could be swung open simply by pulling it upward. She took hold of a recessed handle and pulled at it, lifting the door, revealing the rough ladder below. The ladder led down into a secret basement. Inside, it was dark and uninviting, making it almost impossible to make out the details of what was down there. But, I could make out the outlines of a bookshelf and many supplies, a radio, and a rough-hewn wooden chair.

"Stay down there, with the light off, until the police leave." Svetlana warned. "There is a peephole in the floorboards, at the left-hand corner. You can look and listen to everything that goes on upstairs."

"OK" I replied.

"We will do our best to get rid of them as soon as possible." She continued.

I nodded my understanding and climbed down the ladder.

I tried my best to ignore the dark dampness, but it was hard to do. Spiders love damp dark basements and I don't like spiders. I imagined that they were everywhere around me. What type and how many was the only question. It was too dark to see clearly, however, so I tried my best not to dwell on it. It gave me a creepy feeling, but I tried to focus on something else. I moved the wooden chair closer to the peephole, sat down and waited, hoping no spiders would crawl on me in the process.

Upstairs, Svetlana closed the door and sealed the floor, returning the rug to its original position. With Yasmina's help, she moved some furniture around to make things look more natural. They both sat down, doing their best to seem calm and relaxed, but I knew they were anything but that. They were both tense and alert, ready to deal with whatever was coming, fearing the worst and ready to fight if need be. I placed my hand on my leg, feeling the holster where I knew my 9mm was safely, and it comforted me. The cartridge was locked and loaded.

The sound of a car engine grew until it was loud, and then it suddenly stopped. The car had pulled up in front of the cabin. A moment later, I heard a loud knock on the door. Svetlana quickly stood up and walked over to the door, opening it, and greeted two men in uniform with a smile and a polite tone of voice.

"Good morning, officers. What can I do for you?" she asked.

"Good morning, ma'am. We are inspecting the area. We need to see your documents please, and ask you a few questions. May we come in?"

"Of course, of course." She responded. "Please, make yourselves comfortable. Would you like some tea?"

"No,"

"Maybe, some cookies?" she asked, in a grandmotherly manner.

The policeman shook his head.

"No," he said, again. "We just need to see your passports."

One policeman was tall, with dark brown hair, sharp blue eyes, and a square jaw. He also sported an "in charge" attitude which immediately identified him as the leader. The other was shorter and swarthier, with brown eyes and a round face. Both looked to be in their mid-20s.

Svetlana walked over to a drawer and took out the folder in which she kept their passports and handed it to the tall officer. He opened and examined each one, checking carefully, comparing the photos to their faces. The documents showed that both had voluntarily adopted Russian nationality after the occupation of the peninsula in 2014. After finishing his examination of the documents, the man nodded, slipping the documents back into the plastic folder, and handing it back to Svetlana.

"We need to ask you a few questions." He stated.

"Certainly." Svetlana replied.

"Are you here for the summer?" He asked.

"Yes." Svetlana answered.

"Who else lives with you?" the policeman asked.

"Just my granddaughter, Yasmina." she replied. "But, on the territory, we also have one of my co-workers from the days of the Soviet Union. He has his own cabin."

"Name?" the officer asked.

"Mustafa Azmetov." She replied.

"A Tatar?" the officer asked, as if it was a dirty word.

Thankfully, after the dissolution of the Soviet Union in 1991, starting in 1997, the old Soviet internal passport, which had once included a line for nationality, was replaced by order of then-President Boris Yeltsin and ethnicity information had been officially removed. The officer didn't suspect, therefore, that Svetlana was also a Tatar, because she had a Russian surname. At 68, her weathered look made it harder to tell what nationality she was and, other than the jet black hair, Yasmina looked as Slavic as any girl born in Moscow.

"Yes, I suppose he is," She replied. But, knowing Russian prejudices, and the likelihood that he assumed she was Russian, she added. "But, he's one of the good ones…"

"Where is he?" the officer asked.

"At the moment, I don't know." She replied, smiling. "But, he is also here for the summer and he comes every summer. He lives in the cabin down a little bit, on the right side."

She motioned with her hand to show the way, and then continued.

"There is another man on the territory, Alexander Melnyk." She continued. "We've hired him to make some repairs. As you can see, this place is falling apart."

"This is your granddaughter?" the tall officer asked, turning toward Yasmina.

"Yes. Say hello to the fine officers, Yasmina." Svetlana urged.

Yasmina smiled, looking as sweet as a newborn babe. But I knew she was well-equipped to fight if need be, her knife and pistol hidden under her dress, ready for use at any moment.

"Hello. Nice to meet you." She said with a big smile.

"Hello, miss," the tall officer replied, "How old are you?"

"21, sir."

"Twenty-one? Do you work?"

"I study at the university. I'm majoring in history."

"History? What kind of history?"

"The history of Crimea," she replied.

"Is that so?" he asked, in a suspicious tone, "what do you think of the current situation? Do you like being part of Russia?"

Yasmina knew enough to be careful about answering a question like that. The officer was seeking signs of disloyalty. If she showed any, he might arrest her.

"Russia is our motherland," she said with false sincerity, "The protector of everyone who speaks Russian. President Putin saved us from the Ukrainian fascists."

At this point, however, the officer was no longer listening to her answer. Instead, his attention was mostly fixated with her breasts, and he was looking at her with a lecherous look in his eyes that angered me. Sensing the fact that he was attracted to her, however, Yasmina simply adjusted her tactics and used it against him.

"Most people don't appreciate policemen." She said, flirtatiously.

"You don't think so?" He asked.

She shook her head.

"No," She said, "With all these horrible terrorists, funded by the Kyiv regime, doing all the horrible things that the Americans tell them to do, it's a dangerous job. I can only thank God that there are men still willing to stand up and be counted!"

The officer smiled at that, very pleased with such words spoken by such an attractive woman.

"You are right." He agreed. "People don't appreciate the dangerous job we do."

"My babushka and I do…" Yasmina insisted. "You work so hard to keep us safe. Why can't people understand that?"

"You are very beautiful and charming." He said, continuing to smile.

"Thank you." Yasmina said, demurely.

"My name is Ivan, and this is my partner, Sergei. We're both from Moscow. We've been stationed here for six months." the officer said, blushing slightly.

"Moscow!" Yasmina exclaimed. "How exciting! I wish I was from Moscow. What's it like?"

She took his hand and led him to the couch. He followed without hesitation, and the two sat down next to each other.

"I can't tell you how many times I've dreamed about Moscow." She continued enthusiastically, as if the capital of Russia was the most exciting place in the world. "Crimea must be so boring for you…"

"It's okay," He said. "But, yes, it's different from what I'm used to. Here, we constantly deal with Tatari terrorists, for one example. We do our best to stop them, but sometimes they manage to commit atrocities. Scum! The Americans and their fascist Ukrainian stooges support them in all the bad things they do."

Then, he made a move that greatly annoyed me. I knew that the only thing Yasmina would ever feel for the man was utter contempt. But, I couldn't help myself. He nonchalantly placed his arm around her. I seethed silently at that, in my hiding place.

"It's very scary." She said, making no attempt to crawl out from under his arm. "When I think of those people…oh, I don't even want to think of them! That's what this war is about, isn't it? To defend our Russian world from the people who want to destroy it…like the Americans, and NATO, right?"

"Absolutely," the policeman agreed. "You really are an exceptional woman! Smart, beautiful and patriotic. A true daughter of Russia!"

He gently picked up her hand and kissed it. She giggled with feigned delight, and I watched in awe of her abilities. It was amazing to watch her in action. I never realized, until that very moment, that Yasmina was a skilled actress. Her performance was worthy of an Academy Award.

"Thank you," she said, smiling, "You're very nice, too. You're made from the stuff of heroes. How long have you been a policeman?"

While she busied herself playing up to Ivan, Svetlana was doing her best to entertain Sergey, the other officer. She was not a beautiful young girl anymore, obviously, so there were limits as to what she could do to keep him occupied. She played the doting grandmother. As his companion flirted with Yasmina, Sergey sat with Svetlana, drinking the same tea and cookies that he and his partner had rejected just a few moments before. She left him for a moment, and brought some tea and cookies for the tall officer and Yasmina.

"You know," Ivan said, "All of our work is challenging and rewarding. But, sometimes, it's also hard and dangerous…"

"Oh!" Yasmina exclaimed in awe, "I hope you deal harshly with all the bad people you meet, especially those terrorists!"

"Yes, yes, we do, of course." the man replied.

"I love my motherland!" Yasmina said, without flinching.

He seemed to enjoy hearing that, thinking that she meant Russia. But, I knew something he didn't. Her "motherland" was Crimea and, by extension, Ukraine, NOT Russia. She was telling the truth when she said that she loved her motherland. But, she also hated Russia with every fiber of her being.

"Well," Ivan the policeman said, "You are not only beautiful, but wise and loyal too..."

The Russian police, generally speaking, are not used to fawning treatment, especially not in Crimea. The Russian ethnic group, who are a majority, might otherwise be on friendly terms with the police, but they tend to habitually violate the law in petty ways, usually relating to money and taxes. They do their best to avoid any contact with police. Meanwhile, Tatars greet them with coldness and suspicion. That two unknown women were suddenly greeting them in seeming friendship stroked their egos and helped them forget the reason they had come in the first place.

From my location, under their very noses, I listened and watched. Neither man had ever bothered to carefully examine the cabin. If they had, they might have known I was hiding in the basement. On the other hand, had they been more competent, their lives might have ended somewhat sooner. I was well armed and so were the two women. Thanks to their incompetence, had things gone the right way, the two policemen might have lived to a ripe old age. However, in the midst of his bedazzlement, the tall Russian unprofessionally confided the reason he had come to the rest complex. As he gazed into Yasmina's eyes with adoration, he said something he should have kept secret.

"It's an odd coincidence," he said casually. "Last night, I got an anonymous call on my personal phone. The caller left a message claiming that a NATO spy is hiding inside one of these old Soviet rest complexes. Can you believe that?"

Yasmina's heart must have jumped, but you wouldn't have known it. She simply continued playing along, feigning surprise.

"An American spy?" She giggled. "I don't think so. Sounds like something from a movie!"

The officer laughed.

"It does, doesn't it?" He said, "Supposedly, a group of local Tatar terrorists support him. I know it sounds ridiculous, but we can't ignore the call. We're checking out all the rest complexes. Yours was just the first on our list, because it's closest to the city..."

"Do you know who made the call?" Yasmina asked, keeping her voice steady.

"No," the policeman admitted, "We traced the call to a phone with an unidentified SIM card that we found in a garbage dump."

"Seems like a prank call..." she added.

"Yes. But, we still have to take it seriously," He insisted. "These NATO sponsored terrorists are everywhere now. There was a big incident in Simferopol just a few days ago."

Yasmina feigned incredulity. "Really?"

"Yes," He confided, proud of being "in the know" about information hidden from the general public. "Keep this confidential...but I happen to know that several hundred NATO- sponsored terrorists attacked a prison in Simferopol, freeing a small group of hardened criminals. The attack was carried out with high-tech equipment. And, their leader spoke Russian with an American accent! That's how we know NATO was involved. That's why we're checking out this story. No matter how ridiculous it sounds, it could actually be true."

"Wow!" she exclaimed.

"Yeah," He nodded intently, "But, if we don't find anything, we would look ridiculous, especially because the phone call came in on my personal phone. If it's a fake, I don't want to report it. But, if it turns out to be true, we should get the credit for it, not someone else, because the tip came directly to me. My partner and I decided to check it out, personally, before reporting it."

Yasmina giggled and nodded enthusiastically.

"That was so clever," she agreed.

The officer smiled with pleasure.

"I'm sorry about inconveniencing you," He said, "The moment I saw you and your grandmother, I knew you were loyal. But, we still had to interview you. You understand, don't you? It's just policy now."

Yasmina smiled back.

"Of course," Svetlana interjected, "But, I hope we put your minds at ease. There's no NATO spy here. Can you stay for lunch?"

"Thank you, Svetlana Yurievna," he said, using her patronymic, a derivation of her father's name, as a sign of respect, "And thank you, also, to your beautiful granddaughter. But, we have important police business to attend to."

Then, smitten by Yasmina's charm, with confidence bolstered by her solicitous behavior, he turned back to her.

"We should continue our conversation," He said. "There's a great sushi bar in the city. Will you meet me on Saturday night?"

Yasmina responded with a smile,

"Of course!" she said, feigning sincerity, "I would really like that."

"Your phone number?" he asked.

"Sure," she replied, activating her phone, and displayed the number on her screen.

He looked at the screen, typing the number into his phone. Then, he made a test call. Her phone rang and he pressed the hang-up button and smiled.

"Now, you have my number, too…" he said. "Call me anytime."

"I'll look forward to Saturday night." she said, continuing to smile.

The officer stood up, and his subordinate did the same. They were finally ready to leave.

"I'll see you this weekend," he said. "If you see anything out of the ordinary, call me before that. Or, just call me anyway. Just to talk. But, be careful. There might be a dangerous spy lurking about."

"We'll be very vigilant." Svetlana interjected. "And, of course, we'll report anything that seems unusual."

He nodded, and turned to the door.

But, before he left, Yasmina was thoughtful enough to ask one more critical question.

"Does anyone else know about this NATO spy?" She asked.

The officer shook his head.

"No," he replied. "At this point, it's just the two of us. As I said, we deserve to get credit. If nothing turns up, we'll report it, because we're required to, but with a suggestion that we think it's probably fake. The caller did leave a location, supposedly near Cape Tarkhankut, where he says the spy arrived in a mini-submarine. It's supposed to still be parked there, underwater. Obviously, we can't check that part of the story, so the boss will have to forward it to the Navy. If there's a submarine, they'll find it."

The Russian policeman gazed into her eyes silently for a moment with an idiotic smile on his face. If anyone could stir a man's heart, it was Yasmina. Thankfully, he seemed totally unaware that she was flattering him simply to manipulate him.

"I look forward to seeing you this weekend..." he said, finally.

She smiled and nodded. "Me, too."

He and his partner walked out the door. The two women were left inside the dacha cabin with their hearts pounding. I patiently waited for the two men to leave. My heart was pounding too but for a different reason. I could not let the two police officers report that phone call, which they'd certainly do if I let events take their natural course. They were now a direct threat, not only to my mission, but to my life, to the lives of all the partisans and to the continued existence of the armed resistance. I was forced to act.

I couldn't do it, however, right then and there. Not with Yasmina present. That may seem absurd. After all, she was a resistance fighter who, according to her peers, had been on successful sabotage missions. She also carried a concealed pistol and knife. Yet, for me, she more like a delicate flower. Was I insane? As it turned out, she was far more innocent than you may now imagine. But, I'm getting ahead of myself, so let me step back a bit. At that particular moment in time, although I wasn't happy about it, I knew what had to be done. I was also ready and able to do it. I just preferred to do it outside of Yasmina's sight and awareness. Still, I had to act fast and decisively before it was too late!

13

Moments after the two men left, I was ready to follow them, quickly climbing up the ladder, pushing upward, and forcing the trap door open before Yasmina and Svetlana even had a chance to remove the carpet. I exited the basement in haste. Svetlana rearranged things behind me, putting the carpet back in its usual place. It felt good to be out of that dark damp spider-filled place, but it now felt like the weight of the world was resting on my shoulders.

The two women followed me out, and I turned to Svetlana.

"We need to find that bastard, Muhammad," I said, my voice steady despite the turmoil inside me. "He's betrayed the partisan movement..."

She nodded, even as Yasmina's eyes widened in shock,

"He's bad, but it's almost impossible to believe," She asked, "He's one of us..."

I shook my head.

"Not anymore. He sold us out and put our lives in danger." I said.

"Why would he do such a thing?" Yasmina asked, her voice trembling.

I took a deep breath.

"You know why," I said, simply.

I looked at her, my heart aching at the confusion and fear in her eyes. She seemed so innocent, I wondered whether I needed to spell it out for her. But, if she really didn't understand, it was better to leave her that way. I only wanted her to know that she had been mistaken to urge me to spare his life. Muhammad had gone from being an annoyance and a violator of the norms of decency, to an outright traitor. He had to die. I wanted her to understand this. I intended to kill him this time and there was no amount of pleading for his life that she, or anyone else, could do to stop me.

"It's his jealousy, hatred, and feelings of rejection," I explained, "That turned him into a traitor. But, he can't be allowed to endanger us any further."

Svetlana, who had been silent until now, nodded her head again.

"You are right, John," Svetlana agreed, "We cannot allow him to destroy everything. But, there are others you must deal with, first, as I think you know..."

It was a backhanded way of telling me what she and I both knew, even while seeking to protect Yasmina from the harsh knowledge of what I was about to do. One way or the other, the two policemen had to be terminated and quickly, before they could report what they knew. If they did report it, it would do irreparable damage to the partisan movement. Svetlana did not elaborate. I knew what she meant and she knew that I knew. I nodded and turned to leave.

Yasmina looked at me with worried eyes. I am not entirely sure if she understood what I and her grandmother were alluding to but, perhaps, she did. It seems to me, looking back at things, in hindsight, that she already knew, but I've never asked her directly.

"I'll be back as soon as I can," I said as I left.

I felt an increasing sense of dread but pushed it aside. It was just a new sideshow, not fundamentally different, even if the aim were more deadly, than the freeing of the Tatar prisoners. His actions forced my hand. It was now kill or be killed. If I did nothing, the partisan movement would be destroyed. Its members, including Svetlana and Yasmina, would be captured, tortured for information, imprisoned, and eventually killed. I would suffer the same fate if I were still in Crimea by that time.

In other words, the continued existence of those two Russian cops placed my people in mortal danger. It was only a matter of time before they reported the phone call. Their superiors would, in turn, report a possible submarine parked in the waters near Cape Tarkhankut to the Russian Navy. The only thing that protected the sub was that no one knew it was there or even suspected it. Once a diligent search began, it wouldn't take long for them to find the vessel. Afterward, the partisans and the so-called "NATO spy" (me) would be ruthlessly rooted out.

I rapidly made my way to the partisan's secret underground storage locker to retrieve an AK-74 along with ammunition. I didn't actually intend to use it, but it was a stopgap measure in case of necessity. I searched for a vehicle and saw Sasha's Toyota pickup parked in the dirt parking lot. I didn't need to call him or take the extra time to jerry-rig it. He'd left the keys in the ignition. I jumped in. The roar of the engine cut through the morning silence and I stepped on the pedal, racing down the bumpy dirt road as fast as I could. When I finally reached the tarmac, I increased speed. Scanning the distance for the Russian police car, I finally saw it. Pressing the pedal to the metal, the pickup surged forward and raced past them.

These men weren't traffic cops. In Russia, a separate division typically handles road infractions. However, all Russian police can theoretically issue tickets for violations they witness. But, even if they could not issue a real ticket, it wouldn't have mattered. Ninety-nine percent of people wouldn't know it. Very few Russian cops would pass up the opportunity to threaten a ticket. In Russia, such threats will almost always lead to a cash bribe offer by the motorist. Cash bribes are a large part of the average post-Soviet cop's income. As I'd hoped, their siren wailed as they gave chase. It was exactly what I wanted them to do.

As an obedient motorist, in response to the siren and the police car behind me, I slowed down and dutifully pulled over to the side of the road, waiting. Being somewhat unfamiliar with traffic stop protocol, the two cops made it easy for me. They both stepped out of their car at the same time, and walked up to my car, faces filled with feigned sternness. They were, no doubt, feeling secure in the expectation that a wad of cash rubles, handed through the window, would be offered to take care of the ticket.

I rolled down the window, seemingly reaching for my license and registration. My hand was actually closing around the cold metal of my pistol. Two whooshing sounds, the noise made by a bullet fired from a gun with an efficient silencer, slipped through the air. Two bullet holes appeared, each placed in the forehead of one of the two cops. Both crumbled to the ground instantly. I immediately felt a deep sense of regret, but I pushed it aside.

Terrible things happen in war and, sometimes, the choice is to kill or be killed. I chose to kill. I even weighed the Geneva Convention into the mix. The rules of war are drilled into us. Every Special Forces soldier knows them by heart. Not everyone follows the rules, of course, but that is not the point. We all know them. In this case, I weighed the situation and the circumstances. The definition of a civilian could, sometimes, include police.

But, these particular policemen were not civilians under the definitions section. They were enemy combatants.

All police in Crimea are belligerents according to the Convention. They are acting on behalf of an occupation regime to illegally control a geographic region not internationally recognized as part of their nation. By working to suppress the armed resistance to this illegal occupation, the police in Crimea cross the line from policing into soldiering. As soldiers of the enemy, they are legitimate targets. Until such time, if ever, that the international community deems Crimea to be a part of Russia, this will continue to be the case.

I slipped on a pair of black latex gloves and quickly dragged their dead bodies back to their car and stuffed them inside. It was hurried work, because I knew that, as empty as this stretch of road normally was, another motorist might happen along at any moment. I took their keys and got inside myself. Then, I turned the police car around, making it appear as if they were still heading out of the city. I got out, again, and propped them up into position, in the driver's and passenger's seats, respectively. After first carefully placing a small C-4 plastic explosive charge on the gasoline tank and a detonator. I returned to my own vehicle, got in, and headed back to the partisan base camp holding a remote control in one hand and the steering wheel in the other. I flipped the switch and, behind me, the car exploded spectacularly, flames licking the air. Both the engine compartment and the interior caught fire. Acrid smoke billowed upward into the clear daylight. Having finished the unpleasant work, I continued to drive away, the glow of a burning car in my rearview mirror.

The bodies would be burned beyond recognition. The bullets might, nevertheless, be discovered, if the medical examiner did a thorough job. But, the Russian authorities wouldn't understand who put them there or why. It would all take lots of time to investigate, and in that time we could complete our mission. It would be wise, I decided, to evacuate all the local partisans to Kyiv after that. It would probably be too risky to leave them in place. Svetlana's underground railroad would have to be utilized.

As I drove back, despite using the Geneva Convention to rationalize my actions, I felt a deep sense of unease. I had killed the two Russian cops in cold blood. It was justified and necessary, but that didn't make me feel better. It was cold-blooded and calculated. Something that a Russian officer, in my position, would be proud of. But, I was not a Russian officer and I began to wonder – what still separated me from them? Had I become what I was fighting against?

The answer, thankfully, came to me quickly. I wasn't like them. The Russians knowingly target civilians without regard to the rules of war. I had adhered strictly to the Geneva Convention. If I had not killed the two policemen, their inevitable actions would have killed us. I had to protect myself, the armed resistance, and the woman I loved. I had no choice. In a war, you often don't.

The fact remained, however, that all men have mothers and fathers, uncles and aunts, cousins and grandparents. The two policemen were somebody's sons. Somebody loved them. Somebody was probably proud of them, despite the corrupt and despicable regime they worked for. Were they so different from me? Ivan wanted to date Yasmina. What if I had grown up in Moscow? Would I be like him? Could I have been Ivan?

His mother would cry when she learned the news. Her son would never become a husband or a father. But, ultimately, I did not kill the man, even though I had physically fired the bullet. Vladimir Putin and Muhammad Azmetov killed him. The Moscow regime had illegally seized Crimea and ordered its minions to suppress people. But, I was not angry at the policemen. I was angry at the man who forced me to kill them.

I spoke aloud, saying the words, repeatedly, even though there was no one to listen.

"In war, you do what you have to do to survive."

That said everything that needed to be said. But, I was talking to myself. When a man talks to himself, some say it is the first sign of insanity...

14

I was committed to ridding the world of twisted, rotten-to-the-core Muhammad, a man who claimed to be an Islamist but who was actually an alcoholic, who claimed to love a woman but simply sat down and recorded her making love to another man, and who was a traitor to his people and to the cause of liberating Crimea. The thought of him, what he had done, and what he had forced me to do, fueled my rage. I hated him. I wished I had killed him in the forest. He had earned death, but a clean, easy death would be far too merciful. He had earned a slow death, with plenty of pain, before being granted a final release. As I sank deeper into the depths of the darker side of myself, I fantasized about the ways I would kill him.

I replayed the events of the day, in my mind's eye, and fading traces of remorse and sadness about what I had been forced to do to the two policemen transformed into an even greater desire for vengeance. How could I make that monster feel the suffering he inflicted on others? I had always preferred to believe that such dark places didn't exist inside me. But, they obviously did, and I became so lost in these thoughts that I didn't snap out of it until Yasmina came running, and threw her arms around me, as I arrived at the rest complex again, and stepped out of the pickup truck.

"Oh, thank God!" she cried, the relief clear in her voice, "I was so worried."

Her words gave me a renewed sense of purpose. She buried her face in my chest and the scent of her perfume lightened the load on my mind. When I finally found my voice, it emerged as a hoarse rasp.

"It's over..." I said. "For the moment..."

I gazed deeply into her eyes, and my thumb brushed her cheek, removing a solitary glistening teardrop falling from one eye.

"Let's go inside," I said quietly. "I have a lot to discuss with your grandmother."

Slipping her hand into mine, she led me back toward the bungalow. The warmth of her hand contrasted with the cold reality of what I'd just done. I didn't tell her exactly what I had done, or how I was feeling about it, but in spite of my attempt to shield her from it, as I have said before, I think she already knew. She whispered into my ear, trying to reassure me.

"You had no choice..." she said, softly.

Her grandmother came out and met us before we reached the bungalow. Her face was almost as grim as my own.

"Is it done?" She asked, never having mentioned, even once, what "it" was.

"Yes," I replied. "Now, it's Muhammad's turn."

"Unless and until we find him," Svetlana said, without prompting, "we are not safe. There's no telling what he will do next."

I nodded, knowing she was right.

"I'll find him," I vowed, "and when I do, he won't have a chance to say anything, anymore."

She looked seriously at me for a moment, and shook her head lightly.

"I doubt you will, John," She said. "He knows this area far better than you. He knows a million places to hide. But, if you do, and if you are in a position to kill him, you must not. You must bring him here, so that I can question him. I need to know everything he has done."

I had no intention of following those instructions. I had made that mistake once already, listening to her granddaughter. If I found him, I'd kill him for sure, unless he killed me first. But before I killed him, I'd make him talk. I'd force him to tell me everything. Unfortunately, by afternoon, after very diligent search, I still had no idea where to find him. Back at the base camp, I paced restlessly, regretting sparing his life the night before, but there was no longer anything I could do to reverse it. His treason endangered the entire resistance. But, we all faced the same problem. No one knew where to find him.

As the day wore on, Mustafa finally approached me. Although he was Muhammad's uncle, he and his nephew rarely agreed on anything. Despite that blood relation to the traitor I hated so thoroughly, I trusted Mustafa as a friend. He arrived calm and collected, in stark contrast to my extreme agitation.

"Sveta tells me you want to kill my nephew. Is it true?" He asked.

I took a deep breath, trying to calm myself.

"He betrayed us, Mustafa. He called the Russian police about our operations."

Mustafa listened sternly as I described the police visit, the anonymous call they'd received, the chase, and how I'd been forced to kill the two officers to protect us. When I finished, he was silent for a long moment. Finally, he nodded slowly.

"I don't see why Muhammad would have done this. It makes no sense." He said.

But I knew things Mustafa didn't. I knew what Muhammad's motivation really was. In contrast, Mustafa was unaware of my relationship with Yasmina, and didn't know that Muhammad had watched us make love in the forest. I couldn't tell him this for obvious reasons.

He continued,

"If he did make such a call, he must pay with his life. But, right now, you are condemning him without solid proof. You must give him a chance to prove his innocence. It might have been someone else..."

"It was him," I insisted.

"Simply because you believe something, does not make it true." Mustafa insisted.

"It IS true." I countered. "He has put every single one of us at great risk."

"The issue is not for you to decide," Mustafa stated firmly, "He can only be sentenced by a jury of partisans. To take his life, otherwise, is murder."

I wanted to tell Mustafa everything, confident he'd agree about Muhammad's guilt if he knew it all. But I couldn't. Premarital sex is frowned upon by traditional Crimean Tatars, and despite his surface liberalism, Mustafa was traditional at heart. The truth would humiliate Yasmina in his eyes and in the eyes of her community. Yet if he knew everything, no explanation or trial would be needed. I was sure he would agree. Muhammad was guilty, a traitor of the worst kind.

On the other hand, I could do nothing if I couldn't find him.

"I'll agree to your terms if you help me find him," I proposed.

Mustafa nodded. "Swear it before Allah, Almighty."

"I'm not Muslim." I replied.

"Then by the Christian God you worship!"

"It's the same God, I suppose," I offered, "But, regardless, I swear it before God on pain of my immortal soul."

"Then yes, I'll help you find him. But remember your vow. Breaking it means eternal damnation!"

I nodded.

We set out in Mustafa's tiny Jigoli, that cramped old Soviet relic we talked about earlier, and headed toward the city. Before we left, I had disguised myself with a fake beard and changed the contours of my face, with some special cosmetic putty. That would fool any facial recognition cameras the Russians had set up inside the city. The last thing I needed was for "John Kovalenko, US Army Colonel" to appear on Russian monitoring screens.

Mustafa knew the city intimately and was familiar with Muhammad's haunts.

"We'll start with the mosque," Mustafa said as he started the car.

"Duma-Dama?" I asked.

I had seen pictures of the ancient Duma-Dama mosque in books I'd read to prepare for my mission. In the glory days of the Crimean Khanate, it had been used in coronation ceremonies for new Khans and was still in use. But, he shook his head.

"No. The mosque we go to is unlike any you might ordinarily imagine. The preacher is an extremist who believes, like some other lunatics, that a worldwide Caliphate is about to come into being. He preaches that the entire world will soon live under Sharia law. He is an outcast, forbidden from entering Duma-Dama Mosque, let alone preaching there. He holds prayer in a 4-room apartment. Even that is prohibited, but the Russian authorities ignore him, because he has connections to some Mullahs in Iran, which they are now allied with. Only fools like my nephew take him seriously."

"I get it..." I said.

"Let me do the talking." Mustafa reminded me.

He didn't have to remind me. I knew enough to keep my mouth shut. My thick American accent gave me away instantly and I couldn't shake it off. While many of the Tatars we intended to speak with probably hated Russia and wouldn't betray me, there might be some who would report me to gain favor with the authorities. And, of course, a majority of the city's inhabitants were ethnic Russians. There was no point in taking that chance.

We parked and entered the building. The apartment mosque was on the third floor. We could hear chanting inside even before we reached the door. When we knocked, a man opened it and stared at us blankly. Then, he recognized Mustafa and frowned. It was obvious they knew each other and didn't get along.

"What do you want?" the man asked gruffly.

"I'm looking for my nephew," Mustafa replied.

The man hesitated, then shook his head.

"He has not been here for a long time. Why are you looking for him?"

Mustafa glanced at me, then said.

"We have urgent business. It is very important. Do you know where he is?"

The man shrugged, then said.

"You think he tells me where he goes? He is a loner who keeps to himself. He drinks alcohol and is not a very good Muslim, and that is, in large part, due to the bad influence you have on him. Your loose behavior and disregard for the Holy Koran, Mustafa, have contributed to his problems. Additionally, he is a troublemaker."

"What kind of trouble?" Mustafa asked.

The man looked at him and sneered.

"You know very well what kind of trouble, Mustafa. He is a rebel. A fighter. He fights against the Russian infidels with his own two hands, rather than leaving the matter in the hands of Allah Almighty."

The man shrugged again.

"But, maybe, he will be a martyr someday." He added as if that would compensate for any weaknesses Muhammad might have.

"Some believe he may have betrayed the resistance," Muhammad suggested, "Do you understand what that means? I must find him."

The man gasped, then said;

"Impossible! He hates the infidels. And, he is ordained despite his faults. He will be a martyr when the real battle comes!"

Mustafa grabbed the man by the collar and pushed him against the wall.

"You idiot!" he exclaimed, a fire in his voice. "The real battle is already here! Tell me where he is. Tell me now!"

The man wriggled out of his grasp.

"I don't know where he is," He insisted. "By Allah Almighty, I haven't seen him in days! He doesn't listen to me anyway. Not to anyone. He has his agenda. Contacts. Secrets."

Mustafa grabbed the man again by the collar.

"What contacts? Secrets? What are you talking about?"

"You don't know?" The man seemed surprised.

"What is it that I don't know?" Mustafa asked.

"He speaks with those who believe that the Caliphate will come by the hand of human jihad!" The man replied.

Mustafa looked at me, then looked back at the man, and released his grip.

"Tell me everything. Hold nothing back." He said.

The Imam first shook his head violently and then nodded, the two gestures contradicting one another.

"Yes. Yes. I will tell you," he said, "What you don't understand is that Muhammad is not like you. Not like him..." He pointed at me and then continued.

"He is different. Chosen. Special gifts. A special mission. A vision of the end of the world. Allah works in mysterious ways. He will use Muhammad, with all his strengths and despite his weaknesses!"

Mustafa and I exchanged a look, he shook his head and then turned back to the preacher.

"What vision? What mission? What are you talking about?" he demanded.

The man violently shook his head in the negative.

"No, no! I have said too much already!" he muttered, "I will say no more to a munafiq!"

I later found out that 'munafiq" means hypocrite, a term used throughout the Islamic world to describe individuals who outwardly profess to practice Islam but who are inwardly unfaithful and dishonest. According to the Koran, such people are to be eternally condemned to the lowest depths of hell and can never be forgiven by Allah.

It is a serious accusation and, I think, after being insulted in that manner, Mustafa would have physically gone after the man and beaten him to a pulp had I not deliberately gotten in his way, gently shaking my head.

"He is nothing but a crazy old man." I whispered.

My real reason for holding him back, however, had nothing to do with any sympathy for the Imam. It was simply that, if things came to blows, it might attract the attention of the local Russian police. That preacher had screws loose for sure. Despite surface loyalty to the overall Tatar cause, crazy men might always betray you. And, frankly, I was convinced that he was telling the truth. He knew nothing. He was an idiot and not worth bothering with.

We headed back to Mustafa's tiny car and he started the engine, but before getting back on the road, he turned toward me with a sad look on his face.

"I'm sorry you had to listen to that." He said. "The man is a fool."

I nodded.

"I know that," I reassured him. "And, I don't judge the Tatar people based on one crazy Imam who preaches in an apartment. But, what was that he was saying about a Caliphate, a vision, missions, and the end of the world?"

Mustafa sighed and began to explain.

"He is describing a radical version of Islam. They believe that Allah will soon bring a global Islamic state, or Caliphate, into being. The Caliph will supposedly be the successor of the Prophet Muhammad. They claim the world is about to see an apocalyptic confrontation between good and evil, and their imaginary Caliphate is supposed to play a decisive role."

"That's what ISIS believes…" I commented. "I remember similar insanity coming from a prisoner we captured during fighting in Iraq. Is the Imam a Jihadist?"

Mustafa shook his head.

"No, he is too much of a coward for that," He said. "His group does share some crazy ideas with Islamic State, but he preaches that Allah himself will create the Caliphate. That's the excuse for why they don't need to risk their own skins, actively waging jihad. Instead, they sit in apartment buildings and pray like idiots, waiting for Allah to bring them their Caliphate."

I frowned.

"Well, I guess it's better than ISIS," I commented. "But, how can people believe such nonsense?"

Mustafa shrugged his shoulders and shook his head.

"There are always people who are desperate, angry, and ignorant. Those who want to be told how to live. How to die. If there is a maniac who says something loud enough, long enough, no matter how ridiculous it is, some people will believe."

His words were wise and true. I had seen it myself many times.

"Your nephew is one of those people?" I asked.

Mustafa nodded.

"Unfortunately. And, he gets worse over time, it seems. Because, now, this crazy preacher says he has joined with the others, the ones who think the Caliphate will be brought into being by means of Jihad."

I shook my head.

"As practical matter, that means he can justify anything, even treason against his own people..."

"Maybe...." Mustafa admitted. "But, that remains to be seen. Remember the vow you took...'

"I haven't forgotten," I replied. "But, he can't be allowed to roam free. He can do a lot more damage..."

"I am helping you find him, am I not?" Mustafa pointed out.

I nodded reluctantly. I had made a promise and would keep it if I could.

We drove away and began searching for Muhammad's other acquaintances. The center of Yevpatoriya is a labyrinth of narrow streets and alleyways, filled with tiny shops and unauthorized street vendors. Our first stop was a small tea shop run by a man named Iskander, a burly fellow with a bushy beard, who greeted Mustafa warmly. Regarding me, however, his eyes narrowed with suspicion, as he had never seen me before, and he suspected strangers. I was careful to keep my mouth shut and let Mustafa do the talking.

"Have you seen my nephew?" Mustafa asked.

The man shook his head, his suspicious gaze wandering over to me again before returning to Mustafa. After some small talk, we left, and our next stop was a mechanic's garage. The owner, a wiry man named Ruslan, was elbow-deep in the engine of a car when we arrived. He wiped his hands on an oily rag while Mustafa asked him about Muhammad. Like Iskander, Ruslan hadn't seen Muhammad. We visited more people—a baker, a tailor, a fishmonger. Mostly, they were Caliphate believers. A few were not. But, none had seen Muhammad. My sense of urgency was growing. We were running out of time. We still had no idea where he might be.

After returning to Mustafa's small Jigoli, I felt disheartened. Our leads were exhausted. Mustafa gazed at me somberly.

"We can't predict his next move so it is up to you," He said, "If your suspicions about Muhammad are correct, you must reconsider the attack on the missile storage areas."

I paused, processing the weight of the situation.

"I am certain he is a traitor," I confirmed.

"Then, you have an important decision to make," Mustafa urged.

"I need your input," I replied, "Moving forward poses huge risks, but halting means those missiles will kill a lot of innocent civilians."

Mustafa nodded slowly, showing his understanding of the dilemma.

"We must destroy them," he concluded.

Mustafa was a loyal, brave man I'd grown to admire. It seemed incredible that he could share genes with a scumbag like Muhammad. Mustafa risked his life daily for his people and understood the stakes as well as anyone. Our team was now even smaller without Muhammad, and we were already short-handed. Acting immediately meant we couldn't gather the promised support from Ismail and his Simferopol partisans. Yet Muhammad's treachery left us no choice. I had to either call off the attack and crawl back to Kyiv with my tail between my legs, or carry it out immediately.

We had no time to lose. There was no telling what additional information he might pass to the Russians once he realized his first plan to get me captured or killed had failed. Everything had become much riskier.

"Muhammad is a traitor and a coward and he could contact the Russians again..." I said aloud, for no particular reason, since my position was already quite clear. Perhaps, I hoped that if I spoke loud enough, somehow I could get him to agree with me.

"Even if that is so," Mustafa pointed out, "it is unlikely at the moment. He could not know that the police to whom you think he leaked information are dead. Most likely, if he really is guilty, he thinks he's done enough already to destroy you. And, his natural assumption would be that, if you are not dead or in a Russian jail, you are following your original timeline. If you launch the attack tonight, however…"

The anger inside me kept growing, but his words were sensible. I had never dealt with treachery inside my ranks before. Every soldier I'd ever worked with, in the US Army as well as the Ukrainian armed forces, was honorable, decent, and loyal to the cause, whatever that cause had been. Muhammad was not. He had betrayed his country, Ukraine, and his own Crimean Tatar people. If not for the death of those two policemen, the entire partisan movement, including his own uncle, and Yasmina, the woman he claimed to love, might end up in jail or worse.

What motivated such an egregious violation of everything decent? Jealousy? Revenge? It didn't matter. It was what it was. We were all stuck with the consequences.

"Tonight?" I asked.

"Yes," Mustafa replied, "If we do this, we need to do it as quickly as humanly possible. Whoever leaked the information, whether it was Muhammad or someone else, could leak more information if he knows his original plan didn't work."

I nodded.

"But, first, we must talk to Svetlana…" He said.

It was late afternoon by the time we got back to Svetlana's bungalow with heavy faces. I knocked on the door and Yasmina opened it. I entered with Mustafa by my side and saw that she was already waiting for us, sitting at her worn wooden table, her wrinkled face illuminated by the soft glow of a single lamp. Interestingly, Sasha Melnyk, the electronic whiz, was sitting next to her. Apparently, the two of them had been discussing the situation.

"Good that you are finally back." She said, "You were wasting precious time. I presume you did not find him?"

"Right." Mustafa confirmed.

She nodded, knowingly, and said,

"Did you expect anything else? My sources tell me he has already left Crimea. They say he is in Istanbul."

Mustafa shrugged his shoulders. "It was worth a try…"

She turned toward me.

"What do you suggest?" she asked. "Should we leave for Kyiv?"

"Mustafa and I believe we should go ahead with the mission, but bring it forward to tonight."

"Tonight?" she asked, surprised.

I nodded.

"But, it will be impossible to contact Ismail and…" She said, but I cut her off.

"I have a new plan," I explained. "I think we can be successful with a tiny surgical strike team."

"But, we don't know exactly what he told the Russians…"

"The people he told it to are dead," I suggested.

"He could have told others…" she replied.

"Not likely." Mustafa offered. "If it was Muhammad, as you both seem to believe, you know how much he hates the Russians. We already know what the two policemen were told and we know they did not report it to their superiors. The information died with them. Not even the occupation authorities know the policemen are dead yet, so the traitor doesn't know either. You say Muhammad is in Istanbul? So, if he is the traitor, he definitely won't know yet. We have a window in which to act."

"But, what about Ismail and the extra men?" Sasha asked, "How can we mobilize them so fast?"

"We won't have time," I replied. "I wanted to wait for a missile delivery truck, bringing new missiles for storage. Then, I intended to launch my drones from the outer perimeter of the base after taking out the anti-drone defenses. But, my new plan doesn't require any of that. We can penetrate the outer drone defenses by launching the drones from the center of the base."

"The center of the base?" Svetlana asked, perplexed. "How can we get to the center of the base?"

"We can," I replied, "And, once we're there, we'll be close enough to force open the doors to the bunker, if necessary. We won't necessarily need a delivery to gain entry."

Mustafa began speaking again.

"John has explained his new plan to me, in detail," He stated, "And, I agree with it. But, we must attack right away."

Sasha mused over the last statement, for a moment, and then asked,

"What makes you so sure the policemen are dead?" He asked.

Sasha was, apparently, the only one left who didn't know, even though I had borrowed his vehicle to do the job.

"Because I killed them..." I replied.

A somewhat shocked look appeared on his face. He raised an eyebrow.

"I didn't think Americans could do that..." He commented.

"Sorry to ruin the fantasy," I replied. 'But we're ruthless when we have to be."

He nodded and turned to another subject.

"How would we get inside the base?" He asked.

"With your help," I replied.

"Yes," Mustafa agreed, standing in front of a big map, showing the airbase and its surrounding area, that he had just unfolded onto the table. "John and I have talked about this in great detail."

"We're thinking creatively," I said, picking up where he left off. "I can't release my micro-drones from a distance because of electronic anti-drone defense system will take them down. There's also not enough time to coordinate with Ismail, so we won't have enough men to take out the defense grid."

I sighed, shook my head and then continued;

"But, if we can make it here," I pointed to the center of the base as it was depicted on the map, "We'll be behind the protection zone. The anti-drone screen works on incoming drones coming through this wide circular field. It doesn't extend into the center of the base. It can't because it would disrupt the base's own electronic systems if it did. If we get inside that perimeter, we can be successful. We'll be able to launch drones from the inside, and the Russian defense systems won't even notice."

I traced out the critical areas of interest with my finger and continued.

"I don't really understand..." Svetlana admitted.

"Let me explain it in more detail, then," I said. "Russia's anti-drone defense grid is here. It projects a zone of electronic interference which blocks radio and GPS signaling. Their signal generators are arranged in a circular pattern, forming a doughnut-shaped shell around the base. This doughnut extends about one kilometer in each direction, as well as upward, encasing the base. But, here, at the center, it's like the eye of a hurricane. Everything is calm. There's no radio-electronic interference."

"But, again, how can we get inside?" Sasha asked.

"Sasha, you've hacked into Russia's military computer systems many times," Mustafa pointed out.

"Of course," Sasha confirmed.

"So, we need you to do it one more time." I said.

Sasha scowled.

"You realize that it's never easy to do it," he replied, "And, they continue to tighten security measures. It's harder every time."

"Our goal is to penetrate so deep that we can operate inside the sweet spot," I said, "But, first, Sasha, you need to hack into their military computer system and find out when the next major supply truck is due. You'll need to insert photos into the identification systems, replacing those of the driver and the guard. Can you do that?"

"Maybe...probably," Sasha replied.

I took out another map, unfolded it, and spread it on the table. It was a wider view, showing the airbase as it related to our current location and the road. I pointed to the map again.

"We hijack one of the Russian trucks," I explained. "Sasha and Mustafa disguise themselves as truck guard and driver. I'll hide inside the trailer compartment until we reach the center of the base. Once we're inside, we'll find a safe area, launch the drones, destroy the missile bunkers and get out as quickly as possible."

Sasha shook his head.

"I don't like the risk..." He commented.

"The risk is acceptable." Mustafa countered.

"It's either this, or give up and admit defeat..." I said.

The look on Sasha's face when I mentioned the word "defeat" made it clear that he liked that idea even less than the risk. There was silence for a few seconds.

"Alright," He said, finally. "Supply trucks arrive at the base at all times during the day and night. I'll find out when the next one is due."

"Good!" I said, "We'll need that truck to get us into the base. If all goes as planned, there will be chaos by the time we leave, so it should be a lot easier to get out than it was to get in. We'll get out, abandon the truck and escape on foot."

"And, how, exactly, do we get out?" Sasha asked.

Svetlana crossed her arms, the skepticism was also etched on her face.

"The same way we got in," I replied, "Through the gate."

"Are you sure that three people will be enough?" She asked,

"Well, I wish I had more, but we don't need many if we are on the inside." I replied.

"Who will go?" She asked. "You, Mustafa, Sasha? That's it? Virtually no one to cover your back. With only three men, including yourself, your plan will surely fail."

"As you said before," I reminded her. "I can't conjure up men. I'll make do with what I have."

Svetlana leaned over the table, her eyes seeming to sparkle even in the dim light.

"But, you already have a woman who shoots better than 99% of all men..." she reminded me, referring to her skill as a sniper, which I had heard about. But, I shook my head in the negative.

"No," I said.

"You think I can't fight? Because I'm an old woman?" she asked.

I shook my head. "I didn't say that."

"Not directly, but you implied it," she snapped, laughing harshly. "Do you know I was fighting Russians when you were still in diapers? Even in Soviet times. It's just that no one knew about it."

I was stunned. I had no idea that there had been a Tatar resistance during the Soviet era. The revelation left me speechless but only for a moment. She seized on that moment to press her point.

"Then, it is decided." she stated, unequivocally, "Now, you have four warriors for your mission."

"Five!" came a soft female voice from the corner of the room. It was Yasmina. "I am also going."

"No, Yasmina, I can't allow that," I insisted. "You have to stay here."

"Colonel Kovalenko is correct," Her grandmother added. "Someone must stay to guard the base."

But, Yasmina would hear none of it. She just shook her head.

"John, Babushka, you can't tell me what to do." she insisted, "I am 21 years old and I make my own decisions. Where you go, I go. If you die, I die by your side, fighting."

"No, Yasmina," I interjected. "Someone needs to be here."

"That's a lie." she snapped back, immediately. "You just don't want me to go."

"It is too dangerous," I admitted, finally. "I couldn't bear losing you. And, someone really does need to stay here."

"Why?" She asked. "To eat, drink, and be worried? That's not for me. If you want someone to stay, stay here yourself, John, and I'll carry out your plan without you...whether you like it or not, I'm going with you."

There was a lot more back and forth, but Yasmina was an unstoppable force once she made up her mind. No matter what her grandmother and I argued, no matter how strong those arguments seemed to us, she ignored us. She insisted she was a part of the mission and there was no possibility of leaving her out. In the end, I had no choice but to take her.

Meanwhile, Sasha obtained the information I asked for, after spending less than an hour hacking the Russian Ministry of Defense. His eyes seemed to shine, underneath the wire-rimmed frame, as he told us when and where the next Russian supply truck would pass on the way to the air base.

Svetlana's face brightened. "Gather your gear, everyone. It's time to move!"

Our group swiftly assembled, fully armed and equipped. A mix of anticipation and nervousness hung in the air. We took our position at a strategic point along the road, waiting for the truck. Sasha monitored its progress in real-time on his tablet, keeping us informed. After what seemed like forever, we heard the distant rumble of the approaching supply truck. As it came into view, my heart raced. The moment of truth had arrived.

15

The entire area was covered with the same brownish grassy steppe land typical of the rest of rural Crimea in early summer. We had arrived at the ambush location by means of a small truck that Svetlana arranged at the last minute. It was the property of a rental company owned by a rebel sympathizer, and it was driven by Mustafa. We found some thick bushes growing on the side of the road, and we stopped the truck there and got out.

It was a unique spot where we could hide before waylaying the supply truck. Large collections of bushes were rare in this dry savanna terrain. Each of us was dressed in a fake Russian army uniform, a flak jacket, and a face mask. We waited patiently for the oncoming truck, most behind the bushes, but Mustafa stayed with the truck a bit longer, to move it into position. The plan was to use the small truck to force the much larger military delivery truck into a temporary stop.

"Will it work?" Yasmina asked nervously, in a whisper, showing her unfamiliarity with such operations. She held my hand tightly, seemingly afraid to let go. I smiled reassuringly.

"We've got the element of surprise." I explained. "I've only got one radio wave jammer left, but it should be enough in this tiny area, to prevent them from calling for backup. We just need to take out the driver and the guard. Mustafa and Sasha will take their place and we'll drive right into the center of the Russian base as if we were meant to be there."

Yasmina nodded and tried to smile, but I knew she was worrying. Her questions proved that, despite what I had been told, her participation in past partisan operations were greatly exaggerated, possibly in an attempt to deter her from participating in any more of them. It seemed almost as if this was her first time. Had I known that, no matter what her protests might have been, I never would have let her go. But, now, it was too late to do anything about it.

"What if they check our papers and run our faces through a facial recognition program? What if they recognize we are partisans?" Yasmina asked.

"That won't happen," I reassured her. "First, we'll be hiding inside the trailer. And, if Sasha has done his job correctly and I am sure that he has, both he and Mustafa will use one of the beautifully made fake IDs they've had for a long time. It's Sasha's job to insert the imaginary people, that correspond to the military IDs, into the Russian military's computer systems."

"But, what if the Russians scan their IDs and realize they're not the people who are supposed to be on the delivery truck?" Yasmina asked.

"Don't worry," I reassured her. "As I said, all the existing information about the driver and guard has been switched out and replaced with the details from their fake IDs. If the Russian soldiers at the entry gate scan the IDs, everything will check out. The names, addresses, and other details are fake, of course, but they're in Russia's military database now. If their identities are ever questioned, it isn't likely to happen anytime soon. By the time there's any chance of that, we'll all be long gone, out of Crimea and inside Ukrainian-controlled territory. That's the new plan...'

"I am still a little bit scared." She finally admitted. "But, John. I love you."

I smiled, but I was concerned. It sounded almost as if she wanted to make sure she said it before she died.

"I love you too," I replied. "Just stay calm. If everyone does their job, we'll get in and get out again. We'll save thousands of innocent lives by blowing up those missiles. And, after it's over, we're going to America. You won't be going on any more missions after that, ever again. Do we understand each other?"

She smiled, leaned over, and kissed me. As I spoke to Yasmina, her grandmother was at my other side. She saw us tightly holding hands, which seemed to please her. I was speaking in English to Yasmina and Svetlana had a poor command of English. She probably didn't know exactly what we were talking about. But, nonetheless, she leaned over and whispered to me;

"You remind me of my husband and I when we were young. He was a good man..." And, then, after a short pause, she added, "Life just isn't sweet without him..."

"He was a hero," I said, nodding my head. "And, so are you..."

She shook her head and chuckled under her breath.

"I'm no hero." She commented. "Just an angry old woman who hates Russians. They killed my husband and my son. They left me with nothing but a war…"

For me, the Russians were the enemy and nothing more. I took no satisfaction in killing them. I understood, however, that things were different for her. She had internalized the history of oppression that the Crimean Tatar people had suffered under Russian rule. In the time I had been in Ukraine, I'd seen how they leveled cities to the ground, concentrating on civilian targets to terrorize the population, destroying homes, public buildings and places of worship. I'd seen, first hand, how ruthless the Russian state could be. So, even though I felt no particular animosity toward Russia or Russians, myself, I understood why she felt the way she did.

The problem of Russian ruthlessness was that the elite ruling caste of that nation, whoever they happened to be, whether Tsars or Communists, habitually set a bad example for everyone else. The system was corrupted from the top down. That is as true today as it was in the late 1700s, when they destroyed the Crimean Khanate. The Russian elite call themselves by different names and titles now, but they've retained the same imperialistic attitudes that have been passed on as a sort of cultural birthright.

The idea that Russians had killed Svetlana's son seemed like news at first. But then, I remembered. Her son was Yasmina's father. He had died, one of the many cannon fodder used to fight Putin's war to subdue Chechnya.

"Don't worry," I reassured her, "Soon, we'll destroy billions of dollars worth of their missiles and tons of their ammunition."

"Yes," Svetlana agreed, enthusiastically, "We'll light them all on fire!"

"Fire!" Yasmina repeated enthusiastically.

"Fire!" Svetlana and Yasmina repeated, in unison, in Tatar, the call to arms of the Crimean partisans.

Sasha sat next to Yasmina, but did not join in the call for "fire". He was too fixed on his task. He wiped his wire rimmed glasses and checked his tablet computer again. As the brains of our operation, he couldn't afford to get carried away by emotion. Nothing could interfere with his task of continually tracking the supply truck. He glanced at me, smiled, and gave me a thumbs up.

"Good news and bad news. Which one first?" Sasha asked.

"Bad news," I said.

"The supply truck is running late. It is still about 10 minutes away. We'll have less time to get to the base." he said.

"The good news?" I asked.

"I've figured out a weak spot in their defenses," He explained, "There is a back gate, much less well-guarded than the main gate. Normally, used for emergency vehicles and maintenance."

"Good work, Sasha." I said.

He pointed to an electronic map displayed on his tablet screen and then continued, "See?" He asked, "There's an unmarked gravel road. You can see it on the satellite imagery. It's also on their internal maps."

"That's where we're heading," I said, "You'll guide us since you're the only one who knows the route."

He nodded in acknowledgment.

Mustafa was still sitting behind the wheel of our small delivery truck. Its owner was a loyal Ukrainian, who had willingly accepting Russian citizenship for the sake of appearances. He wasn't an active partisan fighter, but he despised the Putin regime and had been more than willing to cooperate. He would report his truck as "stolen," but not until we had completed our mission. The theft report would ensure that his complicity would never be suspected.

Mustafa moved the truck into position, perpendicular to the road, crossing it and leaving it almost completely blocked. Given the mass of a huge tractor-trailer, in theory it could tear right through the small truck. But, they would only do that if they knew we were there, waiting for them. But, they didn't. That meant they would surely stop. Once the little truck was in position, Mustafa jumped out of its cab, and returned to his place, behind the bushes, by Svetlana's side. We waited in silence as the minutes ticked by. The rumble grew closer. We checked and double-checked our weapons, preparing for the attack.

"Sveta," Mustafa whispered, "we have been through a lot together, have we not? The best and worst of times. We mourned Igor together. We are a family. I want you to know how I feel..."

"Yes, you have been like a brother, always there when needed. You were there when I brought Yasmina here from Moscow. I love you like a brother," Svetlana replied.

He smiled and spoke again,

"We will finish this fight and make our final stand together. We will die with honor."

Listening to fatalistic talk always annoys me, so I injected myself into the conversation.

"Why don't you save those parting words for when one of you is actually on your deathbed? No one is going to die today. We go in, we do the job, and we get out,"

"How will we get out?" Svetlana asked yet again, even though we had discussed it back at the base camp.

"We'll leave through the same gate we got in by," I insisted. "Don't worry..."

I stopped in the middle of my sentence, switching gears.

"Here she comes!" I announced, as the sound of the approaching vehicle came to my ears.

The supply truck finally came into view, a large green vehicle with a red star on its side and a large "Z" painted onto each door, moving slowly and methodically, unaware of the danger that lay ahead. I signaled to the others and we prepared to strike.

"This is it," I said. "The moment of truth! Remember the plan. Stick to it. Remember why we're doing this and what we are fighting for. Freedom for Ukraine! Freedom for the Tatari people! Are you ready?"

They all nodded.

"Fire!" They all chanted in unison.

As the truck neared the place where we had blocked the road, it slowed and stopped. The driver, wearing a Russian military uniform, climbed out of the cab, cursing the unknown person who had parked a delivery truck without a driver, right across the path of his truck.

"Go!" I shouted.

"Fire!" The partisans yelled again, in Tatar, as we all jumped out, from behind the bushes, running towards the man, screaming for him to raise his hands in the air. He raised them without hesitation. Then, Yasmina and I ran to the back of the truck. I quickly opened it and we immediately moved to the side, just in case there was a guard inside. Sure enough, there was a guard, complete with vodka bottle, in true Russian fashion. In spite of drinking on the job, he wasn't slow, immediately opening fire, with wild shots, from the crate on which he sat. He was spraying bullets in all directions, with his AK-74 on automatic mode.

His first cartridge ran out quickly and he had to replace it. This gave me an opportunity. By the time he lifted a new cartridge to snap it into place, it was too late. I shot the man, point-blank, twice in the head. The bullets made a whooshing sound, as they always do, when they come out of the barrel of a pistol equipped with a silencer. He slumped over as blood poured out of the hole in his forehead. Grabbing his dead body by the back of the collar, I tossed him backward, out of the truck, and dragged the body away by the legs, over to the bushes where we'd previously been hiding.

I had to make a quick detour to our small delivery truck to grab a cloth. Back in the trailer, I carefully wiped away all traces of blood from the floor. I knew the truck would likely be inspected at some point, so I made sure to leave it spotless. Afterward, I returned to the bushes and secured the bloodied rag to a sharp branch. The Russians would eventually find it, but by then, it wouldn't matter anymore.

Meanwhile, Sasha had disarmed the driver, tying his hands and feet, before hiding him behind the bushes. I injected the man with an anesthetic. The drug would keep him knocked out for at least four hours, more than enough time for us to complete our mission before he could wake up sufficiently to try crawling to the road, where a passing car might rescue him. The dead guard was already next to him. Mustafa moved the delivery truck out of the way, and left it at the side of the road.

When enough time had passed to let us succeed or fail in our mission, the truck's owner would miraculously find it. He would also "find", free and report the truck driver to the Russian authorities. The driver would be safely returned to the Russians and this showing of good faith would exonerate the truck owner from any suspicion. Unfortunately, the guard was dead. There was nothing I could do about that. There had been no choice but to kill him. But, the small truck's owner wouldn't be blamed and that was what was important.

Mustafa and Sasha removed their masks and flak jackets, and I stashed them deep in the cargo container for possible use later on. We would not enter the Russian airbase with masks on. The fake paperwork alone would have to be sufficient. It was excellent work. A direct link to the Russian Ministry of Defense personnel database had enabled Sasha to replace the real photographs associated with the IDs of the driver and guard with photos of himself and Mustafa.

Sasha climbed into the passenger seat. Mustafa climbed into the driver's seat. Svetlana, Yasmina, and I, together with my equipment bags, found a place hidden inside the cargo trailer. I would have liked to be in the cab, but that was impossible. Too much chance that someone would speak to me and expect a reply. If I gave one, my strong American accent would give me away.

Mustafa put the truck back into gear, and we began moving. Whatever fate had in store would soon reveal itself. We were all ready to accept our destiny, whatever it might bring. Let's face the facts: death can strike any of us at any time, even in places supposedly at peace. What if you take the wrong train, plane, or bus and it crashes? What if you cross the street at the wrong moment? A car runs you over?

Consider the great American general, George Patton, for example. He stood fearless as Nazi bullets and shrapnel rained around him and never sustained an injury. Yet, after World War II, he died in a simple car accident on an American street. Fate rules us all. If you are meant to die, you die. If not, you live. That is what I believe.

The plan was to exit the airbase just as we had entered it, that is, as "Russian" soldiers, as well as people hidden in the recesses of some means of transport, although not necessarily the one we had arrived in. The explosions would come just before we left. I reckoned that the Russians wouldn't know what hit them and complete chaos would rule for a while. By the time they came looking for us, we'd be far away from the air base, safe and secure. It was a bit naive.

16

We approached the air base. The trailer was cramped, but we managed to squeeze behind some big supply boxes in the front. I kept track of the situation outside using a walkie-talkie. Its double-encrypted, ultra-short-range signal connected me to the cab. I pressed the button to speak.

"How are we doing up there?" I asked.

"Almost there, as you can probably see on the front camera," Mustafa replied. "Another 5 minutes and we'll be at the back entry gate."

I pressed the button again,

"Excellent!" I said.

Hooking the device back onto the belt of my uniform, I felt anxious. Success hinged on too many factors out of my direct control. We had to bypass guards, cameras, and base sensors. We needed to find a quiet spot to launch the drones. My job was to pilot them remotely, avoid detection, and guide them into the missile storage area through a window or door. Then, land as many drones as possible on warheads, triggering a chain reaction of explosions. So many things were dependent upon so many other things. If anything went wrong, my entire plan would implode.

Despite being inside the covered cargo trailer, I was actively monitoring our surroundings. My phone connected to micro-cameras and microphones placed around the truck's exterior. That was what Mustafa was referring to when he suggested that I could "probably see." The setup gave me a comprehensive view of our environment, better than what I could see with my own eyes.

A new message came from Mustafa via the walkie-talkie,

"A few more seconds and we'll be at the gate..." he said.

I pressed the button to transmit, "Understood...".

As we moved toward the gate, I monitored our approach. The front camera showed two Russian soldiers at the checkpoint, armed with rifles. Beside them stood what appeared to be an old Soviet-style truck scanner, combining a metal detector and X-ray machine. I recognized it from technical documents I'd studied during my US Special Forces days.

If functional, the massive X-ray machine posed two threats: radiation exposure and the ability to reveal our hidden presence in the trailer. If they attempted to use it, we'd have no choice but to intervene, even if it meant openly attacking the guards on base property. This risky move could jeopardize our entire mission. It was something we would only do if we had no other choice.

Mustafa knew I was watching. He had helped me glue the cameras into position. He sent another message by walkie-talkie.

"Don't worry," he reassured me, "we have our IDs, the original delivery papers, poorly maintained Russian equipment, and basic Russian laziness to count on. Just keep quiet back there. They'll wave us through…"

We halted at the gate. Mustafa greeted the soldiers with a smile through his open window. Meanwhile, the three of us sat motionless among the supply stacks, silent but alert. Our AK-74 rifles were in our hands, fingers close to the triggers, ready for any potential trouble.

Mustafa began chatting casually.

"Good evening, comrades," he said in Russian. "Here is a delivery for the commissary. Mostly, food. We'll be heading toward the storage area."

"Documents?" The soldier asked.

He handed over the two fake Russian IDs and the papers they had taken from the real driver. The soldiers looked them over.

"You are over 3 hours late." One of them commented as he scanned the ID's into an unknown device.

I held my breath, hoping Sasha had crossed every "t" and dotted every "i" when he was creating the fake IDs. Thankfully, the device beeped, and the green LED lit up. He had done his job well. The soldier nodded while handing back the documents.

"Alright, everything seems to be in order," he said, "but we need to check your cargo. It's protocol…"

Mustafa smiled, nodded, and asked:

"You want me to move the vehicle to the X-ray area?"

The soldier smiled and shook his head.

"Are you joking?" he asked, "that thing hasn't worked in centuries. Just step out of the vehicle and open the back.

Mustafa and Sasha exited the cab. The Russian soldiers wouldn't know our exact positions in the trailer and wouldn't be able to see us unless they unloaded the entire trailer. The four men moved to the truck's rear as a group and Mustafa unfastened the lock, even as his hand drifted towards his concealed pistol, just in case.

We had squeezed ourselves between cargo boxes at the front, making it almost impossible for an inspector, at the back, to see us. The brief inspection revealed only food, water, and medical supplies. One of the big boxes, at the back, was labeled "fresh beef."

"It's about time!" he commented, smiling, "Fresh meat! They've been feeding us such shit!"

The two soldiers nodded, fully satisfied that everything was in order. Sasha sealed the back of the truck, snapping it shut. He and Mustafa walked back to the cab section, climbed in and waited for a moment. Then, the soldiers waved them forward.

"Make the first right," one guard suggested, pointing out the way, "about 200 meters, right there. A few hundred meters straight and you will see a man guarding the commissary shipping dock. He'll tell you what to do..."

"Thank you, comrades," Mustafa said, smiling, reverting to the old Soviet method of referring to fellow soldiers.

He drove past the gate. I breathed a sigh of relief. We had passed the first obstacle successfully. I pressed the walkie-talkie button to transmit my voice.

"Good job!" I said.

"Thank you," Mustafa replied.

We prepared for the next phase as the truck stopped near the loading dock. Another soldier directed us to back up, then approached the driver's side.

"You are very late. There's no unloading crew on duty now..." he said.

Mustafa smiled nervously.

"Yes," he replied in Russian, his Crimean Tatar accent thick. "We had delays on the road. Many checkpoints. With all the Ukrainian-sponsored terrorists, everyone is paranoid."

The soldier nodded knowingly.

"Aren't you Tatari?" he asked, as if it were a black mark.

Mustafa nodded. "Yes."

"That's why," the soldier continued. "They probably double-checked you at every checkpoint. So many of you people can't be trusted..."

I feared Mustafa might react angrily to this provocation, but he surprised me, maintaining his composure, continuing to smile without regard to the blatant disrespect.

"Yes, probably," he said, "Many people don't appreciate the benefits Russia has brought us."

The soldier seemed somewhat surprised and had nothing to say in response. Instead, he glanced toward the cargo trailer. Then, he nodded back at Mustafa, apparently satisfied that this particular Tatar, at least, knew "his place."

"You'll have to wait for the unloading crew," He announced, "Night duty won't show up for another half hour."

That was a relief. It meant that the man wouldn't try to open the truck himself. Sasha exited, approaching the soldier with a partially concealed bottle of expensive Beluga vodka. He discreetly revealed it, raising his eyebrows.

"Good stuff!" Sasha said.

The soldier nodded.

"The best!" he agreed.

He leaned closer to the guard and whispered.

"My partner, over there," he said, pointing to Mustafa in the cab, "you know, he's a Muslim. Never drinks alcohol..."

"Not even vodka?" the Russian soldier asked, surprised.

"No," Sasha replied. "It's against their religion, I guess."

The soldier shook his head in disgust at the thought.

"Unbelievable," He exclaimed, disdainfully, "But, I'm beginning to believe anything when it comes to those people. But, I knew a Chechen once. He drank a lot..."

Sasha winked.

"Not this one." He said, motioning with his head toward Mustafa, and then began whispering. "Anyway, I've got this full bottle of vodka and no one to drink it with, and I don't know where I can drink it, off the cameras..."

The soldier's eyes lit up. He glanced around quickly, seeing no one in the immediate vicinity.

"I know places off the camera grid..." He confided under his breath.

"Show me and we'll share it..." Sasha whispered.

"What about the Muslim?" He whispered back. "Can we trust him?"

Sasha nodded and then shook his head slightly

"Yeah, he's OK," He said, "He won't report it."

"You sure?" He asked, "I don't trust those people."

"Don't worry," Sasha insisted, "It's true. He's a damn Muslim, but other than that, he's okay. Doesn't drink, but doesn't care if I do..."

The soldier smiled.

"Alright, then."

He turned, subtly to the left, away from the loading dock and toward the corner of the building, lifting his gun as if he had heard something suspicious and possibly dangerous that had to be checked, with full knowledge that he was likely still on-camera. While no human being was likely to ever review the tape, he couldn't know for sure, so he was putting on a good show, just in case.

"Follow me..." he whispered so that the microphones wouldn't pick it up, "There's a blind spot where I can see my station, off camera. We'll need to drink it fast, though. Can't spend too much time off-camera..."

He and Sasha walked toward the corner together in a manner that implied that they had noticed a possible threat and needed to investigate it. Meanwhile, Mustafa, no longer sporting an idiot's smile, opened his driver's side door, and climbed out of the cab, leaving the motor running, walking around to the back of the truck. The noise of the idling engine masked any whispers we might exchange from being picked up by the microphones. Sasha and the Russian soldier disappeared around the corner.

Inside the trailer, we had prepared our weapons and donned our heat shield/light-bending cloaks. These Ukrainian-made devices primarily masked heat signatures but also slightly reduced visibility in normal light.

Mustafa unfastened the trailer's back door and we exited, partially shielded from cameras by his body being in-between us and them and partly due to the darkness and our heat shields, which would foil infrared lenses. Yasmina, Svetlana and I were fully cloaked and mostly invisible to night vision cameras. I also had cloaks ready for Mustafa and Sasha. They needed to be outside camera view before putting them on.

Meanwhile, around the corner, in the blind spot, Sasha was plying the Russian soldier with spiked vodka, containing a potent, tasteless narcotic developed by Ukrainian Intelligence. It was capable of inducing surgical-level anesthesia for at least two hours. Sasha, having taken the antidote, chatted with the soldier until he passed out. My bags of equipment, including the drones, sat on the floor beside me, and a few minutes later, Sasha appeared, grinning as he swiftly rejoined us, behaving as if he was only approaching Mustafa.

"Good job..." I whispered when he came close enough. "I presume he's out cold?"

He nodded.

I handed him his invisibility cloak but, like Mustafa, he couldn't put it on right away. The current camera angle could only view him from the rear, but once he started putting it on, it would cover his entire body, making him essentially disappear from the night vision camera view. If someone happened to be watching the monitor at that moment, he might wonder how people could suddenly disappear. The moment they could get to another video blind spot, they would both don their cloaks.

"I've also got his ID card, his radio, and his pistol," Sasha whispered in a self-congratulatory fashion. "He was very talkative, by the way, and told me a lot of interesting things before he passed out..."

"Like what?" I asked.

"Like where all the camera blind zones are, for one thing," Sasha said.

"Excellent!" I exclaimed. "Let's take a look..."

Sasha was still carrying his tablet computer. He carried it everywhere. With Mustafa pretending to smoke, he moved behind him. This shielded him somewhat from the camera's view. He opened the tablet's cover and activated the mapping app, zooming in on the base.

"My friend took the trouble of marking a lot of camera-blind spots on this map for me before he fell asleep. Very helpful guy..." He said, pointing to one spot that had been conspicuously circled with his electronic stylus, "There are lots of blind areas, as you can see, but this one seems perfect for you. It's a relatively large, open area, and it's close to the storage facility where they keep the missiles. Before we get there, Mustafa and I can stop at this other one, and put on our cloaks."

I probably had a very surprised look on my face because he continued, pointing again to the screen;

"Yeah, that's right. He even showed me exactly where the missile bunkers are! Here and here!"

I studied the map. There were several roads, buildings, and even a runway between us and our new destination. All of it had to be navigated before we could get there. But, we had plenty of options.

"That's where we go..." I said, pointing to the same spot Sasha had pointed out. "How are you feeling?"

"Not too bad," he said, rubbing his stomach. "The antidote made me queasy at first, but it was over by the time I started drinking."

"Good," I said, smiling and clapping him on the shoulder. "Because you're indispensable. Great job!"

He beamed from the praise.

"Let's go make Putin pay!" he said, smiling, with contempt in his voice.

Sasha's complex background fueled his intense hatred of Vladimir Putin, in particular. His Russian father had brutally abused his Tatar mother before leaving her and disappearing before Sasha turned six years old. Raised in the Tatar community, he had later departed from the usual Islam and embraced Baptist Christianity. But, then, his American-connected church, like many others in the occupied territories, was searched, looted and closed by Russian authorities. Aside from Christianity, Sasha identified exclusively with his Tatar heritage. Destroying the missile cache was an opportunity to strike back.

I turned to the others.

"Alright, people, listen up," I whispered, "We have six drones. Each one has a tiny explosive charge. If placed carefully and accurately, each one can trigger an explosion big enough to blow the whole place to hell. We can destroy all the missiles, but the drones need to be landed in just the right places."

We shouldered our heavy bags and AK-74 rifles, complete with silencers, all concealed under our cloaks. I checked my watch as we set out toward our target, nearly a kilometer away. The night shift would arrive soon, but we'd be long gone by then. Our priorities were clear: stay alert, act decisively when needed, and maintain silence. We had to carefully avoid night patrols as we made our way to the blind zone.

We reached the launch point quickly. It was a small clearing surrounded by trees and bushes, dark and quiet, save for occasional airplane noise. Crouching down, I opened my bags, free from camera surveillance, and quickly assembled micro-drones from snap-together parts. I activated the smartphone app. Meanwhile, Sasha and Mustafa, who had separated out to don their cloaks, joined us a few minutes later.

My first drone took off and headed toward the missile bunker. The high-resolution night vision camera showed everything in its path. Flying low and slow, with minimum propeller speed and almost no noise, I could see the base in exquisite detail via night vision, although it was in a greenish monotone. My camera flew over buildings, roads, fences, and parked vehicles. Anyone out and about might hear the noise, but it was such a low-level background buzz, that they would assume it was a loud bee, rather than a little airplane.

The missile warehouse resembled a low hill crowned by a small tower. Initially, I'd hoped the tower might provide entry to the underground bunkers, but I now saw it was windowless. Covered in shiny panels, it was actually part of an electronic early warning system designed in the old Soviet Union. My tiny drones were slow, low-flying, and microscopic compared to the missiles of the Cold War era. Built for stealth, such objects would normally pose no threat to a fortified missile bunker. While the Russian warning system could monitor flying objects at the center of the base, it was incapable of detecting a modern micro-drone.

A massive set of armored metal doors, large enough for military trucks, were cut into the hillside, leading deep underground. This was a detail not clear from satellite imagery. But, I had assumed there would be armored doors which, I knew, posed the most significant challenge to our success. The likelihood of such doors was why my original plan involved waiting for a military truck carrying missiles, rather than a food truck. Such doors would have had to be opened to store the additional missiles. But, no new missile deliveries were scheduled for weeks. We took what we could get.

I guided the micro-drone to an overhead view. The doors resembled enormous bank vault entrances, thick, robust, and seemingly impenetrable. That was painfully clear. Not even the combined explosion of all six drones at the same time would make an impact. Forcing entry was impossible. I stared helplessly at the display, zooming in to examine the minutest details, but there were no discernible weaknesses. The doors were designed to withstand multiple missile and artillery attacks and they were sealed shut, likely for the night, if not longer. My plan had come up against the first major obstacle.

I shook my head in frustration.

"It's a fucking fortress..." I grumbled, trying to think of a way to open the doors now that we were so close to them.

But, Sasha was watching the video over my shoulder and had some thoughts of his own.

"I recognize those doors," he whispered.

"You do?" I asked.

"Yes," He whispered again. "They're not as secure as they look."

I turned to him.

"What do you mean?" I whispered.

Sasha explained,

"When I hacked the Ministry of Defense, a lot of things didn't seem useful at the time, but I read them anyway. Like the protocol for opening those doors. They're sealed shut, right now, but the guards can easily open them."

I looked carefully at my telephone screen. Two guards stood in front of the doors, looking bored and relaxed, unaware of the danger that buzzed above them.

"Each guard has a card key." Sasha continued. "One of those cards, plus the biometric signature of his hand, can open the doors..."

I felt a surge of adrenaline run through me, as I thought about taking on the guards, instinctively reaching for my AK-74, lying on the grass beside me.

"Not you!" Sasha said, "Remember, you have to fly the drones. No one else can do that. They're the key to mission success, aren't they?"

He was right. It left me with a problem. Sasha was a brilliant ally in a day and age when technology can mean winning or losing. But, he was notoriously weak, in terms of physical ability, at least for a full-grown man. He was slightly built and had no training or experience in hand-to-hand combat. He did have an excellent brain, but that provided little in the way of physical fighting skills.

Mustafa was listening.

"I'll go with Sasha," he whispered.

Sasha smiled and nodded.

"Thanks, Mustafa," he said. They clasped hands, "You're like an older brother to me. We'll do this together."

But Svetlana interjected forcefully.

"No!" she whispered sternly. "Mustafa cannot go. He is needed here. Other than John, he is the only one who served in the military, and who is trained in handling weapons and hand-to-hand combat. He must protect John while he guides the drones."

"There's no one else." Mustafa protested, "I must go."

"You are wrong," Svetlana said, finally, asserting the wisdom and clarity that had made her de facto leader after the death of her husband. "I will go with Sasha."

"You?" Sasha complained.

Svetlana was an amazing lady, fearless and determined. But, initially, her plan seemed absurd. She was an elderly woman, thin, and even weaker than Sasha on his worst day. She would be useless in hand-to-hand combat to subdue the guards.

"No," I said, shaking my head, without thinking first, "That's a crazy idea..."

There was no sign, however, that she intended to back down.

"You have a better idea?" she asked.

I shook my head.

"No, but you're no match for Russian soldiers," I insisted, "I don't need Mustafa to protect me. He'll go with Sasha and I'll take care of myself and, well, I still have you to protect me, don't I?"

"He's right." Sasha agreed.

But, Svetlana interrupted him.

"No he is not," She insisted, "You all discount me because I am an old woman."

"I never said that..." Sasha replied.

"Neither did I," I added, sincerely, "It's just a practical matter."

But, even as I said that, I suddenly realized that Svetlana was right.

"Sasha, Svetlana is right," I suggested, as an idea took shape in my head. "Physical strength isn't a factor here. We don't need to overpower those guards. We'll just have to kill them. A guard's key card and hand will open those doors, dead or alive. Svetlana is an excellent sniper, or so I am told..."

"You've been told correct." Svetlana confirmed. "I need glasses these days, but with my glasses, I can still shoot straighter than almost any man."

Sasha shrugged his shoulders, and the initial flicker of a frown transformed into a smile.

"Babushka..." Yasmina sobbed, throwing herself into her grandmother's arms.

They hugged each other tightly.

"Little Zolotaya..." Svetlana said, brushing away a tear. Zolotaya means "golden" or "golden one" in Russian.

"Where I come from, a woman with your courage and determination is rare." I commented, impressed with her.

"Thank you, John," she said, turning back. "But, again, you are wrong. Just think about the courage it takes to give birth a second time, after all the pain of the first! But, if anything happens to me, you must take care of my little angel, as you promised."

"You don't need to worry about that," I confirmed.

Mustafa looked confused by our exchange. He was unaware of my relationship with Yasmina and the promises I had made. But this wasn't the time for explanations—we had too many other things to focus on. She was 21-year-old, but Yasmina now seemed like a small child as she clung to her grandmother. She was, of course, the same partisan who concealed a long knife, a 9mm pistol, and ample ammunition beneath her clothes. I loved her dearly. But, if she were actually an angel, as her grandmother claimed, she would have to be the angel of death—an avenging force against the unrighteous.

I kept that thought to myself.

"Alright, alright already," Sasha said, impatiently, who, unlike Mustafa, had paid no attention to the talk about my taking care of Yasmina. "Let's just go and do it."

They meticulously adjusted their "invisibility" cloaks, ensuring maximum coverage. They double-checked their earbuds. We aimed for radio silence as a precautionary measure, but there would be pivotal moments requiring swift communication. The base itself provided us with an advantage in terms of detection by the fact that there were a multitude of electronic devices generating radio wave background noise. Our communications, operating on a different wavelength, would be detectable if someone was specifically looking for them. But, in the midst of a cacophony of electronic signals and without prior knowledge of our presence, it was unlikely that we would draw any Russian attention.

"Keep your headpieces on," I urged, "just in case...but transmit only if there's no other choice."

"Ponyal..." Sasha nodded, the Russian military response equivalent of 'Roger that'.

Navigating swiftly and silently, the pair weaved around buildings and down narrow walkways. The bunker hill lay approximately 500 meters away which is not very far. But, the path was interrupted by numerous structures, and there was no choice but to take a winding route. The risk of encountering a Russian night patrol loomed constantly. Adding to that, cameras and sensor devices blanketed the area with surveillance. Every step required caution and precision, in spite of the cloaks that made them less noticeable. Their progress was a tense dance of advance and concealment, each movement calculated to avoid detection while steadily closing the distance. The complex layout of the base turned a short dash into a protracted journey.

Through the drone's camera, I watched things intently. In some sense, I was happy that, despite the high-quality imaging system, I could barely make them out. It meant that it would be at least as difficult for the Russians. Probably, far more difficult, because their equipment was inferior to mine in quality, and they didn't know what they were looking for. In any case,

I tracked their progress as best I could, following ghostly shapes and faint video artifacts.

Suddenly, a three-man Russian night patrol appeared, moving directly towards them. The potential for disaster loomed large. With no other option, I made the critical decision to break radio silence. The immediate threat was more serious than the threat that the radio communication would be intercepted.

"Hacker," I radioed, using Sasha's code name, and I used Russian-style military slang, although I have translated it here, "This is Cossack. I have eyes on three tangos moving as a patrol, grid Papa-Tango-One-Two-Three-Four. Tangos are Oscar-Mike towards your position. Over."

"Ponyal…" Sasha's answer came back to me.

The shadowy figures halted abruptly. Their faint outlines vanished completely as they hid behind a building. They remained motionless until the patrol passed, oblivious to their presence. The danger having passed, they resumed a cautious advance. Within minutes, they reached a low wall, from which they could see the armored entry doors, and took cover.

The guards' negligence was striking. Both men were blatantly disregarding their duties, and were oblivious to the drone's conspicuous buzzing overhead. The guard on the left appeared bored. He was relaxed, casually smoking a cigarette. His companion was engrossed with his smartphone, a clear violation of on-duty protocol. Their disregard for procedure played to our advantage. The helmets and bulletproof vests provided substantial protection to vital areas, but their faces and necks were exposed, presenting an opportunity for a skilled sniper like Svetlana.

Despite her age, so long as she diligently wore glasses, she remained an excellent marksman. She fired two silenced shots, one after another, and each shot met its mark. The two guards simply fell to the ground, blood spilling out of the precise holes just above the bridge of their noses. I don't particularly like seeing people die, not even the enemy. But, they were soldiers, like me, who were unfortunately working for the wrong side. That is the nature of war. As occupiers, illegally posted in a land that is not their own, we had no choice but to kill them.

17

The area immediately in front of the armored doors was heavily covered by the base surveillance systems. The ghostly figures of Sasha and Svetlana suddenly burst out from concealment, dashing directly towards the fallen guards in spite of the significant risk of detection. There was no other option. We could have shot out the cameras, but a sudden loss of camera feed would have triggered an immediate alarm. In contrast, the movement of two shadowy figures might go unnoticed for a while, until someone saw that the guards were no longer standing.

A ghostly apparition, which I assumed was Sasha, miraculously dragged one of the dead guards toward the biometric console. My heart pounded. This was critical time, and time was of the essence. On the right-hand side of the doors, embedded into the hill, was a machine, with a slot for the card and a pad for the hand print. The guard's body and hand moved, as if lifted by an invisible force. The card was accepted. So was the hand. The green light flashed. The body of the dead guard, having done its last service, rolled freely down to the tarmac. The huge doors began to open, slowly revealing the depths of the dark facility within.

There was no time to waste, so I broke radio silence again.

"Get out! Now!" I ordered.

The shadows ran. I turned to Mustafa, who was busy continuously scanning our vicinity with his AK-74 at the ready.

"I'm launching the drones," I said, "their AI programs can take them to their final destinations, but human guidance is more precise, so I'd like to stay here as long as possible."

"OK," Mustafa said. "But, the Moskali know we are on the base, now. They'll be coming for us…"

He was right. We had to assume that those who monitored the cameras had seen everything. The guards falling dead, the ghostly apparitions, the doors opening, and, probably, by now, the fact that I had a tiny drone flying above it all. Even if they were not watching, it was almost certain that simply opening the doors to the missile bunker, at such an odd time, would itself trigger an alarm. If they could triangulate a location, be that of Sasha and Svetlana, or Mustafa, Yasmina and me, they'd attack whoever they could, wherever they could.

"I'm working as fast as I can…" I responded.

Yasmina was serving as Mustafa's backup. She also held her rifle at the ready, looking for movement. We might all die at any moment. But, if I survived, I swore to myself that I would never again let her near anything more dangerous than a mosquito. I would keep my word to her grandmother and quit the Ukrainian Foreign Legion as soon as my contract expired. I would marry Yasmina and take her back to America.

But before I could do any of those things, we both had to survive.

The coordinates to enter the now-open gate into the missile bunker was already programmed into all the drones. It was just a matter of launching them and guiding them as long as possible. Their AI guidance systems also contained images of the types of missiles to seek out as landing spots. I was targeting large warheads and other explosives. In a worst case scenario, if my radio connection was broken, or even if I were killed, the drones could use the programmed information to find targets on their own. It wouldn't be as efficient and precise as human guidance, but it would get the job done.

I had even uploaded a photo of the sign that read "Missile Storage Facility 1" (in Russian) to be sure that, even if I ended up shot and dead in the field, before the five additional drones arrived at the bunker hill, they could still find their way there. I double-checked the settings and hit the launch button. All five additional drones took off and headed toward the one I was using for surveillance. Meanwhile, that was no longer a surveillance drone. It had already dived and made it through the big doors. It was the first to enter, and its two small headlamps lit up automatically in the darkness. The headlamps would drain additional power, and the drone's battery was almost completely drained. But, it didn't matter anymore. The battery only needed to last a few minutes longer. Long enough to land on a warhead, and help with the chain reaction.

After my lead drone reached what must have been the bottom floor, I finally saw the missiles. Row upon row of them, all ready to be loaded onto aircraft, gleaming under the artificial light of the headlamps. Left unmolested, they would be used to commit more atrocities. More killing, maiming, and terrorizing. We had to take them out!

I resumed manual control and carefully landed the first drone on top of the warhead section of a large cruise missile. The battery was almost exhausted, but it was now in place and ready. I turned off the headlamp. The drone would have more than enough energy left for the one final spark that would trigger its detonation. I switched to another drone's video feed. All the drones were dispersing in different directions, guided by their AI systems, which scanned every inch of the facility in search of appropriate landing spots.

Some of the rooms had closed doorways that they could not enter. But, plenty of missiles and artillery shells were exposed. Another of my drones located a target and I guided it where it could achieve maximum damage. Each drone successfully found a target, and I hand-guided each one to exactly the right place, where their tiny explosive force would be most likely to ignite the much larger explosive force of a large warhead.

One drone discovered a room containing nearly 1,000 glide bombs. These weapons were primarily used by close-ground assault aircraft like Su-25s and are devastating at close range due to their low cost, abundance, and ability to carry warheads of up to 3 tons, compared to the 300-500 kg warheads of true missiles. Despite the relative cheapness of each glide bomb compared to cruise or ballistic missiles, a thousand of them represented a significant investment. But, more than that, together they represented an incredible potential explosive force comparable to a small tactical nuclear weapon.

All six drones were in position. My signal feed was already breaking up and I no longer had any aerial surveillance that would allow me to determine why. I didn't need any. I already knew the reason. It had always been just a matter of time before someone activated the closing mechanisms of the armored bunker doors. They were already closing and, once sealed shut, my connection to the drones would be completely severed. But, thankfully, the detonations were not dependent upon my radio connection. They would happen at the time specified, whether my controller app was able to communicate with the drones or not. It was only a matter of time.

I broke the radio silence again and contacted Sasha and Svetlana.

"Hacker, Cossack. Did you reach Whiskey Tango Foxtrot? Over." I asked in Russian.

I was referring to our designated rendezvous point. Whiskey Tango Foxtrot was a camera blind spot, located in the "safe zone" at least 1 kilometer away from the expected blast epicenter. Sasha's voice, however, came back, strained and accompanied by the sound of rapid-fire machine guns in the background.

"We are taking heavy fire!" he replied.

"Hacker, Cossack. Roger that. Rally point at grid Foxtrot-Tango-One-Five-Zero-Niner. Authenticate Bravo-Tango-Seven. Over." I said in Russian.

"Cossack, Hacker... Negative." He replied. "As I said, we are under attack. Situation critical. Out."

"Hacker, Cossack." I transmitted. "I copy your last. We'll relieve you! Transmit position."

A moment later, he sent me the relevant GPS coordinates. The message was encrypted. It didn't much matter if the Russians picked it up. They already knew where he was. It appeared, however, that they didn't know where I was yet. Would they be able to figure it out? To do that, they needed to triangulate our position from the radio signal. If they could, they would scramble troops to our location, to hit us before we moved to relieve Sasha and Svetlana. Obviously, it would be a serious error to stay in one place for too long. Moving quickly was of critical importance. I wanted to make sure that, by the time they triangulated our current location, we were already someplace else.

"We're on the way!" I assured Sasha.

Soon, the drones would explode and trigger the Russian warheads. The chain reaction would be devastating and was likely to completely destroy the bunker hill along with a significant part of the administration buildings at the center of the airbase. All hell was about to break loose. I was counting on that to confuse the enemy. They wouldn't know what hit them. They would likely believe that the number of attackers was far greater than it really was. They might think that they were being bombarded by missiles.

The confusion would help us rescue Sasha and Svetlana, and give us an opportunity to escape. Or, so, I hoped.

I grabbed my AK-74. The three of us headed toward Sasha and Svetlana. While we made our way forward, the earthquake struck. A series of deafening explosions rocked the area, and the ground beneath us trembled violently. The force nearly knocked both Mustafa and I off balance, and Yasmina momentarily lost her balance and fell, before swiftly recovering.

My drones had performed their task flawlessly. They had ignited the expected chain reaction. In the distance, the scene resembled a volcanic eruption. Fire was spewing forth from the earth with terrifying force. Entire sections of the bunker hill were obliterated, leaving gaping wounds in the landscape. Vicious fires erupted from the wounds. Every crack and crevice of the shattered hill bellowed smoke and fire like a dragon's breath.

The missiles and bombs continued to fuel their own destruction, one after the other, each explosion feeding into the next in a devastating cascade. The sheer power was terrifying and a stark reminder of the destructive potential of the human race. We'd just unleashed hell on earth. As we watched the inferno unfold, the magnitude of our success, and the danger we now faced, became starkly clear.

The explosions, one after another, continued. Waves of dirt rippled out as storage areas deep beneath the earth collapsed and air was expelled with incredible force. Even after the bunker hill imploded, more isolated blasts continued inside. The ground repeatedly lifted and fell as virtually all the paved tarmac, located inside the central part of the base, near the hill, crumbled into pieces. Three administrative buildings, close to the center of the base, closest to the bunker hill, collapsed in on themselves, becoming nothing more than mounds of rubble. Dirt kept spewing into the air. Swirling clouds of dust and debris laced the area above the hill and even more munitions continued to ignite and explode.

While the most spectacular explosions had ended, smaller ones continued. TNT doesn't need oxygen to explode, but the underground fires were now being partially fed by broken bottles of oxygen stored for emergencies. These oxygen leaks ignited anything remotely flammable, causing artillery shells in areas we wouldn't otherwise have any hope of reaching, also to detonate. I believe we destroyed all 230 missiles that

Ukrainian Intelligence reported were stored there, as well as the 1,000 glide bombs.

But, even if some of the missiles had survived the maelstrom, it didn't matter. It would take years of digging to excavate the place, and the process, itself, would be exceptionally dangerous. Intact missiles might explode unexpectedly during the process. The airbase was done, finished, ended. It would no longer serve as a base of operations, and that fact sent a wave of satisfaction coursing through me. We had been spectacularly successful. But, there was no time to relish the victory.

Survival was now the top priority. Russians were everywhere, some in total panic and others less so. The odds of escaping the base had grown slim. If we were caught, we would be imprisoned, tortured and eventually executed. Assaulting the guards at the doors had revealed our presence much earlier than my original plan. This allowed Russian forces to make a concerted effort to catch us. The Russians were in a state of total disarray, which worked in our favor. But the chaos wasn't enough to stop them from blocking all the exits. We needed an alternative way out, and I was out of ideas, for the moment.

Rescuing Sasha and Svetlana was the immediate goal. A fully thought-out escape plan would come after that. They had risked everything to open those blast doors and they were fighting for their lives. We had to save them!

"Cossack, do you copy?" I heard Sasha's voice.

"Cossack here," I replied, "Headed toward you."

"Negative. New position. Inside a building near the bunker, behind the curve in the road. Russians have us surrounded. Just get out while you can!"

He transmitted his new GPS coordinates.

"Negative back to you, Hacker. Hold on! Help is on the way!" I insisted.

We moved toward the building where Sasha and Svetlana were trapped. I signaled for Yasmina and Mustafa to follow. We ran across the broken tarmac, dodging searchlights. Our invisibility cloaks helped, but by now, the enemy was wise to our tricks. They were scrutinizing every shadow and video artifact.

We reached sight of the building. About 30 Russian soldiers surrounded it, firing at windows and doors. The shooting paused as a platoon commander spoke through a foghorn.

His voice boomed out with chilling finality:

"You are surrounded. Lay down your weapons and come out with your hands up. There is no chance of escape. This is your last warning."

I cursed quietly as I quickly assessed our dire situation. The Russians wanted us alive, not out of mercy, but for the information we possessed. Our actions—killing their guards and destroying billions in military equipment—had sealed our fate. There would be no clemency.

Their priority was now intelligence gathering. Capture meant imprisonment, torture and extraction of every detail from us before disposing of us. That was the cold, calculated Russian way. I made a grim decision: a clean death in battle was preferable to their "interrogation" methods.

Our options were limited, but the choice was clear: we would not be taken alive. The lull in gunfire, caused by the officer's announcement, offered us an opportunity. Yasmina turned to me and whispered;

"What do we do?" she asked, clutching her AK-74.

"I don't think they know we're here yet," I answered immediately. "So, we attack from the rear. You take the right flank and Mustafa takes the left. I go down the middle, directly after their commander. Lay down cover fire, from each side. I'll try to take him out. Once he's neutralized, there will be a momentary lapse in discipline and a lot of disorder. Hopefully, Sasha and Svetlana will use that opportunity to escape through the back door."

"Then, what?" Mustafa asked.

"Then, we get the hell out of here!" I replied.

She nodded.

"How?" Mustafa asked.

"Let's just rescue them, and we'll get to the details of our escape plan later..." I said. To be honest, I needed to delay any discussion of the issue because I hadn't yet thought it all out.

"I love you." Yasmina said, leaning over to give me a kiss.

There was no purpose in trying to keep our relationship a secret from Mustafa. By now, he probably already knew. Even if he didn't, since we were all likely to die anyway, how could he hold it against us?

"I love you too." I said, returning her kiss. "Now go!"

We split up and opened fire from behind, at the unsuspecting Russians, who vastly outnumbered us. But, they were taken completely by surprise. I headed straight toward the commander, shooting him in the chest, killing him instantly, spraying automatic gunfire at all the soldiers standing around him. Several collapsed to the ground. One dead Russian had several grenades hanging from his belt, and I leaned down and grabbed them, stuffing them into my pockets, figuring that they'd come in handy.

I ran, throwing one of the grenades at the nearest troop concentration, where it exploded, throwing soldiers to all sides, wounding many with shrapnel. It was a good diversion tactic, but one that wouldn't have a long-lasting effect. Reinforcements were already arriving en masse.

"Hacker, Avenger, Cossack here, do you copy?" I called on my radio, again using Sasha and Svetlana's code names.

Sasha's answer came back almost immediately,

"Cossack. This is Hacker. Thanks for the assist. We're on our way out..."

The two ran out the back, dodging bullets, moving towards us, reuniting our entire team.

"Hurry!" I shouted, motioning for them to follow, the details of our new plan of escape forming in my head.

When they reached us, Sasha slapped me on the back.

"Thank you!" he exclaimed.

"No, thank YOU." I said. "That was a great job with the armored doors. This base is history now..."

"But, how do we get out?" Svetlana asked the critical question.

"We get to the choppers!" I replied.

Yasmina and Mustafa continued to fire at Russian troops who had survived our first onslaught, even as we ran for cover. More of them were arriving by the minute. Thankfully, they were still confused and that made them less effective. Some probably thought they were under heavy attack by a superior force, after watching the entire center of their base implode. After seeing so many of their troops slaughtered on our way to rescue Sasha and Svetlana there seemed to be additional confusion among their ranks. Instead of taking full advantage of vast numerical superiority, they were acting cautiously.

"Let's run before the Moskali catch on," Mustafa urged.

His suggestion was sound, but I needed a moment to orient myself. Though I had studied the base blueprints extensively, committing most to memory, I had to quickly figure out our current position and the best route to our objective. Fortunately, aside from constructing the bunker hill, the Russians had made no significant changes since their illegal occupation of the peninsula in 2014. The consistency worked in our favor.

After a brief pause to get my bearings, I led the team through the base, towards our goal. Our progress was repeatedly hampered by a relentless pursuit by groups of an ever-growing number of Russian troops. We returned fire as best we could, but the odds were stacked heavily against us. We were vastly outnumbered and severely outgunned. Our dash through the base became a desperate race against time, each moment bringing more enemies. The tension mounted as we pushed forward. Our window of opportunity was rapidly closing.

We finally reached the corner of a small subsidiary airfield that catered to helicopters. Several were neatly parked in rows. There was only one possible plan of escape and it involved seizing a chopper and flying it out. A likely-looking Mi-24, a Russian attack helicopter that can carry up to 8 people, was sitting a little way off. Unfortunately, the Russians had us surrounded again. We were trapped behind piled crates and sandbags. It was a defensible position, but one from which there was no escape.

Having nowhere else to go, we stopped and sat down, using the crates and sandbags to shield ourselves. Thankfully, we were still dealing with small arms fire. The fact that they had orders to capture us alive is why we still had a chance. At some point, if we put up too successful a fight, they'd get frustrated, and the goal post would shift. They'd either shell us or attack with a chopper. They wouldn't get the information they wanted so badly, but wouldn't help us. We would be history. But, for now, they were still trying to capture us alive.

I tried to think clearly. We needed a chopper. But, how could we get to one? I suddenly realized that Sasha was no longer shooting back at the

Russians. I looked at him and he seemed almost frozen, like he had turned to stone. His back was supported on a crate. Leading to where he was sitting was a trail of blood, and underneath the tarmac was crimson. His eyes were staring ahead as if he were staring at something very fascinating. I quickly moved over to him, sitting down.

"Sasha?" I asked, but received no answer.

I jostled his shoulder to rouse him. No response. I leaned over and felt for his pulse. There wasn't any. Sasha was dead. A bullet had hit him just below the protection of his vest and severed an artery. He had bled out. It was surprising that he'd been able to get as far as he did.

"Damn it!" I cursed under my breath, shaking my head in frustration, feeling a sense of anger and sadness.

He was a good man. Brave and brilliant. He had opened the door, literally, for me to destroy the Russian missiles. Sasha had saved thousands of lives. I had seen brothers in arms fall before, but he was one of the best. It made me very sad, and I closed his eyes with my hand and said a silent prayer. Then, I turned to the others.

"Sasha has bled out," I announced. "He's dead."

Yasmina gasped.

"Oh, my God!" She exclaimed, unused to the idea of death.

I had been told that she had gone on missions and seen death. But, now, I doubted it. It was probably manufactured nonsense designed to elevate Yasmina's participation in the partisan's sabotage campaigns so that she would agree to stay home most of the time. I glanced at Svetlana who, no doubt, was the architect of the deceit. She had a tear rolling down her normally stoic cheeks. The two women hugged each other in sympathy over their loss. A moment later, they parted. But, when Yasmina removed her hand from the embrace, it was covered with blood.

"Babushka, you're bleeding!" She said, alarmed.

Svetlana smiled weakly.

Yasmina looked carefully and then, finding the source of the blood, she cut open her grandmother's blouse with her knife. The old woman had also taken a shot. The bullet had gone in low and upward. Perhaps, it had been fired by a foe who was in the midst of falling to the ground himself. The bullet had missed any major arteries, but was probably somewhere in her upper intestinal tract. Such wounds are excruciatingly painful. They had to be treated by highly trained surgeons without delay. But, there was no safe hospital she could get to for many days. By that time, without professional treatment, she would die an excruciatingly painful death.

I sprang into action, as Mustafa kept shooting at the enemy, keeping them at bay, at least for the moment. I put some pressure on the wound, and dusted instant coagulant over it. I could stop the external bleeding, but I could do nothing to stop what was happening inside her. Svetlana had lived long and seen many people die. She knew her fate was sealed. She touched her granddaughter's hand gently. I think Yasmina realized, for the first time, that her grandmother was mortally wounded and wouldn't survive. She was crying uncontrollably.

"Little Zolotaya," Svetlana said, "I have lived a long and full life. And, I'm not dead yet. I can still take more Racshisti with me to the grave…"

Racshisti is a favorite Ukrainian and Tatar pejorative, applied to Russians. It means Russian fascist.

She tried to smile, but coughed and grimaced from the pain despite her best efforts to hide it.

18

The scene was heart-wrenching. Yasmina and Svetlana sat side by side, a stark contrast between the bloom of youth and fading life. Svetlana's pallor was alarming, her life ebbing with each drop of blood that stained the tarmac. Acid was likely seeping into her abdominal cavity, causing excruciating pain, and yet her resolve was unbroken. She had fought on, wielding her AK-74 with determination, and only stopping when Yasmina's concern overwhelmed her.

She bent over her grandmother, desperately trying to do something. It was futile. Only a well-equipped hospital could offer any hope of saving her life. And, even if there were such a facility within reach, Svetlana's chances would be slim even then. But there was no hospital and surrender was unthinkable. After so many years of fighting, Svetlana was more inclined to face death rather than yield to the Russians. Besides, although surrender might get her a hospital bed, it would lead to torture and eventual execution anyway.

Tears streamed down Yasmina's face, a waterfall of grief and desperation. The sight was almost unbearable. I turned to Mustafa beside me, both of us still alert and uninjured, acutely aware of the stark contrast between our condition and Svetlana's dire state. The situation pressed heavily upon me.

"You once said you were a helicopter pilot during the Afghan war…"

He nodded, and said,

"I was."

"Can you fly a Mi-24?" I asked.

"Of course," he replied, taking another shot at the enemy.

"Good," I said.

The Mi-24 is a large and powerful Russian attack helicopter, heavily armed with rockets and machine guns. The one near us was an easy run from where we were pinned down, and if we made it, it could serve as our ticket out. It was our only chance. But, there was a world of enemy gunfire between it and us.

I turned to the others and said:

"We need to get to that chopper," I said. "Then, we fly it out of here. There's room enough for all of us."

"But, what about the Orcs?" Mustafa asked.

"I'll create a diversion, laying down cover fire," I said, taking out the grenades I'd taken off the dead Russian soldier. "I'll use these. You all run like hell to the helicopter, climb in, and fly away."

It was the best option I could come up with, given the circumstances. I waited for the reaction.

Svetlana looked at me, blankly. So, did Yasmina. Then, Mustafa spoke.

"And, what about you?" he asked.

"I can't fly a helicopter," I said.

"That is not what I meant," Mustafa said. "How will you get to the helicopter?"

"Someone has to stay," I explained, "I'll get there, somehow, but if I don't, take off without me. Take Yasmina and Svetlana, to that chopper. I'll cover you…"

"No," Mustafa insisted, "I am an old man. I'll create the diversion. You go with Yasmina and Sveta. I understand everything now. You and Yasmina are meant to be together."

I smiled at his gallantry, but shook my head.

"You're the only one who can fly it, Mustafa. I don't know how."

Unlike flying an airplane, flying a helicopter involves all four limbs, not just your brain and two hands. I could never fly the M24. Not without a lot more training. We stared each other down for a moment, but before the outcome could be decided, a weak voice from behind spoke up. She spoke with difficulty.

"You are both idiots!" Svetlana snapped, "I am the one who will stay behind."

We turned to her and saw how pale she was, and the blood on the tarmac. We also saw the rifle in her hands and the resolve in her eyes. She cut off our protest, preemptively.

"Don't argue with a dying woman!" She insisted. "You know I am right. I am in terrible pain, frankly, and you know as well as I do that, without a hospital, I'm going to die anyway. A quick death will be a welcome relief. Otherwise, it will be horrible. Take Yasmina and go. It's the only way..."

The young woman listened to her grandmother.

"No, babushka, you can't! You can't..." She exclaimed.

Svetlana looked at her granddaughter, smiling weakly. She then reached out and touched her face.

"Sweet Yasmina, precious girl, I wish I had given you a more normal life. But, don't cry for me. I am not afraid. I want to die! Your grandfather waits for me in heaven. I want to join him there. You love John and should understand how I still love your grandfather beyond life, itself. I want to be with him again. Go to America with John. Be happy. Remember me and remember your grandfather. Be assured that we will be looking down on you from paradise!"

Then, she turned and looked at me, speaking softly.

"You are a brave man. A hero, of America and Ukraine and, now, also of the Tatari people. Love and cherish Yasmina as long as you live. Give me beautiful grandchildren. Name one after me. Promise me..."

A lump formed in my throat. I nodded, but water filled my eyes. A drop spilled down my cheek. Yet, in spite of the grief, I knew she was right. A quick death in a hail of bullets was better than the slow, agonizing death she faced even if we managed to get off the base.

"I swear," I said. "If I live, I will love her until the day I die. I promise you."

Svetlana smiled and nodded.

"You'd better keep your promise, John," She warned, "Because I'll be watching."

An instant later, she winced from the pain, and she added one last request.

"Do me one more favor." She requested. "Give me a shot of that stimulant you keep in your medical kit. I want to be awake and alert, fighting like a demon, and I want to take as many Orcs with me as possible..."

I was surprised that she knew I kept a strong stimulant in my med kit, but apparently, she knew a lot more than I thought. The request was reasonable. Our best chance of getting away safely depended on her staying alert and shooting for as long as possible before succumbing to her wounds. I took out a small vial, snapped off the end, filled a syringe, and injected her with it. Her eyes widened, and her body tensed up as it took effect. We both knew it would accelerate her internal blood loss, but under the circumstances, that didn't matter. The bullet wound was fatal without hospitalization. I passed her the grenades, and she gripped her AK-74 with renewed strength, aiming at the enemy.

Mustafa nodded and then walked over to Svetlana, kissing her on the forehead.

"Goodbye, my friend…" He said. "We meet again when Allah Almighty wills it…"

"Get out of here!" She bellowed. "Or, you'll all die, and my death will lose meaning…"

I grabbed Yasmina, who was consumed with sobbing and clinging to her grandmother, and dragged her away forcefully. We would take our chance at life, even as Svetlana took her chance at death.

The elderly Tatar woman charged the Russian soldiers like a raging bull. Despite being shot at, she kept advancing, throwing grenades and taking bullets without slowing down. Her grenades exploded in quick succession, killing several soldiers and wounding others. The remaining troops were forced to retreat. As we reached the helicopter, gunfire still echoed around us. Miraculously, we seemed to have escaped the barrage unharmed.

Mustafa took the pilot's seat, and I sat next to him. Yasmina took a seat in back of us. We all strapped ourselves in. We could still see the battle through the window. Her grandmother rose back up, even after falling to the ground after being shot multiple times. This was a frightening effect of the stimulant I had administered. She continued shooting like a zombie with a gun and tossing grenades, despite grave wounds, laughing and yelling maniacally while charging toward the Russians. Finally, the old woman collapsed onto the pavement. But, by that time, we were airborne, and on our way out of the airbase. Yasmina gently touched the glass and whispered one last time, voice heavy with sorrow,

"Babushka, I love you…" She said, weakly, her voice trailing off.

As a military helicopter, the Mi-24 didn't have a typical car ignition. But, it does require a key for startup. The overconfident Russians had left the key in place, as it was more convenient to do so. Bullets were still being fired but none could reach us anymore. We flew into the night sky over the escarpment.

There were low hills below as we headed northwest toward Cape Tarkhankut, the same rugged place at which I had first come ashore in Crimea. I had no illusion of being able to pick up my mini-sub and leave the way I had come. But, if we traveled far enough in that direction, we would reach Ukrainian-controlled territory. I breathed a sigh of relief.

We were out of rifle range. But, we were not in the clear. It was only a matter of time before the Russians sent fighter jets, anti-aircraft missiles or both.

It had begun to rain, a rare Crimean summer storm was brewing, and Mustafa turned on the wipers to insure visibility as the raindrops began to fall more heavily. We had destroyed the missile bunker and escaped, but only at a terrible cost. Sasha and Svetlana were dead—two fine people sacrificed for the greater good. They died with honor, as heroes, so that thousands of others would live. But, I had lost two friends, and I mourned them both. My thoughts turned back to Muhammad, the traitor whose actions had forced our premature attack. If not for his actions, I would have had the time to do the attack correctly. I was convinced that things would have gone differently and I vowed to make him answer for his crimes.

I took solace in the fact that Yasmina was safe and sitting right behind me. We still had each other, our love, and our hope for the future. I needed to deal with Muhammad first, because he had to die for his actions. But afterward, I would quit the war entirely and take Yasmina to America.

Despite my general sadness, I managed to smile at that thought. It was a relief to be alive and free, despite our grievous losses.

The moment of relief was cut short, however, by a beep on the radar. Red dots had appeared on the screen, and they were heading straight for us, coming ever closer very quickly. That meant anti-aircraft missiles. They were approaching fast, far quicker than any helicopter could fly, and we were in grave danger! Mustafa's voice crackled through our helmet headsets, cutting through the deafening roar of the rotors.

"We can't outrun or outmaneuver them," he stated matter-of-factly. "I can only deploy the decoy system..."

His fingers danced across the console, activating the chopper's defensive measures. Instantly, a series of flares burst from our aircraft. These simple yet effective devices were designed to confuse the simple heat-seeking guidance systems of the type of incoming missiles that had been launched against us. I watched the radar intently, holding my breath as the dots suddenly changed course, veering away from us to chase the decoys.

Moments later, the sky lit up with small fireballs as the missiles detonated harmlessly in the distance. A mild shock wave rattled the chopper, reminding me how close we'd come to disaster. The simplicity and effectiveness of the countermeasure was remarkable. We had been saved by exploiting the limitations of the missiles' simple guidance systems. The more modern, more expensive missiles, however, did not rely solely on heat signatures to home in on targets. We had inflicted such a heavy blow upon Russia that, inevitably, they would do whatever they had to do to shoot us down. Next, I knew, they would send the best anti-aircraft missiles they had and/or a squadron of jets. Yet, in spite of foreseeing doom, for the moment, I was happy.

"We fooled them!" I exclaimed with a smile.

"Not for long," Mustafa cautioned, repeating what I already knew, "We are still within range of their S-400 defense systems. I won't be able to distract those with decoys. And, we don't have many decoys left anyway. We need to get out of the sky!"

"There are just mountains down there. Nowhere to land..." I commented.

"We don't land," he replied. "We jump. There are 8 parachutes on board. We only need three. I'll put the chopper on autopilot. When they destroy it, hopefully, they'll assume we're dead. We make our way to Ukrainian-controlled territory on foot."

Crossing Crimea, into Ukraine-controlled territory, on foot would be extraordinarily difficult. That was the reason I had arrived by submarine. However, it was not impossible. If adequate bribes were paid to key Russian military officials, anything was possible.

"OK," I replied.

Yasmina hadn't spoken for a while. Normally, she'd be right in the middle of our conversation, offering her thoughts on everything. Her silence was odd. I turned to look at the seat behind me, and my heart nearly stopped. She sat motionless, her eyes closed as if in sleep. But there was blood on the seat, and her skin seemed deathly pale. A cold fear gripped me, a sickening twisting in the pit of my stomach. My mind raced. What had happened to her? How could I not have noticed until now?

"Yasmina?" I called out, unable to keep the worry from my voice.

To my immense relief, her eyes fluttered open.

"John?" she mumbled, sounding disoriented. "What's happening?"

I unbuckled and scrambled over my seat to reach her.

"You scared me. Are you alright?" I asked.

As I examined her more closely, I noticed a dark reddish stain on her shirt near her left shoulder. It ran down the length of her shirt and downward.

"You're hurt. Can I take a look?" I asked.

She winced as she tried to move.

"I... I didn't even realize." She said, weakly, "It must have happened while we were running to the helicopter."

"May I?" I asked, gesturing to her shirt. She nodded, and I gently pulled it aside to reveal a bleeding wound. It looked like a bullet had grazed her, leaving a nasty surface wound. But, she had probably lost a significant amount of blood, which might be the reason she had temporarily passed out.

"Mustafa," I called out, "Yasmina's been hit. It's not critical, but she's losing blood."

As I worked on stopping the bleeding, Mustafa spoke again, his voice thick with emotion.

"Hang in there, Zolotaya. You've always been strong."

Mustafa had known Yasmina since she was a small child, when she had been brought to Crimea from Moscow by her grandmother. She was almost like a daughter to him. The deep affection in his voice said it all.

She managed a weak smile.

As I finished treating the wound, Mustafa's tone shifted, becoming more urgent.

"John, it's only a matter of time before we've got incoming missiles from an S-400 battery. We need to bail out. Now!"

I felt a surge of adrenaline.

"Yasmina, can you move? We need to get our parachutes on." I explained.

She nodded, and a determined look replacing the pain in her eyes. Her courage, I think, was always part of what I loved about her.

"I can manage," She bravely insisted.

Mustafa was already retrieving parachutes from the helicopter's storage.

"There are eight on board. These seem to be in the best condition. Here," he said, handing them out.

I helped Yasmina into her parachute, trying to be as gentle with her injured shoulder as I could. My mind raced. How had it come to this? Where we would go from here? My mission, the infiltration and destruction of the Russian missile bunker, would be hailed as a resounding success by my superiors. The objective had been accomplished. We had sustained the loss of only two team members. Thousands of innocent lives would be saved. But those cold statistics didn't capture the true cost. Those two people had grown dear to me. I blamed myself for making foolish decisions and coming up with a badly thought-out plan that had gotten them killed. Each of their deaths felt like a knife twisting in my heart, leaving wounds that would never heal.

We were seconds away from leaping into the unknown. Yasmina was wounded. The wind howled outside the helicopter. A perilous jump awaited us. As I secured the last strap on Yasmina's parachute, I took a deep breath, steeling myself for the challenges lay ahead.

"John," Yasmina's said, "Whatever happens, I'm glad we're together..."

Her words sent a wave of emotion through me.

Mustafa's voice cut through the helicopter. "It's time. We jump now or we die here."

I took a deep breath, looking at Yasmina. "Ready?"

She nodded, her eyes reflecting a mix of fear and trust. It was abundantly clear that she had never used a parachute before. Taking her first jump while injured would be a doubly difficult task, but Yasmina was up to the challenge, as she always was.

We moved to the door, and I looked down at the low mountains of northwestern Crimea. The trees and rocks glistened with moisture from an unusual spring storm. Heavy rain surrounded us.

"The storm might shield us from their radar," Mustafa shouted over the wind. "It's now or never!"

Without further hesitation, Mustafa jumped first. I gave Yasmina's hand a quick squeeze before she followed. Then, I leapt into the stormy sky. We all floated downward, although I was mindful to keep control over my direction, maneuvering my parachute's trajectory to follow Yasmina. She didn't know how to steer a parachute, and would therefore be carried to wherever the wind wanted her to go. I wanted to land somewhere nearby.

I also kept glancing toward the chopper, keeping it in sight. Suddenly, I saw three missiles strike it simultaneously. The aircraft erupted into a massive fireball. Debris scattered and the shattered airframe plunged towards the ground. If luck was on our side, the radar image of our parachutes would be shielded by the chaos of the thunderstorm. There were no guarantees, but I hoped that the Russians would think we perished along with the helicopter.

Meanwhile, rain lashed at my face as I made my way toward the ground. It was unpleasant, of course, but I felt a glimmer of hope. We had survived impossible odds. Svetlana and Sasha had died, but their deaths were not in vain. They had saved so many people who would never know their names. Now, as we drifted through the storm, towards the hills below, a new chapter was beginning.

I spotted Yasmina and Mustafa nearby, their parachutes stark against the dark sky. We would face what lay ahead together. The future I had dreamed about, with Yasmina, was still within reach. As the ground rushed up to meet us, I braced for landing. Our immediate future was uncertain, but for the first time in a long while, I dared to hope for something beyond survival. Something like happiness…

HOW TO LEAVE A REVIEW

Thank you for reading "A Fate Far Sweeter." We hope you enjoyed it as much as we did. And, if you did, please leave positive reader reviews on retailer websites. The book retailer URLs for this novel, can be quickly found at:

https://books2read.com/A-Fate-Far-Sweeter

Most people do not understand how important a review can be, especially in the case of debut novels. In today's crowded digital marketplace, reader reviews mean the difference between the novel successfully finding its audience or simply vanishing into obscurity. Even brilliant writers remain unknown without them. For new authors especially, your review isn't just feedback—it's their chance to be discovered.

So, post a review and recommend the novel to people you know on Facebook, Twitter, TikTok and other social media. Reviews and social media posts will help spread the word about this book. Every share, every recommendation, every tweet matters—and it means the world to an author!

Thanks for your help!

BE THE FIRST TO KNOW ABOUT JOHN KOVALENKO'S NEWEST ADVENTURES!

Dear Valued Reader,

Thank you for joining us on the thrilling adventure of "A Fate Far Sweeter." We're excited to announce that the next installment in John Kovalenko's epic journey is already on the horizon! Don't miss out on:

- Exclusive updates
- Early access opportunities
- Stay informed about all Planetary Book Company releases
- Join our mailing list now:
- https://planetarybooks.com/new-release-notifications
- We respect your inbox—expect only essential updates about new releases.

Happy reading,
The Planetary Book Company Team

Milton Keynes UK
Ingram Content Group UK Ltd.
UKHW041832121124
451129UK00005B/45